Y NEGATIVE

XX

KELLY HAWORTH

RIPTIDE
PUBLISHING

Riptide Publishing
PO Box 6652
Hillsborough, NJ 08844
www.riptidepublishing.com

Y Negative

Cover art: Jay Aheer, jayscoversbydesign.com
Editor: Carole-ann Galloway
Layout: L.C. Chase, lcchase.com/design.htm

ISBN: 978-1-62649-334-6

First edition
November, 2015

Also available in ebook:
ISBN: 978-1-62649-333-9

Y NEGATIVE

XX

KELLY HAWORTH

RIPTIDE
PUBLISHING

*To those who are finally whole
on the other side
And those who have found comfort
somewhere in between
You are strong
You are beautiful
And we're in this together.*

TABLE OF
CONTENTS

PART 1

EMBER

XX

CHAPTER 1

This would be one of those days, I could tell. One of those days when clients would underpay me, the hot water would run out before I could shower, or some masc would decide I'm looking at him funny and bust my lip to teach me a lesson. It was the stink in the air, that acidic humidity. Made people irritable.

"Hello, this is Ember Dawson, from K Street Repair and Upgrade. Your console will be ready to pick up from the hours of ten to seventeen. Thank you!"

I took off my headset and dropped my head to my hands, my thumbs cupped under the short beard on my chin. *Come on, it's too early to wallow. I can get on with my life; that's what andros do.*

At least it was time to work out. "You ready to go?" I called, shoving myself to my feet and hefting my gym bag.

"Yeah, just a second." Niche's reply came muffled through his door.

Standing at the desk I had sandwiched between the couch and the hallway to the bedrooms, I downed a glass of water mixed with nutritional supplement. Ugh, so bitter. But at least it would sustain me through the workout.

"Let's go." Niche popped an earbud into one ear as he walked past me.

I grabbed my Common and earbuds off my desk and followed Niche out, scanning the hallway for mascs. It was vacant, thankfully, except for the damp, bitter-smelling air. Niche hummed to the song playing in his ear, his unused earbud swinging against his chest. He was wearing his old surrogacy shirt, which hung loose on his frame. I didn't get why he still had his; I had burned mine.

"Let's do three miles today, okay?" He bounded down the stairs to the first floor of the apartment complex.

"If you don't want to go the whole distance, you can wait for me." I pushed open the door at the end of the hall that led straight into the next building over, which was more apartments.

"So I spend the last ten minutes admiring your abs. I see how you like it."

Not this again: complimenting my body as if it made me feel better. "How many times have I told you it takes more than running to get these?"

We passed through another doorway into the gym, masc perspiration pleasing my senses. Continuing past the free weights, I ignored the men staring at us as they lifted.

"Right here." Niche jogged ahead of me and bounced onto a treadmill. I stepped onto the one next to him, stretching as I tapped at my Common. What was I in the mood for . . . Dirty Code has some good beats. I started a playlist, and met Niche's eye.

"Ready?"

He grinned, hand poised over the start button.

"Go!"

We ramped up our treadmills, and the bass line in my ears drowned out his laughter.

Within a few minutes, my body eased into the exercise. Next to me a masc left his treadmill, shooting me a harsh look as he moved to one farther away from us. *Whatever, masc, see if we care.* I increased my pace, reveling in the exertion, then Niche did the same to match my full run.

My pale-blue eyes stared back at me from the gym's mirrored wall. Sweat soon plastered my shirt to my chest. And for the thousandth time I analyzed every inch of myself that I could see—the shape of my jaw, the breadth of my shoulders and rib cage; they mocked me. Five years at the gym and thousands of wattcreds in testosterone in an attempt to bury the origins of my body under muscle. If only that could be enough.

Fatigue caught up to me as I ran. I glanced at Niche, who had already slowed to a walk, a hand on his side. He met my gaze and shrugged. I forced myself onward, mouthing the words that my mind screamed at the mirror. *I want to be a masc . . . I want to be a masc . . .*

When I hit my goal, I stumbled off the treadmill, panting and running my hands through short brown hair, then flicking sweat off my fingers. I scanned the gym. A few men wore wide smiles as they traveled from one group of machines to the next, their conversation lost to the music in my ears. One masc performed multiple pull-ups on a high bar, and the effortless working of his arms, the serenity of his demeanor, was beautiful. What I wouldn't give to look like him. What my body wouldn't give to be under him— No, wrong. I couldn't think that.

Niche's hand rested on my shoulder, and I pulled out an earbud. "Weights next?"

I tore my gaze from the glistening muscles of the masc on the high bar. "Yeah."

We settled at a bench, and I led Niche through our regimen. We lifted, and I focused on breathing steadily, and the comforting strain in my muscles.

A pair of mascs left their machines and started toward us. One of them was Loren, who I had ogled the past several months, his shorts revealing sculpted thighs and calves, his shirt hiding what I knew were perfect abs, the kind I wished I could have. He smirked right at me, malice shaping his cheekbones and sweat spiking his light-brown hair.

"What do we have here?" he said to his comrade. "Two little andros pretending to be men."

I couldn't say the same for Niche, but there was nothing little about me. Loren and I were almost the same height and build. I put down the weights and stood.

"Let's check out the high bars, Niche."

As I turned from them, Loren grabbed my arm. "Leaving before we get to say hello?"

I tried to pull away but his grip was tight enough that the motion simply stung my skin. His brown eyes pierced mine with a malicious edge never present in my fantasies. This probably wouldn't end how I had fantasized either.

"Yeah, I don't think so," Loren growled, yanking me toward him and grabbing my hips. The other masc laughed as Loren pressed himself against me. "This is how your kind says hello, right?"

Damn it . . . I blamed the hormones when my face flushed, and I stifled a moan. Loren shoved me toward his friend, who twisted one of my arms behind my back before I had gotten my bearings.

"Damn, you should have seen his face!" Loren's friend exclaimed. "I think he likes you."

At least he had the decency to call me "he" instead of "it." For a moment I struggled, and then he wrenched my arm and pain shot through my shoulder. I hissed to keep from shouting.

"Ember!" Niche gasped.

Loren cocked an eyebrow and knocked my forehead with hard knuckles. "What's wrong with you? Do you think you're a masc? 'Cause I doubt there's a dick in those shorts."

"There could be if you're inviting yourself," I quipped.

Loren snarled and pulled back his arm. As he swung, I clenched my abs as hard as I could, and his fist landed square in my tensed gut. *Nice try, asshole.* Pain blossomed, and I fought my captor's grip, so he twisted my arm harder.

"Let him go, please!" Niche tried. They ignored him.

"Are you het?" Loren asked, like it was illegal. With reactions like this, it may as well be.

I coughed a laugh. "What difference does it make?"

He punched me again, and again I anticipated his blow, though just barely. He narrowed his eyes and shook out his hand.

Niche let out a whine, then the bastard dashed out of sight.

"Why do you need this guy holding me down?" I challenged. "Don't think you can beat me in a fair fight?"

Loren's friend crowed with laughter.

"Know your place and stay in it, andro." Loren's fist flew at my face, and my nose exploded with pain.

Loren's friend shoved me to the floor. As their chuckling receded, I pushed myself up to hands and knees, the green tile speckled bright red.

Letting out a groan, I sat down with shaking limbs. "Niche?"

Hands gripped my shoulders, and I recoiled.

"It's just me; it's me," Niche soothed, helping me up. "They left. Let me get you a towel or something."

I wiped my nose, smearing red on my arm, and the familiar metallic flavor tainted my taste buds. Loren sure had gotten close to breaking my nose. I breathed slow and deep, trying to brush off the shock.

Niche returned with a small towel, and I cleaned up as well I could.

Then he put a hand on my arm, which I shoved off.

"Why do you act like this?" he asked. "If you keep daydreaming you're a masc, it's gonna get you killed."

Not this again, Niche. Where had my Common gone? Ah, it was under a bench. I retrieved the device and sat down.

"Why do you inject?" I countered.

He shrugged, sitting next to me. "It's what a Y negative does when he's finished his damn service for society. Become an andro."

"Well I don't inject to be an andro."

"It's a daydream, Ember. Sometimes I daydream that I can jog outside and not be fried under acid showers. It's never gonna happen."

"Yeah, it's a daydream. And when I'm living it, you can eat your words."

Niche let out a sigh and retrieved our gym bags from beside the treadmills. "Let's hit the showers."

It was definitely time to rinse off this sweat and blood. We crossed the gym and entered the changing room, then continued past changing and showering mascs. I averted my gaze so my voyeurism wouldn't start another fight. Once in the andros' section, Niche tapped his Common on a sensor outside the shower stall, then shed his clothes and got in.

I lingered near the waist-high mirror that ran the length of the changing room. My red, swollen nose looked ridiculous, and my mustache still held flecks of blood. It wasn't the first time I had seen myself like this, and it probably wouldn't be the last.

Pulling off my shirt, my lower abdomen jiggled. Like I could ever be fond of my abs when they were obscured with this loose, scarred skin. The jagged silver lightning bolts of stretch marks radiated out from my pubic hair to my belly button, the result of six surrogacies.

I resisted the urge to grab the hated skin and twist. Like that would help.

My gaze slipped up my torso, past healed gashes from fights with mascs, to the thick scars that lined the bottom edges of my pectoral muscles, where my breasts had been removed. So much of my body was a disgusting reminder, after I had tried so hard to forget. And when I pushed down my shorts, I looked away; that was a difference I didn't need to be reminded of.

A tap of my Common paid for my shower, and I soon shivered as the lukewarm water ran down me. The water washed away more than just the grime as the pain in my abdomen eased up and the knots in my muscles loosened. I'd survived another morning. That had to count for something.

My body ached when we returned to the apartment. Niche stepped to his bedroom and I to mine. I pulled the sweaty clothes out of my bag, tossing them on the piles strewn around my unkempt bed. Yeah, I'd get to laundry eventually.

But first, my least favorite part of the day: figuring out what to eat. The cupboards held only a few cans, packages of various grains, and some nutrition supplement I could lay claim to. That was it? Damn it, the in-counter chiller held mostly Niche's stuff too. I put a bowl of oatmeal in the radiator and peeled an orange as I waited for the oatmeal to heat.

Each orange slice burst with tang, bringing to mind the time Dad had taken me to one of the greenhouses he managed, and I'd gotten to try an orange right off the tree. Seeing the miles of greenhouses, learning that all our food was grown under glass, had been staggering. Now living away from home, and eating an orange that cost five wattcreds, it was impossible to forget. As had been my glimpse past the greenhouses, at the endless dead plains. I couldn't believe this world had ever been different.

Breakfast in hand, I settled at my desk to start work on a customer's circuit board. If only business wasn't so sporadic. There'd been one month where I'd earned ten thousand wattcreds, and had enjoyed the smell of fresh cooked food every night: pasta, lentils, snow peas, potatoes. Lately, I barely managed my six hundred wattcred rent. Thus the supplement to look forward to when what I had left ran out. Ah, the beauty of being self-employed.

I propped the circuit board up in a stand so I could replace outdated components with better ones using a tiny soldering gun. My vision aided by a magnifying glass, I positioned a capacitor with a pair of tweezers, then soldered its connections. As it set, I shoveled down oatmeal, bland without expensive honey.

A few more components and connections later, that project was completed. I tapped at my keyboard and donned my earpiece, then left the customer a message, cringing at the sweetness in my voice. Okay, on to the next job.

Rubbing my nose, I sat back in my chair, recalling the day with a hesitant chuckle. I shut my eyes, and memories of the mascs at the gym flashed. It didn't matter how much I was beaten down, did it? I was still attracted to them.

I shifted in my chair, and fought off a wave of arousal with a slow exhalation. My body itched for the confidence and energy that followed a testosterone injection, which mascs probably felt all the time.

But not me, since I got to be part of the lucky fifth of our population who lacked the Y-gene cluster on either of our X chromosomes. Every time I heard the word "andro" it reminded me that I was pretending, like Niche had said—daydreaming I was a masc. But this wasn't pretend for me. It was the life I wanted to lead.

There was a knock at my front door, and I rose to answer it.

"Mr. Johnson, how are you?" I said as cheerfully as I could stand.

He was about six inches shorter than me, sporting a gray wrap and a shaved head. "Is my console ready?"

Some small talk. I retrieved it from my desk: a newer Askeron 2200M, a shiny silver box that fit in the palm of my hand.

"It's now overclocked and with an advanced heat sink. You'll be pleased to see its performance rivaling a 4400."

A lump formed in my throat as I waited for him to pay me. He finally reached for his pocket, and my shoulders relaxed. "Three hundred, yes?"

"Three hundred fifty," I corrected.

He frowned. "All I have in my account is three hundred wattcreds."

I hid my sudden anger. "I'm—I'm sorry? We agreed on three fifty."

Mr. Johnson stared up at me and slowly crossed his arms. I knew this game. Father played it. He had taught me to lose.

My muscles tensed. *I could beat the shit of out you.* With a breath, I strained to keep my face calm. I couldn't afford to lose future business. "Oh . . . all right. Three hundred." I handed him the console, and he stuffed it in his pocket.

He held out his Common, and I changed his invoice fee on my own device and scanned his screen. Our Commons chimed.

He mumbled a farewell, and I shut the door, my hand on the doorknob white-knuckled. I thrust my Common back into my pocket. Three hundred . . . the bastard. That hardly gave me a profit over the cost of the upgrades.

"Did you get ripped off again?" Niche called.

"Yeah."

"You're too polite! Get some balls, eh?"

Niche knew just what would cheer me up. "I'll have you know I almost have enough for rent." I settled at my desk, considering the profits for my current jobs. "Yeah. I only need another two hundred wattcreds after getting my next shot." I rubbed the crook of my arm, an almost unconscious caress.

One of those days, indeed. Wanting to purge masc injustice from my mind, I got back to work.

The week crawled by, and sleep proved to be difficult with my shoulders aching. My nose bruised nicely, making my customers double take. Too few customers. As the week drew to a close, I wished I had an extra day. For that much more income, for a chance to have extra creds for food. Most of it would be going to the injection I was about to buy. Things usually weren't quite this bad, but all the small jobs I'd had lately didn't add up to enough.

"Did you make it?" Niche was sitting on the couch with a bowl of popped corn, watching a televid playing on a monitor in the living room.

"Yeah, I get to eat steroids this week." At least he laughed. I left the apartment, and took the inner hallways through the buildings on my street, still not wanting to brave the weather. A business outlet resided a few blocks away: past the gym, through two more apartment complexes, a ninety-degree turn into the grocery store, my eyes to the floor the entire time. Finally, I entered the two-story mall. Through the skylights, the sun shone dull yellow, obscured by light-brown clouds. Men traveled the walkway; some moved with the speed of imminent business, sashes or robes flowing in their wake, and others took their time. A few were tailed by younger children, whose fates as Y negative or male were indeterminable at that age.

My destination was FitStop, an outlet that advertised vitamins, supplements, and various accessories for the gym regulars. I'd never been able to afford testosterone from a doctor, so here I was, shopping under the counter like most andros. I trusted this shop to be clean, though. They hadn't proven me wrong thus far.

A short, buff masc named Glen idled at the counter, and he greeted me with a nod.

"The usual," I said.

"You sure I couldn't interest you in a deluxe cocktail this week?" He had been pushing this on me more often lately. As far as I was concerned, the word "cocktail" shouldn't apply to a testosterone injection, even if the stuff was synthetic. I shrugged off his words, and snatched the thumb-sized vial off the counter.

"Don't forget to tell your little andro friends about me. You know my shit works just like you want it."

I faked a laugh, nodding in agreement and farewell. He always threw that closing pitch at me, probably due to the few times Niche and I had come in here together. But Niche was the only andro I could stand to be around. There wasn't another Y negative out there that hadn't been ridiculed into forced mental oblivion. They were all dumb and horny and fake. Of course, that included myself.

Right now, however, I was itching for my injection. I returned to the apartment and shut myself in my bedroom with shaking hands. Unlike the surrogacy hormones, which had been injected into my thighs, this stuff was intravenous. That was one advantage of synthetic hormones, at least. I liked that shooting up didn't make me as sore as those shots had—completely worth the steeper learning curve.

After giving my needle a sterilizing flush, I slipped a rubber strap up my arm and tightened it above my elbow, then drew up the vial's amber contents. I bit my lip to keep myself from trembling as I eased the needle's tip under my skin and pulled gently on the plunger to test my placement. Satisfied, I pushed in the plunger, releasing my breath through my teeth as I imagined the steroid pumping through my bloodstream.

My mind calmed as I sharpened the needle before putting it back in its canvas bag, all the while my legs bouncing as shivers shot up and down my spine. These reactions were still psychological at this point, but I didn't care. The drug would do its job, and that's what mattered.

A few minutes later, I emerged from my bedroom and searched through the cabinets for some sort of dinner. Niche's, Niche's, ugh.

"Hey," Niche greeted. He had changed outfits, now wearing new pants that tied up the sides, the fabric imprinted with a faint yellow hexagon pattern.

"You going out tonight?"

He tapped at his Common with one hand and played with the strings on his hip with the other. "Probably. Zell wants to hang."

At least he wasn't bringing his boyfriend back here. The walls were too thin for that. I stared at the floor, and then idiotically opened my mouth.

"Do you . . . think I could borrow a can of—"

"No." He peered at me from the middle of the living room. "You never pay me back for whatever food you take."

"Come on, man, I haven't had a big gig in weeks. I'm looking at two days, maybe three before I have enough . . ."

"Absolutely not." He grabbed a black jacket off of the couch. "Don't make me label everything and keep count. You're the one who chose to eat steroids this week."

I went to respond, and then the first flames hit me, a blossom of pleasure and light-headedness. I gripped the counter and released my breath in a controlled hiss.

"Looks like you already ate." Niche pulled on his jacket, walking past me.

"Like you'd ever be late shooting up."

He paused at the door, and his expression hinted at pity. "No, I can't say I would. Every week on the dot. I've never missed a single one."

"Then you see where I'm at here."

He sighed. "Don't touch my stuff, Ember. I'm sorry."

The front door closed, and then the flames licked through me, adding desire to the hunger.

I satiated the latter with a glass of supplement, then settled at my desk, pinching the skin of my arm while the flames erupted into a blaze within me. So I had to live off supplement? This was worth it. I ran my hand down my arm, the tingling contact making me shudder.

This called for some music. Soon the punchy sounds of Aperture Riot hit my senses, and I mentally pushed aside the shit in my life. Asshole clients, mascs, injustice, all easily ignored so I could enjoy my weekly rush. I savored this feeling: the power, the churning confidence. This was what it felt like to be a masc. This was what I spent my creds on, even if the rush only lasted an hour. A smile curled my lips as I unbuttoned my pants and hair tickled my fingertips. The steroids hadn't helped my pseudo that much. But I could still get off just fine.

CHAPTER 2

Reality hit me early the next morning with the growling of my stomach. I lasted through the morning's gym run, repair projects, and halfway through my client calls before I slammed down my headset, marched into the kitchen, and stared at Niche's food in the cabinet. He was at work. Would he really notice if something went missing?

I picked up an apple, heavy and shiny, its skin swirling red and green. *Would he really notice...?*

Damn it, this was embarrassing. But a few more days without a solid meal would start to wreck my build. There was an easy way to prevent the muscle loss, though arguably, it would be far more embarrassing than stealing my roommate's food.

A groan escaped me. "I could call my parents."

I could already hear Father's harsh lecturing... but if enduring it resulted in enough wattcreds to last me a few weeks, it was worth it, right? I paced with arms across my chest, my breathing deep. It was worth it. Or maybe Niche could— *No. Just call them.*

So I did. And then Father insisted on talking to me in person, and Dad decided he'd make an elaborate dinner as it had been so long since I had visited. This was a mistake. A horrible, futile... but fuck if Dad wasn't a good cook.

After rushing through the rest of my client calls, I changed into cleaner clothes: a blue tank with the silver pattern of circuitry decaled on it, dark-silver pants with black stitching and a black drawstring in front. The old clubbing outfit looked much newer than the rest of my wardrobe.

Out in the apartment complex entryway, I eyed the hazy sun through the front door's windows. I zipped up my jacket and entered the muggy atmosphere, an uncomfortably hot breeze rustling my hair.

With a swipe of my Common, the last of my wattcreds went on the bus fare to get within running distance of my parents' neighborhood. The crowded bus was standing-room only, with a disproportionate number of andros accompanying me on the ride. If we were paid better, we'd have vehicles; damn how I'd love to have my own car. I could do house-call repairs, and just thinking of the income made me angry.

Half an hour later, I stepped off the bus and jogged down the street, suppressing the instinct to choke out the thick, wet air I forced into my lungs. The dull turquoise sky gave me some comfort though: no rain clouds. Familiar locales summoned memories that tightened my chest. There's where I punched my first masc, at the age of seven. His friends threw me into that storm ditch around the corner. And there's the steps of the middle school, where my friend Jacquel tried to kiss me. I had been eleven, already confused and frustrated.

I turned down my parents' block, slowing to a walk. The houses where my elementary school friends used to live came and went, though now with a lack of toys tucked under the front porch. It had been only a year and a half since I had visited, but these memories were like opening old wounds. I approached my old house—two stories of acid-etched metal with a solar panel roof—and knocked on the door.

My younger brother Steph answered. He smiled and beckoned me in as he caressed his swollen abdomen, his pale-green shirt stretched tight. The doctors were going to confine him to a hospital wing any day now. The sight of that round belly tied my gut in knots.

The house hadn't changed—still the same narrow hallway, the dull metal walls with their peach hue. The doorway to the living room revealed the same yellow-brown couch and a newer, larger monitor. I realized I hadn't yet said hello.

"Your hair's getting long," I said. His brown hair, a few shades lighter than mine, was almost to his eyes, and shaggy in the back. Why did Father let him wear it so long? Probably Dad had insisted he wear it as he wanted.

"You . . . you look great," Steph said, and I sensed envy in his voice. Now that Sable was done with his surrogacies and had started injecting, Steph was the only pure Y negative in the family. He still had to deal with our youngest brother, Valence, a genetic male, as a constant, mocking reminder of what he could have been. I was damn thankful I got out of the house before Valence got older. I wouldn't have been able to take it. Hopefully he wouldn't be here tonight.

"Ember." Dad came into view down the hall. He wore a simple tank and pants in muted beige, along with a gentle smile. "Look at you. Business doesn't seem that bad."

I returned the smile, but muttered, "It is."

"Come in, sit down. It's so good to see you." Dad ushered me into the living room, and I eyed a platter of mixed veggies, crackers, and dip on the side table. Steph plucked a carrot from the platter and crunched down.

I chose a broccoli floret, smothering it in tan, creamy dip, and popped it in my mouth as casually as I could. Ohhh, the earthy flavor of hummus.

Dad joined me on the couch. "Tell me, how is everything? You were distraught when you called."

I swallowed down a cracker. "Well, it's like I said—"

Father joined us from the kitchen. "You've come begging to us?" He wore a red patterned shirt over dark-gray slacks, large boots clunking with his gait. His hair was much grayer than the last time I had seen him.

He scanned me, and I stood as he approached, inclining my head to meet his gaze. Looking him in the eyes was the only way my brothers and I had learned to satisfy his desire for our attention.

"You haven't visited in almost two years," Father said. "You say your self-employment isn't as fruitful as you had hoped."

"Alex, please," Dad tried, still on the couch. Steph took a few delicacies from the platter and retreated, watching from the kitchen doorway.

Father exhaled and continued. "Yet your desire for assistance has a fundamental flaw."

I narrowed my eyes, unsure where he was going with this.

"I wouldn't dream of helping you when you're using as heavily as you are."

My jaw dropped. "You think I'm trying to spike? I'm not stupid enough to get hospitalized!"

"Yeah? I'd like to see a regular andro get muscle like that."

This was about as close to a compliment as I would ever receive from my father. But his intent was not kind.

"Muscle like this is from hard work, Father. Hours a day. I'm not spiking."

"That's hours a day you could be spending with your business!" he countered. "Or better yet, getting a real job with a steady income!"

"I'd like you to show me a company that will give a Y negative the same wage as a masc," I said, breaking eye contact to glance at Dad and Steph. Dad was shaking his head but remained silent. Steph simply clutched his abdomen and stared at the floor. Like they usually did when Father got like this.

"And you think being self-employed fixes that? I'm shocked you get business at all."

"The quality of my work tends to override the mutation of my chromosomes."

"Clearly not enough."

Dad must have seen my lips curl into a snarl, and finally intervened. "He's not here to be patronized."

Father threw his hands up and turned away from me, and Dad cleared his throat.

"Let's just have a nice dinner and then we can continue discussing this tonight, okay?"

Father didn't respond. He strode past us to the hall, and ascended the stairs.

Dad exhaled and stood, smoothing out his shirt. "I'm going to finish dinner. Ten more minutes."

As he left, I collapsed onto the couch, and Steph sat next to me. I stuck another floret in my mouth.

"This was a mistake," I mumbled.

"Dad's so happy you're here though; he hasn't stopped talking about you since you called."

"So he's been inadvertently riling Father up all day."

"Pretty much."

I laughed, and Steph grinned for a moment before he scrunched his face and put a hand on his abdomen.

"Big kick?" I asked. He nodded. "How far along are you?"

"Eight and a half months."

The memories came over me too suddenly to stop them: The hospital rooms, the blinding pain, the exertion, exhaustion. The infant's cries before it was ushered out the door to masc parents. The hormone injections to ready my body for the next implantation. The ache in my gut, where something was lost that I could never get back.

"But this is my last one!" Steph added.

I made myself smile. "Then the fun really starts."

"Dinner, boys!" Dad called, just like when I had lived here. Steph and I meandered into the kitchen, and I was greeted with familiar polished metal countertops and dark alloy cabinets. The school art on the wall around the table was gone, replaced with designs painted on strips of fabric. Then someone bounded down the stairs.

"What the fuck, Ember's here."

And there was Valence, an inch taller than me and with a face like Father's when he was young. A real masc, with wide shoulders and a full beard.

"Duh, where have you been all day?" Steph lamented, getting a plate off the counter.

Valence approached and squeezed my bicep. "Nice."

I glared at him. "I thought you went to college."

"He comes home some nights because he can't cook for shit," Steph declared. I got in line behind him to fill my plate with flatbread, beans, and sautéed bell peppers and tomatoes. My first well-rounded meal in weeks.

"Steph, don't swear." Dad sat at the kitchen table, which held the same handblown glass vase it had always carried.

"You didn't tell Val not to swear, and he's younger!"

Dad hummed innocently, and Steph and I joined him at the table. Valence soon followed.

"Father's shut in his office," Valence announced, casting a sideways glance at me. "He that mad at you already?"

"I'm just that good at getting him mad." I picked up my precariously filled flatbread and took as large a bite as I could manage. The flavors exploded on my taste buds—hearty earth, bitter plant, smooth and salty and seasoned—a moan buzzed my shut mouth. Steph giggled.

"What?"

"You're acting like you haven't eaten in a week."

I took another bite, succumbing to caloric ecstasy again.

"A week, Ember?" Dad asked.

Valence chuckled. "He's a supplement-chugging andro, what do you think he can actually afford after shooting up?"

Dad dropped his silverware with a clatter. "Valence!"

I bit my tongue and tensed.

"That's the problem isn't it?" We all stopped and turned toward the voice as Father entered the kitchen. "What he can afford. Isn't that right, Devin?"

Dad cleared his throat. "Your father—and, well, your brother—has a point."

I stammered into action, eyeing the rest of the dinner on my plate. "The issue is not affordability, it's the economy. If I get the kind of business I used to—"

"Ember," Dad cut in, "have you considered decreasing your usage? At least until your business picks back up?"

My shock at Dad's words escalated to anger when he gave Father a shrug.

"Do you think using is a luxury? Like owning a car? Do you truly believe I should let my entire identity erode because of a slump in business?"

"It was just a suggestion," Dad pleaded.

"It's not an option. You both have no idea how hard it is to live as an andro, let alone a Y negative." I gestured to Steph. "Yet you fucking raised three of us. I can't believe you've kept yourselves so blind to what we endure."

"Oh, you think it was clear skies the whole time we raised you?" Father snarled, and Dad gasped. "Driving you to doctors' visits constantly? Dealing with your mood swings?"

Valence sat back in his chair, watching the show with a smile on his face. I forced myself to look away from him, and met Father's eyes. "Don't you fucking dare."

"Alex, stop it," Dad demanded as I spoke, but Father wouldn't be deterred.

"I know what you're going to say, Ember. How about the wattcreds we were paid to compensate for having negatives? It all went right back into caring for you. And you—what about the compensation for your surrogacies? Where is that? Straight into your veins the moment you left home?"

My throat seized as I struggled to respond. Dad stood and glared at Father, his pale eyes fiercer than I had ever seen them. "You told me our discussion would remain civilized tonight. How is this at all civilized?"

"He's a grown man and should be able to support himself! You think my father ever would have helped me? So why should I help him?"

"You know damn well why," Dad said through clenched teeth. I couldn't believe this. Was he suggesting they help me merely because I was Y negative?

"Do you want to know why I'm not helping you?" Father returned his attention to me. "Because you aren't willing to make sacrifices. If you can't support your alternative lifestyle, you have to give it up."

"Alternative! Fuck! You make it sound like I have a choice. I didn't have a choice about that"—I thrust a finger at Steph's belly—"so I don't have a choice about this." I held out my arms.

"Anyone would be honored to help mankind as you have," Dad said.

I shook my head, trying not to let out the desperate laughter within me. "Don't give me that surrogacy propaganda crap. No one would choose to be Y negative! And you two are walking evidence no one wants to bear one—you kept having kids until your genes gave you a male!"

Valence coughed a laugh, then gave me a smug look. Just two steps and I could punch him in the face. Two steps . . .

"Ember, that's not true," Dad insisted, but his heart clearly wasn't behind his words.

I released a sigh and glanced at Steph, who sat quietly, like the good little Y negative he was expected to be. "Have they not stopped acting like this?" I asked. He nodded, his cheeks flushing. "Fuck, I'm not dealing with this."

I shoved the rest of my dinner down and strode toward the front door still chewing. After I pulled on my jacket, Dad put a hand on my shoulder.

"I'm going home," I said, more harshly than I meant to.

"If you truly need the wattcreds, I'll transfer them to you."

"Forget it, Dad."

"I'm serious. Do you need a thousand?"

I shut my eyes. After all that, I couldn't request so much from them. "I can scrape by with a hundred." Given the income from my current projects, I was short that much from making rent and getting my next injection. It wouldn't be planning ahead. I'd need some good business, or supplement would continue to sustain me.

I opened my eyes to Dad tapping at his Common. Mine chimed.

"I love you, Ember."

Mumbling a reply, I pushed the door open, stepping out into warm twilight.

The "good business" remained beyond my reach over the next few weeks. At the mercy of the ebb and flow of the market, I barely kept up. With my work hours dwindling, I spent long sessions at the gym, running out my frustrations, cursing at my reflection, and burning calories I couldn't replace. I drank down chalky supplement, glass after glass, but it only took the edge off the hunger. Niche noticed the difference in me as my mentality worsened, and he grew even more distant than usual. I kept myself from stealing his food. Call it stubborn pride.

The afternoon before I was due to inject, my console beeped that I had an incoming call. I greeted the client with far too much excitement.

"Uh, hello . . ." the customer responded. "I'm looking to upgrade my hard drive to a point six?"

"No problem, bring your console over and I'll have it done in a day. That'll run you two fifty."

The customer grunted. "I'm pretty sure I'd only be spending one fifty at the Tronic downtown."

Yes, because he'd have to install it himself and would be buying a used part. Fucking Tronic, making me have to cut prices. But that was the name of the game. The fear I thought had vanished when my phone rang rattled in my empty gut. "How about I make you a deal: two-hundred wattcreds. You know Tronic would charge you more than that to install it too."

The customer hummed. "You're quite right."

"What's your name?"

"Kat Sanders. That's Kat with a K. I'll be over soon."

I hung up and buried my face in my hands. By the time someone knocked at my door, I hadn't moved. Niche had just walked into the kitchen, and he leaned on the counter to watch.

I donned my fake smile and pulled myself to my feet. *You can get through this, just keep smiling.*

As I scanned the man standing in the doorway, I raised my eyebrows. He was an andro, wearing a purple, loose-fitting robe that cinched at the waist, which emphasized wide hips and skinny arms. His jaw was even less angled than mine, and he either couldn't or didn't want to grow a beard to hide it. He looked me over, the same air of surprise gracing his features.

Perhaps our common origin would allow him some compassion when paying me.

"You called about your hard drive?"

His eyes snapped back to my face, and he nodded, procuring his computer from a shoulder bag. "Can you have it ready by tomorrow evening?"

"Of course. I'll need fifty as a deposit." He frowned briefly, but then paid me.

"Until tomorrow." He nodded again in farewell. I spent an extra moment watching him walk away, his hips swaying in that characteristic Y-negative fashion.

"Well that's good at least," Niche announced, and I shut the door and met his eyes.

"Yeah, business."

"No, he likes you."

I shook my head and laughed. Niche stepped up to me, his arms crossed.

"You would feel better if you went out with him."

"How many times do I have to tell you I'm het?"

"Don't be absurd," he said. "The sooner you give up on that nonsense, the happier you'll be in life."

A hissed retort gurgled in my throat, but then I thought about it. "Okay, want to make a bet out of this?"

He narrowed his eyes at me, but a smile tugged at his mouth.

"Pay for my next injection," I said. "He asks me on a date, I pay you back and go out with him. He doesn't, I don't."

"That's a lot of creds. I'll only agree if you actually go out with him if he asks—no backing down, got it?"

"I'll go, I swear." Ugh, what was I getting myself into?

Niche pulled out his Common, and tapped at it for a moment, then mine chimed.

"You couldn't afford your next injection, huh?"

"Not until after the andro pays me." I glanced at my Common—he had transferred a hundred and fifty wattcreds into my account. The creds were beautiful, sitting there. Too bad they weren't really mine.

He sighed, scrolling through his Common. "You've been miserable for weeks. Don't think I haven't noticed. I hope you have some damned fun."

"Yeah, fun," I murmured, as Niche sauntered into the living room.

The idea of going out with an andro made my skin crawl. But it wasn't like I hadn't before. It wasn't like I couldn't again. As long as I was high enough to forget the truth.

Well, I had some shopping to do. After a short jog past the mall, I entered a wholesale electronics distributor and approached Trace, a younger salesman who was a bit shorter than me, the bright yellow sash across his chest awkward on his thin frame. Our common professions had allowed a tentative friendship to form over the years. He noticed me and started to smile, but the smile faltered.

"Hey, Trace," I said, stopping at his counter and propping my elbows on it.

"You got an order for me?" he said blandly, and I hesitated at his distant demeanor. Why did I try being friends with an exin when his mood swings were just as bad as a Y negative's? Exins might be lucky enough to have the Y genes, but they were screwed over by faulty X chromosome inactivation. Maybe his mood today was a result of that.

"Just a point six hard drive," I responded. "Business has been slow."

"Sorry to hear that." He checked the shelving behind him and brought me a small box. I passed my Common over the scanner, leaving just Niche's creds in my account. Trace sighed and broke eye contact. He shifted from foot to foot, and finally I gave in.

"Hey, are you all right?" I asked, my voice low.

Trace shook his head, staring at the counter between us. "I'm fine, it's just been a rough week."

"Anything you want to talk about?"

He met my gaze. "Next time, Ember. You have a good day."

With a shrug, I left the shop. Exins often didn't like talking about their condition, especially if it was bad enough that they had to shoot up. "Take care of yourself."

I headed across the mall to get my steroids, my mood tainted by Trace's. Niche's words echoed back: being het was nonsense. Yeah, I had gotten enough black eyes and bruised ribs to prove that true. But I'd also sucked enough dicks to know it wasn't unanimous. I wasn't alone.

Maybe one day even I'd believe that.

exploring my freedom; I'd forget what those andros were until I'd pass my hands over soft stomachs and between legs and feel myself. I had known it wasn't what I wanted. But their own hands would travel and fingers would penetrate wet flesh, and I'd be too high to care.

I pulled Kat closer with the firm grip of my hand below his navel. My tongue started right below his ear, sweet plums and tangy grapes teasing my taste buds as his conversation waned and he rubbed my outer thighs.

"Sorry guys . . ." he said, his voice fuzzy beneath my inebriation and the buzzing of the music. "Give us an hour . . . maybe two . . ."

With a surge of adrenaline, I sat up and shoved Kat against the couch. He shuddered beneath my hands, and as I kissed him he arched his back and pulled me toward him with eagerness I hadn't experienced since my last time in a club. Eventually, I let him catch his breath while I licked his cheeks, his eyelids. He moaned and the sound both startled me and urged me on.

"Kat . . ." I whispered. He looked up from my onslaught and met my gaze with half-shut eyes. "I have a bit of a fetish."

"Go on."

"Uh . . ." I smiled. "You happen to be a boy who will . . . take it?"

He shivered beneath me and gave me a smile. We snorted another set of lines, and then he led me away from the group. Through blurry vision I noticed other andro pairs scattered around the booth. None of them had removed clothing, but there were unbuttoned flies here and pushed-up shirts there. I'd say I had missed this, but it would clearly be the drugs and my arousal talking.

Kat gestured at a vacant couch, and I took a seat. He straddled me and eased my index finger through a loop of the tie on his pants. I yanked it loose. As it unraveled, I wasn't surprised when the lacework curled between his thighs, stopping far enough up his backside for him to spread his legs unhindered once I pulled the cord through its holes. Dark hair only partly obscured a dainty pseudo and folds of skin. The sight didn't necessarily turn me on, but I would make it work. He slipped off of me and lay back on the couch, so I went with him. The lingering paint in my mouth sweetened the taste of him as I listened to his soft moans, and after a few moments of him playing with my hair, I sat up and searched my pockets. I plopped a strap-on onto his chest, and he exhaled. The toy sported only a moderately sized member, but andros usually couldn't handle much more.

"You were serious!" he breathed. I simply smiled. Next best thing, right? I got onto my knees on the floor, and Kat sat in front of me.

"Go easy on me?" he asked, his anticipation or the drug making his tone erratic. "I haven't done this very often, I don't know how well I'd—" I shut him up with my mouth against his, and simultaneously I unlaced my pants.

The moment I got the toy in place, excitement pulsed through me. I flipped a switch, and the vibrator's buzzing was immediately lost to the booth's music, though the sensation tickled down my thighs and all through my abdomen. He wrapped his legs around my waist, and as I pushed the toy into him, he let out a startled cry. I eased deeper, pulling his hips toward me.

I kept my pace slow, the vibrations making me shiver with each movement. Thrusting my pelvis against his thighs, feeling the warmth of his body, greatly pleased some carnal part of me. The part of me that yearned so badly to feel like a masc, to be a masc. But as the J-seven high swirled and faded, Kat's groaning and occasional swears fueled the self-hatred writhing in my core. There was no enjoyment in my motion, no connection between the arousal and my mind. I didn't care about the andro beneath me, and he didn't care about me either. This was just bodily pleasure covering up the hollow ache.

Regardless, I continued. Soon Kat switched from scratching down my arms and under my shirt to rubbing his pseudo in time with my motion. After a few more minutes, he grabbed a fistful of my shirt and yanked me down. I panted into the crook of his neck while his staccato voice buzzed in my ear. I kept up my pace, riding that sweet edge of oblivion until his legs squeezed my waist and his free hand dug nails into my shoulder, clenching in time with his excited swears, his body's tremors. When his throes subsided, he sucked in a breath and gave me a wide smile.

Dizziness muddled my return gesture, and I flopped next to Kat and struggled to unclasp the strap-on's buckles. He grasped my hands, placed them at my sides, then finished removing the toy before shimmying my pants farther down my thighs. I caught a silly grin on his face as he stooped low enough for me to feel his breath between my legs. His slick tongue twirled against me, and I lost it within moments. My head slammed into the couch's back. I pulled his hair, I screeched.

After I calmed, he lifted his head and laughed. "Ah, a screamer." His thumbs traced small circles on my inner thighs. "That was too fast. Think I can squeeze another one out of you?"

I growled and shoved his head back down.

"Ember, you wanna go to the gym?"

I blinked, my head throbbing. Damn it, not a hangover. After lurching out of bed, I stumbled to my door. "Yeah, lemme get dressed..."

"Hungover?" Niche smiled at me.

I rubbed my eyes. "Yeah." I fumbled for my gym shorts and running shoes.

"You must have had fun; you didn't even give him the chance to lick you clean."

I emerged from my room and turned into the bathroom. Half of my face was a greenish hue with smudges of navy. Some of Kat's purple was smeared around my mouth too. I dampened a towel and washed the paint off. If only I could wash away the memories too.

"Well? Good time?"

I shrugged, heading toward the kitchen to try to cure my headache with a glass of supplement. "I guess. Good sex, mostly."

"You're not even going to try to get to know the guy?"

I rolled my eyes at him.

"I swear, you've had more one-night stands since I've known you than I've had dates my whole life."

I finished my glass. "Never more than a stand."

"And whose fault is that?"

We stepped down the hall. Mascs' faults, for not wanting me. The world's fault, for making them feel that way. My fault for getting off on denial and boring myself deeper into this hole.

I couldn't do this to myself again. I couldn't give in to temptation just to hate the consequences. But at the same time, I couldn't keep on under the pressure, with a fruitless job and empty gut. A vacant bed and heart.

What choices did I have here? How could I keep pushing forward when everything remained the same?

PART 2

JESS

xx

CHAPTER 4

his was the last gift Dad would ever give me: a cup of water in my hand—distilled water from his now-cremated body. My brothers whispered to each other as Uncle Cal spoke to the gathering. Father, my brothers, my uncles and cousins, all held identical delicate cups. The rest of Dad's reclaimed water would flow to the edges of Kansas City to water the crops.

I had thought I could handle all this, but knowing he would reenter the system, help our world grow, got to me. I blinked back tears. *Why did you have to leave us? Father doesn't understand half your research; he hardly cares enough to understand me.* Heath squeezed my waist, and I leaned against him.

Uncle Cal gazed at the cremation chamber as his words faded, the chamber's heat still emanating into the hall around us. Lit above by skylights, the crematorium walls were painted with geometric shapes and gradients in purple, blue, and green. I appreciated the vivid colors offered to grievers, though I wasn't sure how much it helped. The celebrant idled to the side of the chamber, wearing pale red fabric that wrapped across his chest and draped to the floor. He held a dark metal urn, polished to a shine, and stood in silence.

Father's voice caught my attention, and most of us looked his way. You don't run a corporation unless you can turn heads.

"I'd say we were no more than Jess's age," he said, gesturing his cup in my direction. The last few days had left him with dark circles under his eyes. "So we've both snorted ourselves into orbit. Tori gets the great idea for us to drive across town and watch the sun set over the greenhouses. We drive off, giggling the whole way 'cause we can't stop ourselves."

Uncle Boyd snickered. "And then a cop pulls you over."

A smile tugged Father's stubbly cheeks, and the expression looked odd on his usually cold and serious face. "Nope. We're at the last intersection before the edge of town. Tori runs a red light, and out of nowhere comes this bus. I scream; he cranks the wheel; and his truck swerves, misses the bus, skids through the intersection and stops facing the same direction we started from. I can still hear Tori's voice, whooping and hollering that he didn't kill us, honking the horn and revving the engine." Father paused, shaking his head. "Finally he looks at me, his eyebrow cocked, and says, 'And you thought this was a boring idea.'"

The men laughed, and I couldn't help but smile too. Father waited for them to calm. "Enough of my asides. Go ahead, Roan."

Dad's youngest brother raised his glass toward the cremator. "Brother, you were a gentleman of the finest order. You got caught screwing the neighbor boy at fifteen; I came home countless times in high school to find you had ditched, yet still you passed with higher grades than I ever could have. Then you broke a lot of men's hearts before settling with this schmuck and coercing him into raising three kids with you."

Father chuckled and clasped his shoulder.

"You taught me to work hard and fast in order to still have time for fun. I'll miss you," Uncle Roan finished.

Father cleared his throat, then his gaze met mine. "Jess, please say a few words."

I swallowed, and beside me, Heath shifted on his feet. What do you say at your dad's funeral? What do you say after three months of watching him wither from cancer, knowing he was going to die before his time?

"Dad," I started, my throat threatening to shut tight. I could do this like they could, yeah? "Dad. I think I can forgive you for all the times you gave my clothes and toys to Jayne and Joule. And for the tough curfew." Father chuckled, and I breathed with relief. "But really, I want to thank you. You encouraged me to follow in your footsteps, you taught me everything you knew—not just how to shave." I smiled, tugging at the hair on my chin. "You showed me the Outskirts, the beauty of the wilderness. I will keep walking where you stopped, making footprints in dirt and marsh and grass. Maybe one day I can live up to your legacy."

I didn't know what else to say so I let my voice die, and a tear ran down my cheek. I stiffened and wiped it away. Father embraced me, patting me hard on the back. Then Jayne stepped forward and held up his glass to speak, and I let Heath hold my hand, his fingers entwining with mine.

Joule went next, and his voice cracked as he spoke. As he finished, we all turned back toward Father.

"You want a serious speech now?" Father straightened the dark-blue sash around his shoulders. "All right. Tori, we had thirty wonderful years together. You were a fantastic parent to our three sons, and your research has helped us all more than we can yet tell. Most importantly to me, you were always there. You told me you loved me every day, and I will always love you too."

The tenderness and sadness in Father's face amazed me. I had never seen him so human. Definitely not the stark businessman he usually was.

The celebrant raised his head and gazed out at our group. "We are all here on borrowed time, with borrowed resources." His gentle voice hushed what murmuring remained. "But our lives here are no less crucial. Tori Cameron contributed to mankind in many ways, making the most of what he borrowed from the universe. He is part of the cycle again, the same water and energy that has been stored and used countless times over countless millennia. Let part of what sustained him sustain you now."

"To Tori," Father said, raising his glass to his mouth.

"To Dad," I echoed, the others following suit. I squeezed Heath's hand tight and tipped the cup, the familiar blandness of distilled water hitting my senses. His water. Dad's. As Joule collected the cups from each person, Heath kissed the stubble on my cheek. I breathed deep. I didn't want to cry.

The celebrant held the urn toward Father and spoke. "May the rest of Tori's sustenance fuel lives and perpetuate love."

Father nodded and then clutched the urn to his chest. "Always."

It was over. Family members left in groups and couples, their voices mingling, mixed with laughter as the stories of Dad's life started up again amongst them. I turned to Heath and buried my face against his chest. It wasn't manly to cry, but I wanted to believe there was an exception to every rule.

The months of waiting, dreading that this day would come, now behind me. What came next? Getting on with my life?

How?

The professor droned while I doodled at the bottom of my notes, sketching grasses and shrubs and hills. My ambition was out there, not here in class. Especially today when I was already well versed with the material. The screen flashed with the next economics subject, and I pretended to jot more notes. A twisted tree slowly formed on a hillside, leafless, reaching, struggling in the sunshine, drowning in acid. I wanted to go back to the wild. The end of the month couldn't come soon enough.

As the professor discussed his last subject, students around me began to fidget. I switched off my tablet and slipped the stylus in its slot.

"I find it necessary to remind some of you that the final is in two weeks," the professor added, the screen now showing a calendar. "On Wednesday we will cover the last of our material, and next week will be review sessions."

Good. I didn't want to go, and wouldn't have to. Though I wouldn't tell Father that, of course. I filed out of the classroom with the others, and we scattered in the glass hallway, the sunlight blocked at regular intervals by the solar panels above the glass. Taking my time walking to my last class of the day, I wished my motivation would return. Men passed by me—when had the fashion trend become wearing skintight shirts? If I could tell whether they shaved their chest hair, they needed the next size up. I chuckled to myself, and shuffled into the class, preparing myself for an hour and a half of doodling. It was physics, usually one of my favorite subjects. But I wasn't with it today. I just wasn't here.

Only ten minutes passed before I had to get out of there. I strode down the hall, in shadow, light, shadow, light. Outside, hot, sticky air greeted me. I mounted my electric scooter; maybe Heath could help me find myself.

The central office of Father's company wasn't too far from campus. A few miles past apartments and businesses, and then through a security gate where the guard knew me well enough that I didn't have to show identification. The sun glinted off custom solar panels in the shape of the letters *CamCo R&D* mounted on the office's front face. I parked next to Father's car, a bad idea if he happened to leave early. But that was unlikely, and I wouldn't be long.

Without the wind blowing past me on the bike, the warm humidity smothered, seeping through fabric and hair with just the slightest sting of acid. Striding around to one of the back entrances, I swiped myself in with my Common.

Heath sat at his console, one leg sticking out into the aisle as he typed away. I walked by, purposely catching my foot on his shin. His head shot up, and then he smirked.

All I had to do was raise my eyebrows at him, and his holoscreen was off in an instant.

"Let's ditch this joint," he whispered as he walked past me. I followed him out, some of the other workers raising their heads as I walked by. They recognized me as Mr. Cameron's son, all right—hopefully they wouldn't tell Father about me ditching class.

Back in the sun, Heath hooked his fingers in my front pockets and pulled me to him. "So we're both skipping the hard work and going straight to some hard play?"

"Can we eat first?"

Heath smiled, and his mustache tickled my lips as we kissed. "Fine."

At this time of day we were fools to be outside, as attested by the forming sweat stains under my arms. I drove my scooter with Heath squeezing my hips. And after I parked, he tried to hold my hand, but something about the implied commitment made me stick my hands in my pockets. So he went for my back pocket instead, occasionally squeezing, making my pulse accelerate.

We entered a small café, the air cool and fragrant with spices. A short, skinny andro hardly out of his teens seated us, and asked for our order. And with the voice he had, you'd think he hadn't started injecting yet. Heath's brow furrowed as we gave our requests, and when the andro left, he turned back to me.

"Hey. How are you?"

I squirmed in my seat. "I don't know. I want to say I miss him but. . ."

"But what? You can damn well say it and you know it."

Yeah, I knew it. But that didn't ease the tension in my chest.

Heath shrugged. "Come on now, be real. If it were my dad? I lost it bad enough when—"

"Yeah." I didn't want him to get started. "At this point I just want to keep moving forward. Finish my credentials and my internship."

"Your father will love having you at the labs all day."

That was the understatement of the year.

Our food arrived, and Heath dug into his pasta with the fervor I had come to expect from him. It was the same way he tackled a line of J-seven, the same way he pushed me down in bed. I ate slowly, watching the muscles of Heath's jaw flex under blond stubble.

At the labs all day . . . it's what Father thought I wanted. Dad had been the one to teach me to care for the environment stations, where I had found my true passion. Just a few more weeks, and I'd be back, as I intended to be every season for years to come. As long as Father let me.

CHAPTER 5

Heath played video games as I tried to study. He broke my concentration with grunts or outright laughter, the rhythmic tapping of his fingers on the control pad barely audible. There was something about the way he slouched in his chair that gave me enough of an erection that it was getting difficult to keep studying.

Once again I felt a void that I could only explain with the notion that I didn't want to commit to someone. He was a good friend and a good lay. That's all.

How could I tell him that?

I renewed my focus on the ecology of the northern regions. Not even thirty seconds later Heath threw his control pad across the couch with a shower of swears.

"Finished already?" I took his mumble to mean yes, and shut off my tablet and joined him on the couch. His console's screen flashed *game over* above a space scene depicting colorful ships and planets.

"Get over here," he muttered. That's all he really had to say to make me reach out to him. He slipped a hand up my jaw and kissed me hard. I gripped the fabric of his shirt in tight fists while he struggled with the tie of my pants, and my skin grew hot as my mind narrowed its focus. I needed Heath's ferocity, to forget about class and forget about the labs and forget about Dad.

I broke away from him long enough to manage the word "bedroom" before his tongue found mine again. He let out a half moan that buzzed my mouth, and then we stood, leaving my pants in a heap on the tile. We broke contact and traveled the few steps to his bedroom, ditching shirts and boxers on the way. I collapsed onto his bed, and he climbed on top of me with that smirk on his face, the one that hopelessly turned me on. A wave of excitement drew me close to him, and for a while we kissed, hands pulling chest hair and erections pushing against each other's thighs. He shed my stress and worries as his skin slipped against mine.

"Damn, I needed this," I breathed.

"You and I both." He sucked at the stubble under my jaw and my eyes fluttered shut. Then he yanked at my hips, which I had quickly learned meant "get on your knees." So I did.

Heath was the first man I had been with who put himself so consistently on top. However, I didn't mind; his experience made him damn good at it. He stayed gentle while my body adjusted to him, and picked up the pace as soon as I craved it. And one of his hands cupped and squeezed and tugged as the delicious burning of his thrusts increased in intensity. I knelt before him, moving my hips in opposition to his, my face buried in a pillow, moaning.

"Right there, right there . . ."

Definitely a damn good lay. His grip around my dick tightened and his synchronous motions unraveled me like acid-worn fabric. I fell apart, and he shoved me down and kept up his rhythm even after I wet his hand. I think he liked when I came first, because my body was tight and he could grip my hips with both hands and lose himself. It didn't take him that much longer, and I pushed against him, reveling in his nails digging into my skin and the soft groans escaping his throat.

We separated, crumpling onto the bed in a tangle of limbs. Our gazes met, and he ran his fingers through my sweaty hair and smiled. I woke up an hour later to his snores, with that hollowness in my gut again. An uneasiness that led me to just lie there and stare at his bedroom wall. And that was how our relationship went.

My father typed at a console, and the holoscreen projected onto one of the walls so we could all see. He opened a video-chat program, and as usual, it took forever to connect. A windowed wall to the right of the screen showed a fourth-floor view of buildings covered in gleaming solar panels. I blinked away the glare, and caught Heath raising an eyebrow at me from across the metal table.

Finally, two faces joined us on videoconference from Atlanta: Gene and Kacy. As they smiled and waved, I felt punched in the gut—with as long as they, especially Gene, had known Dad, they should have been at the funeral. But the weather between Atlanta and us hadn't allowed it. Gene had practically raised me alongside Dad out in the wild, and seeing him brought Dad's absence from this table into sharp focus.

Gene had been promoted into Dad's role as chief field ecologist a few seasons ago when Dad retired from field work. With Kacy as a seasoned mechanical technician, and Heath's networking skills, I was the only one in the room without full credentials, besides being the president's oldest son. But unlike any of CamCo's interns, I knew what the damn I was doing, especially when it involved maintaining the environmental stations.

"We're rapidly approaching another opportunity period," Father proclaimed. "Preliminary weather reports are looking good, and we're hoping for mostly clear skies. Gene's told me he's drafted up the goals for this season's field research. Go ahead, Gene."

With his voice distorted from the usually shoddy signal, Gene described what we would be looking for as we trudged through the marshes. A few times he cut out entirely—couldn't Father's techs get a better connection to Atlanta? Gene would go over his itinerary again when we got there, so I didn't fuss over the details. I kicked Heath's shoes lightly, and he puckered his lips and stroked his beard. *Damn faker, he's paying as much attention as I am.*

Father's chief technician talked about preparing hardware and software upgrades for us, which was always a good thing. However, there was a caveat this year, and soon enough, Father brought it up.

"We need to hire a new computer specialist for your group," he said airily. I knew what he wanted: for me to volunteer myself. But his not-so-subtle method of egging me to work on my leadership skills just grated my ears, especially when he had yet to invite me to any executive meetings where I might learn what a leader actually does. However, in this case, I did want to choose who would join us.

"I think I can handle hiring someone." If only I could say these things with more confidence.

Father raised an eyebrow at me, and I shrunk in my chair as the weight of his gaze soaked in. He nodded. "That's a great idea. You're on it, Jess."

Heath kicked my shin. I met his eyes, and he opened his mouth enough for me to see him twist his tongue. It was our way of making fun of the other person for kissing ass. In return I clenched my jaw hard. *Stop it or I'll bite that tongue off.*

Meanwhile, the chief technician was rattling off the job requirements for the new specialist. I scribbled them into my tablet. Heath straightened in his chair and stared at the table, his silliness sobered.

For Heath, time at the stations likely meant a vacation from reality, even if he still had his work duties. But for me, the stations allowed for the most real experiences a man could face. The land, the elements. The disaster-that-was lurking in forgotten history, evident by the acid, by what creatures remained.

But this year was different: Heath and I were a couple now. I didn't want to know how that would change things. The few years we had gone together, something crazy had always happened. Last year especially. Something crazy would probably happen this year too, sure as rainfall.

Just a few more days until finals, and what was I doing? Not studying enough. And not finding a replacement computer technician either. I wasn't sure where the time had gone. It had passed, though, as my beard had grown out a bit. Heath caressed my jaw, and I felt as much as heard his nails scratching through coarse hair.

"The new guy at work is pretty hot," he said, one hand continuing to caress as the other tapped at his Common on his lap. "You can tell he works out. Very nice ass."

I grunted in response. Typical Heath.

"You've seen him, right?"

"Maybe?" I managed, my fingers swiping across my tablet to flip through pages of notes. My free hand fiddled with extra discs in my lap: a bunch of textbooks, and transcriptions of old-world encyclopedias that Dad had given me. There was no way I could focus on studying with Heath's fingers distracting me, just no way.

Heath hummed along to the music playing through his console. Something by a college band, unpolished and missing that truly catchy quality. He was probably thinking about fucking that new guy. And I didn't really care.

"So who are you going to hire?" he asked. His hand had moved to my arm, fingertips tracing swirls across my skin.

"Are your two topics related?"

Heath snorted. "They could be, I think he's a tech guy."

"I'm going to go with someone I've worked with before."

"Like who?"

I shrugged. "The company hires third-party techs all the time for this kind of thing. Contractor guys, you know? Like the guy who set up Gene and Kacy's office. Or the guy who got us that tower array last year."

"He was an outside guy? I assumed he was one of Hale's lackeys."

"In Atlanta?"

Heath waved his hand. "Well that sounds fine. Do that, then."

The mediocre beat filled the gap in our conversation once more. Glancing at my notes, my gut churned. I didn't want to study. Turning off the tablet and making Heath think about me instead of the new guy would be much more fun. But then just as quickly the thought left me, replaced by the guilt of a cup of water.

I had to study, for Dad. And I had to do my job, for Dad. It wasn't so much an obligation but a dedication. He wanted to see me succeed, and succeed I could. If I could keep myself on task.

For him, I could damn well try.

There's nothing quite like taking a test when you know the material. My confidence returned as I filled out my answers, as the stress of the semester lifted from my shoulders. This was the last final, and then I was done, and summer would be here, and I could escape.

I tapped the Submit button on my tablet as many around me were still working, then I stood and nodded a farewell to the professor.

Anticipating my speed, Heath was already waiting outside the classroom for me. I kissed him fiercely, so happy to be free. After a few moments, I withdrew and he sucked in a breath.

"Great, now I'm hard. Quick go in the closest bathroom?" He raised an eyebrow.

I smiled and mockingly stroked my beard. "Are you defining 'quick' as less than a minute here?"

He gasped, and then something behind me caught his eye. His eyebrows lowered.

"The fuck?" he whispered.

I looked over my shoulder to see that an andro from my class had just emerged from the final, stopping a few feet away from us to put his tablet in a woven shoulder bag.

"Hey, Heath, let's get going," I tried.

He still approached the andro, who froze and focused on the floor. As Heath stopped in front of him, the andro clasped his bag, easing the strap back onto his shoulder.

"You aren't going anywhere, are you?" Heath asked, his tone deep, almost sultry.

"Just going my way, brother." His voice was hardly distinguishable from ours.

I tapped Heath's arm. "You don't have to do this every time."

Heath shrugged me off, using the movement to step forward and grab the andro by the wrist.

"Who on this acid-bathed earth do you think you are?" he hissed, and the andro shook his head, still looking down. Heath tugged the andro toward him, dragging him past me to the classroom's outer wall. "Now you stand up straight right here and answer my damn question."

"I don't . . ." the andro attempted, and I just stood there like an idiot, trying to summon the courage to act.

Heath glanced back at me. "You've been going to school with an andro and you didn't tell me?"

"Didn't even notice him," I muttered, still unable to move. All my confidence drained through my feet into the cement.

"How can you miss this?" Heath flicked his fingers against the andro's throat, where his Adam's apple wasn't. "Or this?" and Heath pinched his hip. The andro ripped his arm from Heath's grip and lunged for freedom, but Heath got his other arm around the andro's neck and pulled him into a choke hold. "It's day and night to me." He smirked and yanked the andro toward me.

"Come on, man, give a guy a break!" the andro whined.

"I would if you were one," Heath laughed. "Go on, Jess."

I knew why Heath did this to andros, as I knew why my brothers did, my friends and cousins too. They all had to out-macho each other by kicking those who were already down. But violence like this would always be despicable to me.

"You know I don't hurt people," I managed. "And neither should you."

Heath shoved the andro against the wall, and then let go. The guy ran, and Heath shook his head. "Why the damn are you so soft?"

"It's called empathy." I exhaled. "Probably one of the best things Dad taught me."

As a smile softened Heath's features, he ran his hands down my arm. "You better be happy I like you."

Our fingers entwined, and I released a relieved sigh, but the tension in my gut lingered. "And you better be happy I tolerate you."

"Asshole."

We walked down the glass hallway, the late-morning sun already quite warm. Yellow-tinged clouds floated past the solar panels above us. This was as good of a time as any to tell him.

"I've picked a technician."

Heath squeezed my hand. "Oh?"

I waited for his gaze before continuing. "You have to promise me that you'll behave."

He smirked. "I'm always on my best behavior."

"Just now you weren't," I pointed out.

"Oh, come on! Who gives a shit about a—" His eyes narrowed. "No. You didn't."

"I said promise me."

Heath's set jaw said it all. This was definitely going to be a crazy season.

PART 3
EMBER

XX

CHAPTER 6

There's nothing like living on supplement to test a man's resolve. Determination alone drove me to make it through each day and each job—and each meal Niche ate in front of me. A quiet Monday morning found me reorganizing my tools for the tenth time, Niche working his way through a bowl of oatmeal while watching a televid. But it wasn't the oatmeal that bothered me, it was the fresh blueberries he had casually mixed in.

I focused on my tools. One millimeter screwdriver, one half millimeter, three different soldering wires . . . damn it.

"How are the blueberries this season?" I asked, sweeping the tools back into the drawer.

"Don't torture yourself."

Pressing my lips to my teeth, I exhaled. "Ffffuck you."

Niche chuckled. "Catch, asshole."

He threw a blueberry at me, and I yelped and cupped my hand over it as it hit my chest. I popped it in my mouth and savored the burst of sweetness.

"Oh, oh, they are good," I breathed.

"And I bet that's how you sound when you have sex," Niche joked.

I ignored him. And then there was a knock at the door. I answered it, and eyed the man that stood outside with interest.

"Uh, hello, Mr. Dawson?" He was a few inches taller than me, with dark-brown hair falling right above his eyebrows, and the kind of jawline I would kill for, just squared enough to prove his genes. His black jacket was worn, the fabric broken and frayed across the shoulders and down the arms, like it had been in rain. I repressed a shudder at the thought.

"Hello." I rested a hand on my hip. "Can I help you?"

"Yes, I do hope so." He smiled over a well-trimmed beard, and stuck his hands in his pant pockets. "I'm looking to hire you."

I returned the smile, as a weight lifted off my shoulders. His demeanor told me this was going to be something big. I opened the door farther, and gestured for him to step inside. He complied, and I glanced at Niche before leaning on my desk and crossing my arms. Niche watched us silently.

"What can I do for you? I offer a full range of upgrades and repairs to anything from Commons to radiators."

"You don't recognize me, huh?" he asked. I frowned and shook my head. "My name's Jess Cameron. You helped me a year ago. I needed a current amplifier for a communication tower antenna. Hah, you do remember."

I had nodded with a chuckle. It was a part that took me weeks of searching to dig up at a reasonable price. "Don't tell me you need another one."

"No. I'm actually thinking of something much more involved than that."

I raised my eyebrows. The couch creaked as Niche sat up to listen in. Couldn't he leave and let me do business?

"My father, Hale Cameron, owns CamCo Research and Development," Jess started. "He's in Kansas City, but his researchers get their information from several stations between here and there. At each station are towers and sensors that take readings on weather fluctuations, along with soil sampling equipment. And along with the machines are the accompanying computers and programs to run them. Everything needs to be serviced twice a year: instruments need to be cleaned and calibrated, software needs to be updated, stuff like that.

"I've been in charge of the servicing crew for the Arkansas stations for a while now. It's a lot of travel, but you get to leave the city and enter the wild."

His monologue paused, and I took the opportunity to speak. "I assume you'd like me to join you."

"That's the general idea. My previous electronics specialist isn't available. I'm offering you his place."

"How long will we be out there?"

"About a month."

I bit my lip, and Niche inhaled sharply. Besides rent, I would need to buy at least four vials before leaving. It had been years since I had enough creds to do that. "And the pay?"

"Five thousand wattcreds for the whole month."

I coughed. "Fucking serious?"

Jess shrugged, with the hint of a smile. That was enough creds to entice me to try almost anything. Like leaving Atlanta? Though the prospect was strange, it excited me.

"What do you think?"

I exhaled, hoping my next words wouldn't cancel the offer. "I'm interested. But I'm going to need twelve hundred up front."

"I'll have my father wire the wattcreds to you tonight."

I couldn't stop the relieved chuckling that escaped me as I held out my hand.

He shook it. "I'll come pick you up in two days. I hope that's not too soon for you."

I smiled broadly at him. "Not at all."

After Jess had gone, I regarded Niche with my mouth hanging open.

"You lucky bastard," he admonished. "But I'm glad it's not me."

"Why?"

"It's a whole different world out there, from what I hear."

What he wasn't saying was that "different" meant "dangerous." But this much pay was an opportunity of a lifetime. "Good, I could use a change."

True to Jess's word, I had the wattcreds by the next morning. Within the hour, I remembered how satisfying it was to have a full stomach. And then I had the pleasure of reliving how happy I got when I could buy more than one vial at a time. Maybe my bad luck streak was over.

Of course, I was about to spend weeks with unfamiliar men, likely domineering mascs. I would need all the luck I could get to not end up with another broken nose, or worse.

I transferred Niche my half of the rent, he as happy as I that my finances for the next several weeks were taken care of. The rest of the wattcreds from this job would cover another two months—longer if business was better when I got back. I packed the few clothes I needed into a shoulder bag, along with my entire collection of tools: magnifying glasses, tweezers, pliers, screwdrivers, a soldering iron and wire, and data cards filled with console diagrams and software just in case. Was I seriously smiling? Looking forward to this?

My optimism reminded me of when I first left home, my veins full of confidence, my account full of surrogacy wattcreds, and my head full of dreams. It had eventually been eroded by reality as I'd learned the truths of the world and grew up. But I guess some of that youthfulness still survived.

Sure, youthfulness—I rubbed my arm with a chuckle—or testosterone-induced cockiness. It didn't really matter.

The next morning, Niche surprised me with a hug before leaving for work. "Take care of yourself."

I nodded, gripping his shoulder. "I promise not to get myself killed."

He smiled, and left.

Jess was not alone when he came to pick me up. A blond man with a full beard accompanied him, dressed in a tight, dull-red tank and a pleated skirt to his knees. He scrutinized me with a gaze as sharp as needles.

"And Ember, this is Heath Mills. He's the communications specialist for our team."

Heath hardly nodded a greeting to me as he inspected the small view he had of the apartment past my shoulders. "Whatever you say, Jess," he muttered. "Let's go get the lovers so we can hit the road."

Heath turned away, and I lifted my bag onto my shoulder, trying to smile at Jess.

"Gene and Kacy," Jess said as we left my apartment.

"The lovers?"

"Yeah. The other two members of our team. They got together shortly after meeting each other during the research season a few years ago."

"That's nice." At least I had some warning before I was assaulted by public displays of affection.

Jess and Heath jumped into a large all-terrain vehicle, its wide frame bouncing on wheels that were thickly reinforced with woven metal. The ATV's roof and hood sported hinged solar panels, and from bumper to bumper, it was covered with dried mud and the pitted pattern of rain. They really couldn't keep it any cleaner than this? How bad was it out there? I climbed into the backseat, which was equally dirty, and stuffed my shoulder bag between crates that took up most of the enclosed cargo area.

"So Jess tells me you've been working with electronics for a while," Heath said, and I caught his narrowed gaze in the side-view mirror as Jess pulled into the street.

I played with the seat belt. "I've had my own business for five years, but I've fiddled with spare parts as long as I can remember."

"Do you know anything about the equipment you'll be working on?" he asked, steady and skeptical.

Jess merged onto a major thoroughfare that would take us to the west side of town. I glanced out the window at large, tan clouds dotting the sky.

"Just what I needed to know to understand the part I got you guys last year," I admitted. "But give me manuals or schematics and I'll figure it out pretty fast."

"Sure you will," Heath grunted. Jess turned onto city streets, entering a neighborhood not too far from my parents'. Small houses lined the road, some with front yards decorated with rare rocks or metal figurines. We drove by a group of children drawing pictures on the pockmarked cement with large, brightly colored crayons.

Jess stopped in front of a single-story house and he and Heath had hopped out of the car before I had the chance to open my door. I followed a few paces behind them, and kept my distance as they knocked on a door. A tall, lanky man with a shaved head and large nose answered, and he hugged his teammates in turn.

"Another season!" he said before looking back inside. "Kacy, are you ready?" Then he noticed me standing almost at the street. He gave me a surprised look before the expression turned pained. "Adin's replacement?"

"Yeah. That's Ember."

"Okay." He stole a glance at Jess, and then nodded at me. "I'm Gene Garner."

"Nice to meet you," I mumbled. Another man leaned against the house's doorway now, talking to Heath. Kacy stood a foot shorter than Gene, with a slightly darker complexion to go with his dark-brown hair and mustache. He peered at me.

"Kacy Nash. Nice of you to join us." Huh, his voice was higher than mine.

"Well," Jess started, "let's get going. We have quite a drive ahead of us."

"How long of a drive?" I asked. We piled into the large vehicle, and Kacy and Gene shoved their luggage over the backseat.

"Two days; longer if the weather turns bad," Jess said. That didn't sound appealing, especially sitting so close to mascs. But I'd survive.

As Jess drove off, I wondered when anyone was going to point out the obvious about me, but presently no one paid me any notice. I pulled my Common out of my pocket and took advantage of these last few minutes with signal to check my mail one more time. Nothing. Sticking an earbud in one ear, I spent a few minutes staring at passing buildings accompanied by rhythmic melodies.

"So Ember . . . Tell us about yourself," Gene said. I reluctantly turned my attention to the men as I stopped my music.

"Well, I've been building and repairing consoles since I was young." I paused. "Um, I like going to the gym." *Damn it, what do you want me to say?*

Gene nodded, looking down. The awkwardness of the resulting silence thickened the air.

"Kacy and I have been meaning to go to the gym. It's impressive that someone like you goes," he finally attempted. I rolled my eyes and let the conversation wane again as Jess turned onto a wide road that would take us to the edge of Atlanta. We passed a billboard for a clothing company, displaying a handsome masc sporting a muted-gray vest that hung open to reveal his perfect muscles. Because obviously the universe needed to give me another reminder that I was different.

"Is no one going to say it?" Heath, of course it'd be Heath. He twisted to look over the passenger seat at me. "Do you people really shoot up once a week?"

My face grew hot as Kacy and Gene stared at me.

"I'm sorry, Ember," Jess muttered.

"It's okay . . . And yes, that's right." I pinched the skin of my forearm, hoping the discomfort would keep me calm. Heath faced forward again, snickering. I had to redirect this conversation. "So how about you guys? What do you do?"

"I have certificates in meteorology and geology," Gene explained. "I'm writing a research paper on how soil acidity affects plant life."

"Is the land improving?" I asked. The buildings of Atlanta retreated, replaced with acres of greenhouses filling the landscape to the horizon. Sun sparkled off the glass, bright and blinding. Dad was working somewhere out there . . .

Gene laughed, hints of exasperation in his voice. "It's too early in my research to tell."

"In other words, no," Heath offered.

"Inconclusive, Heath." Gene sighed, and rubbed the top of Kacy's thigh.

Kacy placed his hand over Gene's. "I'm actually a mechanic," he began. "You get good at repairing rain damage when you work on cars. So when Jess was looking for someone to upkeep the stations and their solar panels, I qualified."

I hummed, but my gaze kept slipping outside. The landscape no longer had glass roofs, but was now an endless expanse of ruddy tan grass, dotted with the occasional twisted tree. I shivered. This was the farthest I'd ever been from home.

Heath pushed his palms against the ATV's roof. "I guess I'm next. I'm one of CamCo's programmer lackeys. Jess would complain about the network going down, so I thought I'd come out here with him. You know, take care of shit he should be able to do himself."

"Fuck you," Jess bit out, and the others laughed. "I just finished a certificate in radiobiology. My father wants me to take over CamCo when he gets older." Jess maneuvered the vehicle around a pothole in the road. "It's pretty amazing when you're out there, in the wild, seeing the scars of our past. You wonder if the land will fully recover, then you see that life is trying to refill all the niches mankind blew apart."

Jess's words stirred a yearning within me for a world I had only read about but never seen. I thought the land was dead, that it couldn't recover. Now my certainty clashed with his hopeful tone.

"Damn, that was way too deep." Heath's voice snapped me back to reality. "Let's lighten the mood a bit." He pressed a few buttons on the vehicle's dashboard, and vibrant music pumped out of the speakers. Gene and Kacy bobbed their heads to the beat, humming along. I didn't know it, so I slumped in my seat, resting my head against the back and staring out the window again.

Outside of Atlanta, the road degraded severely. Its broken surface rattled the ATV's suspension, bouncing us in our seats. The men talked intermittently over the music: Gene explained physics concepts to an amused Kacy; Heath and Jess talked about bands. I kept silent.

We passed low hills, windblown trees, and murky brown rivers of water laden with acid. Then Jess drove by the rusted-out frames of buildings. The metal beams were bent, mangled, and weatherworn, now twisted abstract sculptures of lost human ambition. I imagined the buildings new and whole, glass windows shining in the sunlight, and people strolling on the sidewalks that had long since eroded away.

"Okay, who else is hungry?" Heath asked, and there was unanimous affirmation. He passed around granola bars. As I nibbled on my bar, the others casually ate their fill and returned to their conversation; they likely had never gone hungry. Had never tried to make a little last.

The beaten-down road stretched ahead of us, on and on after each low hill. It was like a long, huge treadmill, like this was the same land looping over and over. Going nowhere. And to the north, thick brown clouds hung over a distant range of low mountains, their darkened hue failing to affect my resolve. Storms came in and blew through; that was just a part of life.

A few hours after we left the city, a sign stood in the dirt ahead of us. Something had been painted on its washed-out front.

"'Welcome to the Outskirts,'" I read as we drove by. I frowned at my fellow passengers, but they wouldn't meet my gaze.

Finally, Jess commented. "Don't mind that, Ember."

What was that supposed to mean? Why was there even a hand-painted sign in the middle of nowhere? It was difficult to not mind it, given his uneasy tone, but everyone's silence held my tongue.

It wasn't much longer before Jess stopped the vehicle, and the men chatted about their favorite actors as they all hopped out of the ATV, took a step or two, and urinated. My cheeks grew hot, as I had to go too, but I hated the lack of privacy. Mascs might occasionally hold doubt whether or not an andro was actually an exin, but one's behavior in a restroom always cleared that straight up. Jess and Heath climbed back into their seats, but Gene and Kacy took an extra moment to stretch and walk around.

Fucking damn, I hated the awkwardness. *I should just get out, it's okay . . .* As the lovers joined us again, Jess started the vehicle.

"Jess, just a minute," I mumbled, then I slipped out, ducked behind the ATV and squatted. Ugh, me with a bunch of mascs. What was I doing out here?

I rejoined the others, and Heath muttered something. Jess hit his arm with the back of a hand, and we resumed our journey. The hours continued to trickle by, and the clouds ahead of us got progressively closer.

"Yeah, we're gonna catch up to those," Jess mused.

Heath clicked his tongue. "Let me know when to fold up the solar panels."

"Does it rain a lot at the stations?" I asked, and the others fidgeted as they seemed to remember I was in the vehicle with them.

Gene answered me. "About as often as it does in Atlanta. The winds are a bit rougher though, so storms will come in faster."

"Hope you like showering in acid." Heath laughed. "You'll get stuck out in it more than a few times."

The others chuckled, but it wasn't as lighthearted as they were probably trying for.

"We have plenty of neutralizer if that happens though," Jess added. I wrinkled my nose, recalling the stuff's metallic scent. When I was much younger, my brothers and I had forgotten our jackets one afternoon when a storm rolled through. The rain had stung, but the neutralizer had stung even worse. It had been worth not getting scars from the rain back then. But now? What were a few more scars? What was a bit more pain?

Within the hour, the brown clouds swept over us, and the light dimmed to a weak yellow. Heath pushed a button on the dashboard, and a series of whirs and clanks resulted in the solar panels folding in half, their undersides reinforced with metal that showed heavy wear from the rain. Kacy lifted himself up to check the panel on the hood of the car.

"Yeah, those backs have to be replaced soon." He noticed me watching him, and cleared his throat. "The main station, we call it Headquarters, can do that too. It's much cheaper to replace their backings than to replace the actual energy cells."

"Of course, occasionally they don't get folded up in time," Heath cut in.

"That wasn't my damn fault!" Kacy retorted. "Adin was supposed to—" He stopped. I frowned as Gene shifted in his seat and Jess took a deep breath, adjusting his grip on the steering wheel. I waited for someone to elaborate, but then the rain erupted around us.

It fell with a whooshing hiss, splashing off the windshield and dripping down my side window. I shuddered. Jess drove slowly now, as the ATV didn't have the solar power to supplement its batteries. Heath turned up the music in an attempt to drown out the sound of the rain, but it didn't help much. I was able to make out more ruins through the gloom, including a few lone poles—lampposts I figured—following parallel to the road. Next to me, Kacy rested his head on Gene's shoulder, and they talked softly, their hands entwined. I sighed, wriggling in my seat until I was comfortable. I leaned my head back, and shut my eyes.

It was another hour before the rain let up, and Jess pulled over. I took this opportunity to step outside, and stretched my arms and legs while Jess wiped the windows with neutralizer. I spent a few moments running in place. The air was just as muggy, smelling more like dirt and acid than Atlanta did. Heath took the driver's seat when we got back in, and as the vehicle's tires began sending rocks rattling off its undercarriage, Jess twisted in the front seat to look back at me.

"How are you doing?" he asked. Perhaps I didn't look all that comfortable huddled against the vehicle door, my arms across my chest.

"I don't think I've ever been in a car this long."

"I figured. You're doing good so far." He sort of half smiled, and I inwardly winced at how handsome it made him look.

"Yeah." I looked away from him, and he apparently took the motion as an end to our conversation.

Jess and Heath started talking about some televid I had never seen, while Kacy griped to Gene about customers that demanded outrageous upgrades to their cars—I could have shared instances with my own business, but I couldn't bring myself to speak. This was the most time I had ever spent with mascs who were not my brother or cousins, and when they weren't belittling me, their conversations were weirdly normal, and not what I had expected. Normal had never been my strong point. Fitting in with them seemed out of the question, regardless of how much part of me wanted it. I put my earbuds back in to drown out their music. This day was a shitty start to what was in all likelihood going to be a frustrating month.

CHAPTER 7

My eyes fluttered open the moment it started getting light outside. And then Kacy mumbling in his sleep a few inches from my face startled me the rest of the way awake. I shuffled away from him, and an ache pulsed through my back. Yeah, sleeping in a reclined seat had been just as uncomfortable as I had imagined. I left the ATV as silently as I could, and leaned against my shut door, surprised by the cold. A light breeze brought the smell of dirt, and I could just barely taste the lingering bitterness of acid in the moist air.

I let my gaze travel up the road in front of me. It continued on, somewhat downhill until it disappeared into morning mist.

Soon the horizon brightened, the pale blue shifting to pink and yellow. I had never been so far from everything . . . no people, no buildings, no cars, no talking, no advertisements, no gym-goers staring me down. It was lovely.

As the sun's light warmed me, the others began stirring. They climbed out of their seats, and Heath passed me to open up the back hatch.

"What were you doing out there?" he asked with a laugh.

"Enjoying the vacancy."

Jess nodded at that. "Eat some breakfast, we'll be hitting the road again in a few minutes."

I complied, uncomfortable at the thought that I was taking more of their food. But there wasn't any way for me to pay for my own . . . whatever was at the stations, or whatever they brought, would be all we'd have access to out here.

We hit the road, and the sun climbed up the sky, obscured by thin clouds that thickened gradually. Gene was of the opinion that it would not rain, so they left the solar panels open.

Through the haze and horizon obscured by mirage, I could make out the abandoned frames of buildings. As we approached, the twisted metal increased in apparent size. Soon we were driving past them, large, multistory sculptures made by damaged nature. There were so many of them, the streets between them reduced to stretches of rust. This ruined city appeared as dense as Atlanta, and I wondered if in another millennium, Atlanta would be reduced to this as well. A shiver ran down my spine.

Abruptly, the ruins ended, and we approached a large bridge, its rusted metal showing surprisingly little degradation. Jess pulled to a stop before its muddy surface. The derelict sections of an older bridge stood about a half mile away across the expanse of water. My jaw dropped as I recalled maps I had studied during my education . . . This was the Mississippi River. Its brown water churned endlessly ahead of me. Stretching on toward the horizon, it flowed past the crumbling bridge and out of sight. Jess left the vehicle, and the others followed suit. I grimaced at the thought of braving the weather, and, with a groan, I stuck my Common in my pocket and climbed out too.

The humidity was almost unbearable this close to the river, and I inhaled with effort. My skin felt immediately as damp as it would be after I'd been running for an hour. And with the air reeking this badly of acid, I wouldn't have been surprised if my throat started burning within a few minutes. Coughing, I followed the men onto the bridge, curious why we had stopped instead of simply driving across. Jess and Heath scrutinized the surface of the bridge, occasionally jumping on particularly dirty sections. Ah, they were looking for weaknesses.

"Are we going to check the whole length?" My voice sounded flat against the whistle of the breeze and chirping of insects.

"All six thousand feet, yes," Heath replied. "We just drove across two weeks ago, but the ATV is fully loaded this time, and there's been a bad storm through here since then." He kicked at a muddy dip in the metal, and wedged up the paneling with the tip of his boot.

"Kacy, mark that spot," Jess said, and Kacy pulled a spray can out of his shoulder bag and drew a green X by the panel in question.

They kept going, and I tailed them for more exercise. Then, without prompting, Jess elaborated on the situation.

"Just one of the many things my father takes responsibility for." He pointed at a slab of metal that was cracked along the whole length, one side sagging dangerously. "That must have been the snap we heard on our way over, Heath."

After at least half an hour, we were most of the way across. I let the men carry on, and I wandered to the edge of the bridge and gazed at the river flowing slowly to the south. The cloud-diluted sunlight danced off its wavy surface, gold on murky brown. It was so wide . . . wider than any body of water I had ever seen. I had never been to the ocean, despite its closeness to Atlanta. There was no reason to go unless you worked at the docks.

Beyond the river, a bush-speckled wasteland stretched as far as I could see. How much farther did we have to travel? Now that we had driven for hours and had gotten nowhere and seen almost nothing, I couldn't believe how big the world was. Atlanta to Kansas City, everything that I was familiar with, was a mere fraction of what was out here. Is this what filled the rest? Empty land, dirty water, and dead seas?

The others had made it across the bridge, but hadn't started back toward me. I jogged after them, noticing the shiny silver roof of a building on the approaching shore.

Jess and Heath were hefting a large metal sheet between them as I approached. Kacy emerged from what was apparently a warehouse with a welder in one hand and a tinted face shield in the other.

"Ember, you wanna drive the ATV to the first X?" Jess asked. "We need it to power the welder." I nodded, and Jess tossed me his crowded key ring. "It's the one with the black top." Picking out the right key, I jogged back to the ATV, the keys jingling loudly. Well, he trusted me with his ATV. That was something, right?

On the east shore, I climbed into the driver's seat with a giddy laugh. It had been years since I had driven a car, and this was definitely the largest I'd attempted to drive. Switching on the engine produced a smooth electric hum. After testing taps on the accelerator and brake, I drove to the first weak spot we had found, a few hundred feet onto the bridge. My reward for not crashing was a few minutes enjoying the air conditioning as the others converged.

When Jess and Heath put down their burden, Jess motioned for me to get out. I complied, and tossed the keys back to him.

"Go help Gene carry another sheet over here," Jess told me, so off I went.

With each panel we repaired, we inched our way across the bridge. I carried my fair share of metal, and thankful nods from Jess and Kacy in particular hinted at budding respect. Whether that would last . . . we'd see. Finally, with the job done and the ATV on the west shore, our journey resumed.

We left the river and soon saw nothing from horizon to horizon but interspersed groves of dark trees among the scrubby grassland. Definitely unlike orchards under glass, the trees I was familiar with. Eventually, the sun began to set, and my manual labor left me relaxed, almost sleepy. The sky faded to orange through the haze of partial cloud cover, the sun's rays lighting the clouds' bellies gold.

"Damn I'm starving . . ." Kacy moaned, and he tugged at his partner's sleeve. "You'll have to make your stir-fry tonight."

Gene laughed. "But of course . . . we've earned a treat today, and I'm sure our newest member will appreciate it too."

His tone promised a meal akin to my dad's, and I smiled.

"No eating-for-two excuse, okay, Ember?" Heath added, causing Kacy to burst out laughing and elbow me in the ribs. I stifled a grunt, my face flushing.

"That was in incredibly poor taste," Jess announced.

"Come on, I'm joking with the guy. Trying to get a rise out of him! Thirty hours with us and he's said about as many words."

"What do you expect?" Jess muttered, and Heath gripped the steering wheel with a grumble.

After a few moments, Jess spoke again. "Ember, look—"

"Fuck you guys," I spat. Their resulting silence wasn't really any better.

The land was shrouded in blue shadow when we stopped at a metal fence. Jess unlocked a gate, and Heath pulled the ATV in. Barbed wire appeared to line the top of the fence, though in this light I couldn't tell for sure. As we continued, the vehicle's headlights illuminated a one-story building with a sloped roof that featured a number of antennas and instruments jutting into the sky. Its metal walls were rusty. I grabbed my bags, and hopped out of the ATV. Then, Jess sprinted ahead. He looked flustered as he fiddled with his keys and unlocked the door.

"What is it?" Heath called.

Jess pointed to his right before disappearing inside. We followed the gesture to a broken window.

"Fuck," Heath groaned.

"I wonder if gusts blew the window out . . ." Gene strode into the building, and Kacy followed him.

Hopefully rain hadn't destroyed expensive equipment. I wandered inside to discover an open floor plan, one half of the building a single large room. Metal beams crossed the ceiling, and desks and equipment lined the wall with a long conference table in the center. On the back wall was a large tack board with the words *Arkansas Headquarters* along the top. It all appeared untouched by wind or rain.

I approached a wide doorway that I assumed led to the living quarters. Flustered voices and the clanking of various kitchenware drifted to my ears.

Kacy rounded the doorway and shrugged. "Not much rain damage but a nasty breeze knocked stuff all over the floor."

I nodded at this, motioning that I wanted to move past him to see for myself.

Kacy ignored my gesture. "You like techie stuff? Check all this out."

As he showed me around Gene's chemical analysis equipment, Jess's voice resolved into a few words: ". . . take anything."

My curiosity swelled, but I didn't want to press matters. And then Jess and Heath joined us, Jess's cheeks red.

"Come on, let's get the rest of our stuff inside."

One of the crates we brought in contained more variety of food than I had seen in the past few months. Electronic equipment and battery packs filled another. I organized the electronics in piles by my sides, filling up a mental inventory as I went. Jess and Heath stacked the other crates near the front door.

"Look, he's giddy." Heath patted Jess on the shoulder. "I guess you did pick the right guy."

"Are you fucking kidding?" I exclaimed. "I've never gotten to work with so much stuff." I held up a video card. "This is worth five thousand wattcreds! And this one..." I showed them a microprocessor. "Eight thousand! Jess, where does CamCo get so much funding?"

"I'm glad you're enjoying yourself." Jess gave a polite smile. "Actually, I have something else for you. Hand me your Common."

I did, and he plugged it into a console. Beside me, Kacy and Gene were dragging the food crate into the kitchen, discussing what we should eat. Their casual talking couldn't quite hide their shaken nerves. Trying to ignore them, I picked up the package of a heat sink I had only heard about but had never worked with ... I'd finally opened the box by the time Jess handed my Common back to me.

"Two thousand pages of manuals and research papers and then you'll be an expert on all this stuff." He smiled as I thumbed through the table of contents.

"You have until tomorrow morning," Heath announced. I eyed him, and he cocked his head to the side. "How else am I gonna trust you with my console?"

Jess exhaled slowly. "I think they got most of the shit off the floor in there ... Hey, Ember, let me show you around. First of all, this is the conference room. Through here is what few amenities we have."

Relieved to stop meeting Heath's stern gaze, I put the Common in my back pocket and followed. Past the doorway was a kitchen and dining area. Pieces of broken glass still glittered on the linoleum, and plates and pans were hastily stacked on the counters and table as Kacy and Gene organized. Next to the kitchen was a lounge, with a couch sticking out from one wall, and a small display and console in the corner. Jess led me toward a hall past the lounge.

"That door's the bathroom ... We have to recycle our own water here so please use only what you need," Jess lectured, gesturing to each location as we meandered down the hall. "This is my room, that one is Gene and Kacy's, and the last one is yours and Heath's."

Heath came up behind us, wrapping an arm around Jess's shoulders. "I think I'll crash in your room if that's cool."

I scrunched my nose at his lack of tact, but what struck me was Jess's expression following these words. There was reluctance in the pursing of his lips, the frown in his brow.

"Yeah, that's cool." Jess regarded me. "Guess you get a bedroom to yourself."

"Good." I opened my door and flicked on a light switch to reveal two twin beds separated by a pair of desks. Florescent light reflected off the metal walls, allowing a little light to go a long way. I stepped in. A previous occupant had scratched notches into one of the desk's edges. Running a finger across the grooves, I sighed. It was very minimalist, which I liked.

When I left my room a few minutes later, I glanced into Jess's now-open door. There was a desk covered with schematics, data cards for a Common, and a newer console. A pile of clothes sat in one corner beside the single bed. I raised an eyebrow at that. It had been obvious that Jess and Heath were friends outside this gig, but . . . hmm.

I started when Heath spoke from right next to me. "What're you looking at?"

"Nothing." My gut clenched. I averted my gaze and pushed past him, sickened that our tones had already taken on the bully/victim cadences.

Gene was preparing dinner, and I settled at the table as he chopped vegetables. Beside me, Kacy took off his boots and propped his feet on the table, leaning on the two back legs of his chair.

"How much work we got planned this season, Jess?" he called, and Jess walked in from the conference room and sat across from me.

"No talk of work until tomorrow." Jess ran his fingers through his hair. "That drive is too long for me to function afterward."

"Gene seems to be functioning just fine," Heath countered, joining us.

"Gene can spend a ten-hour day stomping around the bogs and still have the capacity to write reports when he gets back," Kacy pointed out. "He's a superman."

"You would say that." Gene laughed.

Kacy sighed. "I guess after this . . ." He glanced at the broken window. "We can justify waiting a bit."

I couldn't keep quiet this time. "What's the big deal?"

The others all stole glances at Jess, who stared at the kitchen table, his elbows propped up and his fingers on his temples. He scrunched his eyes shut. "I don't know what's got you waterlogged."

"Right," Kacy agreed. "Want me to at least board the window up until I can fix it tomorrow?"

I shook my head, already tired of them separating me, being secretive around me. "Don't brush me off."

"Just fucking drop it." Jess stood and left the kitchen, and Heath followed him out.

I sighed, the sound muffled under an eruption of sizzling as Gene dumped his chopped vegetables into a pan on one of two hot plates installed into the counter. I could just barely hear Jess and Heath talking in the conference room.

I resolved to ignore them, and read on my Common until everyone returned for dinner. Gene had prepared a potato hash with mushrooms and bell peppers, and as I dug in to my share, the garlic and herbs pleasantly complemented it. I told him so, and he smiled proudly at his dish.

Around me, the others relaxed as well. As we finished, Kacy and Gene exchanged excited glances, then stood, their hands clasped together.

"We have an announcement to make!" Gene smiled widely at his partner. I instantly knew what they were going to say. And the warm room seemed suddenly cold.

"Go on," Heath prodded.

"We've hired a surrogate," Kacy exclaimed. Jess and Heath clapped and cheered their congratulations, while I put down my silverware and pushed my chair away from the table.

"I assume this'll be your last season, huh?" Jess added, and Gene nodded.

"For a while, at least. It was a hard decision to come to," Gene mused. "But I'll return now and then to continue my research."

"You're of course welcome anytime," Jess said. "This is wonderful. When is the surrogate due?" Just the word made me want to gag.

"We only got this started recently. He has another seven months." Gene then looked straight at me. "If you're willing, I have a lot of questions for you."

"No." My hands collapsed into fists as I stood. "Damn, no."

Gene gaped at me, and Kacy frowned. I left them, shut myself in my room, and crawled on one of the beds, tucking my knees under my chin.

Heath's ridicule was to be expected, as was Jess's distant air. That I still reacted so negatively to them was frustrating, but I simply couldn't help it. This, however, was different. I had not expected a fucking couple surrogating a damned child. Those ignorant, happy faces brought back memories of doctor's visits, symptoms, derision . . . and their singling me out shattered all hope of being one of the guys. For the next month I would be akin to a kitchen appliance to them. How long must a baby cook for? At what temperature, and with what kind of heat? Must the tool be cleaned between usages?

Is the tool even still a human being?

I shuddered, trying to swallow down a sob. There was a knock at my door.

"What do you want?" I rasped.

"To apologize."

I pulled open the door and leaned against the doorframe. There stood Gene, with Jess a few feet behind him.

"I understand it's a sensitive subject," Gene said. "I figured your knowledge would be available. Is it not?"

I sighed. I hated him assuming that I was a retired baby factory and nothing more, especially because he would never ask me the questions I wanted to answer. He'd never let me give the only answers that really mattered: You crave food that doesn't exist. You're sporadically and violently ill for weeks. Your friends stay away from you so they aren't seen next to your bulbous form. Eventually, they stop coming back.

That familiar sorrow pulsed through me, a vacancy I could never hope to fill. I looked up to see Jess furrowing his brow.

"I'm tired," I told them. "I'll see you tomorrow."

Gene seemed to deflate as I shut the door. Returning to my bed, I tapped the Common's screen. Spikes of anger or embarrassment flashed through me, enough to make my gut ache and my hands tremble. How could I fit in with these guys? Shut up and keep my head low?

Yeah, right. I opened my Common's calendar, and scanned the four weeks of this trip. That would be a long time to lay low. I tapped the Tuesdays, my injection days, which highlighted a neat little row down the month, like they always did, dividing my life.

The muted whooshing of the wind was broken up by a creaking whir—but the mechanical noise had stopped by the time I realized what it was—the solar panels closing on the roof.

No more than a few minutes later, the rain started. The metallic patter gave me nothing but unease. Everything was different and strange. Here I was, hundreds of miles from my life.

I felt alone.

CHAPTER 8

I groggily opened my eyes, and muffled voices from the next room over caught my attention, their intonations of pleasure making my gut seize with discomfort and longing. This must be the lovers living up to their name. With a grimace, I stood, my stiff muscles demanding exercise. No gym out here . . . I'd have to make do. Leaving my room, I joined Heath and Jess by the kitchen table.

"Good morning, Ember," Jess said. "Hope the rain didn't keep you up."

After my nod in reply, Jess and Heath resumed their conversation, so I scanned the ceiling for any kind of pipe or beam I could grab to do pull-ups. There were none in the living area, and venturing into the conference room, I was again disappointed. The room had one tall wall due to the sloped roof, lined with windows at its top, which revealed a cloudy sky. After a few moments, I returned to the kitchen.

"What do you guys do for exercise around here?" My shoulders slumped as they replied with blank stares. Here was better than nowhere, so I hopped forward into a lunge.

Jess spoke up. "You'll get all the exercise you want as we repair the stations. There are sensor arrays scattered across miles of bogs, fields, and forests."

"Are they all over the area?" I asked, stretching forward and putting my palms on the floor.

"Over a hundred square miles around Headquarters, yeah."

I settled on my back, then began counting crunches. "How . . . many?"

"I think we're down to eight buildings, three towers, and a few dozen remote sensors," Heath answered.

I hummed in response, the strain in my muscles just starting to wake me up. "Hey, could one of you stand on my feet?" Jess gave me a confused look. "Sit-ups, yeah?"

Heath snorted a laugh as Jess complied. I counted, and my cheeks burned from more than the minor exertion of my body. Jess was watching me, and it wasn't a disgusted, "get out of our damn gym" sneer like I was used to.

"How long are you gonna do that?" Jess asked.

"As long . . . as I . . . can stand," I replied between timed inhalations.

"Well, I gotta admit," Heath said, "it's not every day I see an andro exert this much effort."

That's it, masc. Patting Jess's calf so he would move, I leaned forward into a plank. "How many push-ups can you do, Heath?"

After my first ten, he laughed, and joined me on the floor. He did five, and was then grunting from the effort. I finished my second ten.

"I don't think I can do nearly that many," Jess admitted.

"What's going on in here?" Kacy entered the kitchen. He was shirtless, showing off a dusting of dark hair across his chest.

"Ember challenged Heath to a push-up contest," Jess stated.

And thirty. I sat back on my feet, then stood, shaking my arms and steadying my breathing. "He calls me an andro like it's something dirty and wrong. It's not. It's—" I shut up, my cheeks going hot, then I thrust a finger at Kacy's chest. "You mascs use the word to divide us."

Heath laughed, and climbed to his feet. "Kacy's a damn exin."

"Bastard!" Kacy snapped, lunging at Heath, who shoved him back with a malicious smile.

"One step up from an andro, at least," Heath jeered. Kacy sighed and crossed his arms.

I scowled at Heath, and then regarded Kacy again. Exin, eh? This probably explained his voice. I scanned up his body and found he was looking right at me.

"I'm not bad enough to inject," he explained with a shrug. "You say the words divide us, but we're all more of a spectrum."

Y negative, andro, exin, masc. He had a point, a point that I had thought about before. However, it had one glaring error. I glanced below his navel briefly. "There's still a division."

Jess planned out our schedule on the tack board, consulting notes and lists. Every few days, we would be traveling to a different station in the Outskirts.

"How long have these buildings been here?"

Jess settled at a desk and booted up one of the consoles. "My father likes to tell me they've been here over a hundred years, but I doubt it. Though his father owned the land before him."

"So eventually you will?" I sat on the edge of the desk.

Jess typed at the console for a moment, a smile brightening his features. "I hope so."

The screen displayed a long stream of numbers, and several graphs. Every second, entries were added.

"That's data from the stations," I guessed.

"Yeah. Wind, air pressure, precipitation, seismography, pH levels of standing water and streams. Analysts say it's still too acidic for food crops."

The numbers ticked by. What had happened here? Had there been a bomb, meteor, or volcanic eruption? Would we ever know?

"Is it really getting better?" I asked, recalling the conversation from our trip here.

"Ecologists predict that the acid level will stabilize." He closed the program and started up another. "The problem is, it probably won't happen in any of our lifetimes."

"But there is hope."

He met my gaze and cracked another smile. "The earth's been through worse. It recovers, nature adapts."

I nodded and glanced out the windows at blue sky streaked green with thin clouds. It was nice to think of the world recovering, even if I would never see it.

"Jess, are you talking science at him?" Heath asked as he joined us from the living quarters. "You think he understands it?"

I didn't even dignify that with a response.

"He can follow me just fine," Jess replied, and Heath faked an angry look before turning from us to consult Jess's schedule. He pointed at a specific date.

"Twenty-four, now?"

Jess sighed. "Twenty-five, asshole."

I raised an eyebrow, and Jess noticed my confusion and laughed.

"That's my birthday. We tend to celebrate by getting high. Well, he does, mostly."

My gaze switched to Heath. "Do you regularly . . .?"

"Sometimes we like to relax. Nothing crazy." He approached me, and put a hand on his hip. "Do you?"

I rotated a palm up, and his gaze flicked to my forearm. "One drug's enough."

He grunted. "Once a week, right? For how long?"

"Over five years." I traced a finger down the center of my forearm, the skin lightly bruised from my last shot.

Jess hummed. "Does it hurt?"

Hurt what, my body? Or my psyche? "Not really."

"I've heard it gives you a high," Heath said.

"In a way."

"What's it like?" Jess asked. *Like I can answer that without feeling embarrassed.* Too late, my face already felt hot.

"It feels like you can do anything," I mumbled.

"Or anyone?" Heath mocked, and I blushed and hunched my shoulders. As he left us, chuckling, I looked up to Jess's raised eyebrows and soft smile.

"Sorry to take you from your fellow negatives for the next month," he said. When I frowned, his smile faltered.

"I don't like other andros," I explained.

"You don't?"

"Well, I mean, I do, but not like—" Oh for fuck's sake. "I'm het."

Why the damn did I tell him that?

He looked away. "Oh."

As Jess typed at the console again, I wallowed in the awkwardness churning my gut. I sat at the next desk over, and got my Common back out, hoping he would forget I said anything at all.

Pale-purple light of a new day reflected off the metal walls, tables, and cabinets. The satisfying ping of completed system upgrades echoed within the conference room as I continued some semblance of structured exercise. The beeping faded into a silence disrupted when I launched into jumping jacks. *Damn, I want to run.* Maybe today I could find a good path to follow outside.

All right, new processors in the two oldest machines should finish my upgrades. There had been processors in the crate Jess had brought in, but it had been unpacked.

I searched a few of the desks, but they weren't there. Next came the cabinet between the receiving module for sensor data and the server rack. I dug through drawers and finally found the boxes I sought. Heading back toward my desk, I caught movement out of the corner of my eye.

There was something on the ground almost the size of my hand. I stared at it, taking a step closer. It scuttled a few feet away from me, and I shrieked, dropping the processors in my arms as I leaped back. Never in my life had I seen anything like it.

Jess rushed into the room wearing only his boxers. "What's wrong?"

"What is that thing?" I whined, pointing at it.

Heath joined us, further dressed than Jess. The thing scrambled toward me with a horrible rhythmic motion of its legs.

"Fuck!" I screeched, pulling myself onto a desk.

"That's quite a spider," Jess said, a smile forming on his face.

"That's a fucking spider?" I exclaimed, my feet now safely off the floor.

"It's okay, Ember, he'll only kill you in half an hour if he bites you," Heath teased.

"Fucking serious?"

"They don't have shit like this in the cities. Forgot to mention that job perk," Jess chuckled. Heath took delicate steps as he neared the spider, and then in one swift motion jammed the heel of his boot straight into it.

"Luckily the little shits aren't all that fast." Heath rubbed his boot in the squished carcass. Gross. Remembering the processors, I retrieved them from the floor and put them on my desk. I better not have broken them.

"I feel sick," I mumbled. Heath approached me with a grin on his face, and I resisted the urge to shudder again.

"Glad I could save you from the spider." He slapped my shoulder hard. I shrugged off his touch. "Hate to see how you'll react with some of the nastier critters we'll find in the bog week after next."

"It's not that bad," Jess assured me, his arms across his bare chest.

Heath leaned close to me, and whispered, "I didn't know andros could still scream like that."

I stormed away from him, turning the corner into the living quarters.

"What the fuck, Heath?" Jess's voice was muted but angry. "Why do you have to treat him this way?"

I pressed against the lounge wall and listened. Gene was halfway out of his bedroom and he stopped, an eyebrow raised.

Heath replied just as forcefully. "'Cause he's a fucking andro, why else? You don't think his reactions are hilarious?"

"I'm sorry I don't share your sense of humor," Jess hissed. I took the few extra strides to my room, glancing with reddening cheeks at Gene, and shut my door.

"Thanks for trying, Jess," I whispered, but some mascs would never learn.

CHAPTER 9

"**Y**ou mean we have to get real work done?" Heath donned a jacket as worn as Jess's, its green fibers bleached and frayed. The thrum of a power drill echoed from Kacy working on the roof.

"Yes," Jess snapped. I suppressed a snort. He had been short with Heath ever since yesterday.

"You better keep up with us," Heath said to me, undeterred.

I hefted a backpack of equipment, and narrowed my eyes at him. Jess picked up his own bags, and put on a brimmed hat.

"Come on." He led the way outside. "We're going to Station One today."

The sun hit me sharply, and I shielded my eyes against the glare. We climbed into the ATV, and as Jess backed it out of the garage, Gene opened the gate to let us through. He sat next to me, and we started north on a road, which, like the others, was only distinguishable due to tire tracks. The scenery didn't change much from gently rolling hills with yellowed grassland and groves of scraggly trees.

It took about an hour until we could see the top of a com-tower on the horizon. We stopped at the tower's base, and I studied its rusted metal supports that stretched at least two dozen meters into the sky. A small building hid behind the tower made from gray-brown metal, all its gleam etched away.

"Welcome to Station One," Jess announced after we had hopped out of the ATV. Heath unlocked the station's door. The roof sported the same solar panels as Headquarters, but a metal cage enclosed them. The cage caught my attention for more than a few moments as I tried to puzzle through why it was there. Surely it wasn't protecting the panels from the weather.

"There's some equipment inside the station to check, and then there are sensors a half mile to the east and west." Jess gestured to each side. "They'll probably need some work; they get damaged pretty heavily by the rain."

We stepped into the building, where Heath was already typing at one of the consoles. Gene filed past us to a counter on the far wall. On it sat many devices I had never seen; Gene switched some on. I pulled myself onto a black metal stool at the console beside Heath's and opened up a diagnostic.

"Ahh, only twice a year do I get to feel at home," Gene mused.

Jess responded softly. "I agree."

Home to them, maybe. The bitter smell of acid permeated everywhere, and a layer of grime dirtied the stool, counters, consoles—pretty much everywhere the metal had lost its gleam. I'd say they should take better care of it all, if it was "home" to them, but most likely the acid didn't let them.

Not quite halfway through the day, I finished with Station One's consoles, switching seats with Heath frequently enough to provoke scoffs and glares.

"This one's reading two point four," Jess called, and Gene hummed and jotted in a tablet. Jess retrieved samples from a cup of soil that had been dissolved in water, inserting them via dropper into receptacles in the equipment. I could appreciate their focus, but had no idea what any of it meant.

"And finally, three point eight."

Gene nodded and wrote.

Jess rubbed his hands on his pants, and gave me a nod. "Okay, Ember. Let's get going."

Back in the sun, I squinted as Jess and I walked along a worn path in the scrubby grass. A few gnarled trees dotted the horizon, and the thankfully clear sky resulted in heat made unbearable due to the humidity. My lungs rebelled against the thick, hot air.

"Not like the city, huh?" Jess asked, and I raised an eyebrow at him.

"Not at all."

"I like it out here. Give yourself a few weeks, you'll like it too."

Yeah, we'll see about that.

We approached a sensor array: a collection of dozens of delicate instruments. Another cage encased the equipment; Jess unlocked it and lifted its front face.

"Why is everything locked up?"

Jess put his key ring away and hesitated. "My grandfather used to tell me stories about wild animals on these plains. I guess the defenses against them have become a habit."

It was a good answer, but it didn't sit well with me.

Jess pulled open his backpack. "Let's get started."

I spent the next few hours replacing corroded wires, broken circuit boards, melted cases, miniature solar panels and their associated storage cells. Jess tested the functionality of every component as I worked. Finally satisfied, we traveled back to Station One, and checked in with the others.

"Ember, you're getting sunburnt," Jess said, plucking Heath's hat off his head and handing it to me despite Heath's protests. I felt silly wearing it, but smiled at the consideration as we stepped back into the sun, and headed in the opposite direction to resume our repairs. The next sensor array looked as worn as the last.

"It's a miracle any of these were working at all," I commented, tossing crumbling wires onto the ground.

"We are usually down to ten percent functionality the month before repairs."

I grunted and soon gathered my equipment. Jess locked the cage, and we began walking back. Rolling my shoulders, I wiped sweat off my brow with my sleeve and scanned the horizon. There was something off to the right, farther north.

"You see that?" I gestured. Jess stopped.

"Fuck." He produced a small pair of binoculars from his backpack, and peered through them. "Fuck, we're going."

Jess picked up his pace, and the edge to his voice scared me. The com-tower was visible in the haze ahead of us, but it would still take a few minutes to reach it. I glanced over my shoulder at the mysterious object, and jogged a few strides to catch up to Jess, grabbing his arm roughly.

"What the fuck is going on? What is it?"

Jess grimaced at me, looked back. "That's a scavenger. We have to get back to the ATV."

A what? He resumed his brisk pace, and I strode alongside him. Tingling fear constricted my chest.

"So we're not alone out here?" I scanned the otherwise empty scenery, wondering where you'd run if you were in the middle of nowhere.

He didn't answer. We reached Station One, and Jess banged on the station's door and bounded toward the ATV. Gene peered past the doorframe.

"Pack up, now." Jess's tone was unquestioningly urgent, and Gene must have gotten the hint. In less than a minute, Station One was locked up and we were returning to Headquarters.

"You guys saw scavengers, huh?" Heath asked, with a surprisingly sober tone.

Jess nodded. "Just one. He had a rifle across his back." In the moment of silence after this statement, my pulse picked up. A weapon . . . We could get shot? "We're starting the firearm rule early this year."

"Does Ember . . ." Gene started, but Jess grunted, so he glanced at me. "There's . . . a group of people. A tribe. I don't know what you'd call them. They have an encampment about forty miles northeast of Headquarters."

"They raided the kitchen?" I deduced.

Gene nodded. "Food is scarce here, as you can imagine. They've been getting more desperate over the past few years."

"Why are they out here?"

Jess shook his head. "They couldn't make it in the city, or they just didn't want to."

"Crazy, wild men," Heath muttered.

We arrived at Headquarters, and Jess called to Kacy on the roof. "Come down, we're having a meeting."

Upon hitting the conditioned air, I removed my jacket and hat. Beside me, Heath didn't stop at his jacket, removing his shirt too. He caught me looking at him, and threw his shirt on the ground.

"I hate this damn weather," he spat.

I shook my head. Crazy men, Heath had said . . . with rifles. That was a great combination.

"What's the firearm rule?"

"Do you know how to use a gun?" he asked. I shook my head. "I'm not surprised. Do you think you'll be able to learn?"

Well this hadn't been in the job description. I hadn't even touched a gun before—it wasn't the sort of thing Father had allowed when I was growing up. Despite the situation, a thrill ran up my spine at Heath's words. Handling a gun was something I never would have otherwise done back home.

Kacy joined us, the knees of his pants stained brown-red from rusted metal. Gene settled at the conference table, and Heath and I followed suit.

Jess paced from the conference table to the message board, his hands on his hips.

"I assume we're not telling Hale," Heath said.

"We don't need to bring him into this. They've got to keep under the treaty. We can handle it," Jess hissed.

"Can we?" Heath challenged, his voice rising. Kacy stepped past them to talk in a hushed voice with Gene. I frowned at Heath's tone. This definitely did not seem as simple as Jess was making it out to be.

"Jess, what exactly happened?" Gene ran a hand over the stubble on his head, just long enough now for me to see the color as a lighter brown than his beard.

"We saw an armed scavenger about two miles north of here," Jess explained. "But they know they can't mess with us."

"A lot of good the treaty did last year," Kacy mumbled.

Jess shot him a glare. "I still trust it."

Kacy shrugged. "Screw the treaty and tell your father to take them out."

Jess went to answer, but I spoke over him. "Are you really that barbaric?" Heads turned in my direction, and I pressed my palms against the table.

"Sorry, Ember, but I don't think you get it," Jess said. "They negotiate with bullets, so we have to speak their language. In years past, if we saw them getting close, we would practice shooting targets and wear firearms when outside. It was a reminder that there's two sides to this, and if they stayed away from us, we'd stay away from them. Then we wouldn't see them the rest of the time we were here." He sighed. "They'd never broken into Headquarters before."

"At least all they cared about was the food," Gene pointed out. "They didn't try to break through to the conference room."

"Yeah, this time," Kacy countered.

The men carried on talking, and I tried to figure out what I thought of this. I couldn't go home, not without gravely inconveniencing one of them to drive me. But being in a potentially life-threatening situation was pretty inconvenient for me, to say the least.

However, despite the risk, I wanted to stay. Maybe to see if I was man enough to tough it out. Take my chances. Even if that involved putting my trust in men I hardly knew. What did I really have to lose? All that was waiting for me at home was a bunch of electronics and a roommate with his own life. I refocused on the conversation.

"They know we're here now, so they'll keep their distance." Jess stared at the floor, his eyes stern, as he said this to the others. Like he was trying to reassure himself. "Let's arm up."

Jess and Heath stepped away from the table and down the hall; in the time they were gone I attempted to quell the nervous churning of my gut. They returned with long-barreled rifles that were as dirty and acid-marked as everything else out here. Gene and Kacy stood and claimed their rifles, and Jess appraised a fifth rifle before holding it out to me. I pushed to my feet and took it reluctantly, but embarrassed by that reluctance, I hefted it firmly to my chest. As the men grabbed boxes of ammunition from a shoulder bag Heath set on the table, Jess fixed his eyes on me.

"I know this isn't what you signed up for."

"But it's what I got, and I'll see it through." I tried to keep my voice steady. Jess gave me a relieved smile, and handed me one of the small boxes.

"Who's up for some target practice?" He motioned for us to follow him out.

The large rifle sat awkwardly in my hands as I stepped back into the sun. Jess was headed toward the gate. Heath caught up to us, a small crate in his arms full of empty cans painted green, his rifle already slung over his shoulder. We walked along the outside of the surrounding fence until a gently inclining field stretched before us, the Headquarters at our backs.

"Last one to hit a can has to wash dishes for a week!" Kacy challenged as he pressed rounds into his rifle's magazine.

"You're on." Heath carried the crate over a dozen strides away, and placed the cans on top of it. From this distance, they were mere specs.

I cupped a hand over my eyes. "Are you serious?"

"Yeah. Here, I'll give you the basics." Jess spent a few minutes pointing out all the parts of the rifle, and had me load it myself as he loaded his. "These are simple machines, ancient in design, but their reliability continues to prove itself. They're bolt-action, so every time you fire, you're going to follow it with this." He pulled on a lever, which made satisfying clicks as it moved. I copied him clumsily.

Heath snickered. "You think you can handle all that, andro?"

I didn't dignify him with a response.

Jess raised his weapon and fired. The rifle was much louder than I had anticipated, and I flinched at the shock of it. The shot echoed distantly, and my ears rang. Jess had missed the cans, and he adjusted his scope and aimed again. This time he sent a can flying. The others clapped, then took turns firing. Heath hit his target quickly, as did Kacy. Gene took his time adjusting and aiming, and eventually hit a target as well. I tried to imagine them shooting people instead of cans and my gut lurched.

They now waited for me to go. Following their lead, I peered through the scope at the last standing can, took a deep breath, and straightened my back. *They're all looking at me . . .* I released my breath and fired.

The rifle boomed right next to my ear, and it recoiled, slamming against my shoulder. I yelped, and shakily lowered the rifle from my face. My hands fumbled trying to pull the bolt. Damn it, this reminded me of school, and Heath and Gene's whispering to each other was all too reminiscent. My second shot was off, so I adjusted the scope as well as my sweating hands could manage. The third shot missed. *Damn!*

"Are you trying to hit the targets?" Heath jeered, muffled in my ringing ears.

"Suck pseudo," I bit back, and brought the green can into my sights. When I pulled the trigger, nothing happened.

"The bolt," Jess said, and I hastily loaded my next round—I was probably blushing brilliantly.

The rifle's report shook me. The bullet grazed the can and sent it spinning, and the men cheered. I turned back to them, and for a fleeting moment, felt like part of the group. One of the guys. Too bad it was under such a morbid circumstance.

Jess nodded at me. "Good job. Let's set them up for another round."

A few days later we traveled to Station Two with rifles on our shoulders. The station sat at the edge of a forest, an almost-copy to Station One. I made quick work of the consoles, and then Jess and I took care of the sensor array outside Station Two. As we worked, he asked me about my business, and soon we were debating operating systems and comparing Common upgrades to pass the time.

Thick clouds obscured the sun, and the brown sky melded with the brown land, the color of acid erosion. Those clouds held the temperature and the humidity close to the ground, like a blanket trying to smother us.

The next array was a mile into the forest, the last another mile after that. We set out, and I eyed the dark woods, the breeze carrying with it the sound of chirping insects and rustling leaves.

"Just watch your step out there, I don't want any twisted ankles," Jess warned. His meaning became apparent as I stepped over the trees' exposed roots.

The thick trunks and dark leaves blocked the sun but not the heat. I pushed aside a branch that hung across my path, and then pulled my hand away with a yelp. Sticky sap coated my palm.

"It's their defense against the acid," Jess explained. "Shit-tons of sap. Smell it."

"Neutralizer!"

He tipped his hat with a smile.

The path then led us to a fallen tree, and we scrambled underneath it through piles of crumbling leaves. Soon we reached the first array, and as we worked, the rust and dirt accumulated on our clothing and hands.

"I could use some of that sap about now," I laughed, rubbing my stinging fingertips together.

"You think this is bad?" Jess smiled. "Wait until you see where we're working next week."

With that array complete, we plunged deeper into the woods. My apprehension grew with each step as the meandering path scrambled my sense of direction. At least, I assumed we were following a path, though I couldn't see it in the dirt, bushes, and roots. I just had to trust Jess to lead me.

After a few minutes, Jess held out a hand, and I paused. He approached a clearing in the trees, where a decent patch of sunlight was visible.

"We're good," he called, and I joined him at an array that sat near the edge of the clearing. He scraped a patch of dirt from in front of it into a jar. "All the trees make this dirt surprisingly neutralized," he explained. "These are usually our highest pH samples."

We installed wires and solar cells until I ran out of needed replacements. Satisfied enough, we started back.

A rustling in the trees made us brandish our rifles. From the source of the sound came a cloud of chortling insects, their wings reflecting the dappled sunlight.

Jess exhaled and slung his rifle back over his shoulder, shaking his head. "Scared the shit out of me."

We stepped over crisscrossing roots. "We wouldn't really see one of those wild men out here, eh?"

He curled his lip uneasily. "You never know."

We met up with Gene and Heath at Station Two, and then Jess drove us back to Headquarters in the brighter yellow-brown sky of afternoon. We pulled in past the gate, and I caught a glimpse of Kacy positioning a sheet of metal on the roof. How he worked in this heat, I had no idea. Stumbling inside, we gasped for conditioned air and shed our guns and damp jackets.

"Two down." Jess wiped his forehead with a sleeve as he placed his rifle on the conference table. "Six to go."

"At least we didn't run into any of our friends today." Heath sighed as he joined Jess at the table. "But it is definitely time for a shower."

I averted my gaze as he pulled Jess's shirt off with a laugh, disregarding Jess's grumbled protests. Trying to ignore them, I settled at my desk, and began emptying my shoulder bag of my tools and parts I hadn't used.

"Not in front of everyone," Jess said over the sound of skin on skin, and then there was the pop of a kiss.

"Since when did the andro become everyone?"

I glanced up to find Jess pressed against the conference table, Heath gripping his waist. My face went hot, and I refocused on putting away my supplies.

"Get off me," Jess insisted, and he gave Heath a shove.

Okay, this was getting too physical. I pushed away from my now-cluttered desk, leaving them to their scuffle as I shut myself in my room.

I tinkered with one of the processors I had dropped the other day, soldering on new pins to replace ones that had bent in its fall. An hour later, I appeared to have made progress, so I fixed myself a plate of veggies, beans, and flatbread. While in the kitchen, Kacy and Gene ignored me. Jess and Heath were elsewhere.

Not long thereafter, I prepared my injection and pushed the drug into my veins with reluctance I didn't want to analyze. I wanted to blame the sourness in my gut and bitterness in my throat on breathing in acidic humidity all day, but I knew their origins were mental. The relationships I struggled to form with the others, the payoff at the end of it all, that payoff tainted by the threat of scavengers . . . This was harder than I thought it would be. *Stop it; I can't let myself care.*

I sat on my bed and read any article I could focus on, but focusing soon became difficult as my imagination wandered and my body began to burn. I kept reading. "Over the past two decades, the weather fluctuations have been surprisingly consistent . . ." I recalled Jess, shirtless, pressed against the conference table. I shook my head. ". . . there has been speculation that the periodic release of sulfuric acid helps fuel this pattern, though the origin of this release is unknown . . ."

With a groan, I pushed the Common away. The burning within me was too much to take, so I put out the fire to try to clear my head. But my skin tingled with imagined contact—him beneath me, tilting his head back, that stubble just begging for my tongue. Fuck.

Is that what this is? I like him? Seriously? I don't want . . . Okay, it was futile to stop the fantasies, but I had to keep this shit to myself. One slip, and I was going to get myself killed.

CHAPTER 10

The next day, a patch of noon sun lit up a keyboard before me, and I clasped my hands together as the console booted up. The processor worked!

"Knew I could fix that bastard," I exclaimed. Stress tests would be good though, to make sure, so I queued some up.

Soon satisfied, I meandered into the kitchen, to find Gene and Kacy sitting down for lunch. Gene gestured at a pot of chili on the hot plate.

"Help yourself."

Settling at the table with a bowl in my hands, I eyed the lovers skeptically. I stuck the spoon in my mouth, enjoying the heartiness, the spice. *Damn, Gene.* After a few more mouthfuls, I paused.

"So . . ." I began, hesitant to really talk about this. "You have questions about the surrogacy process."

Gene stirred his bowl and smiled. "Actually, we want to hear about your experiences with the infants."

I blinked at them. They had to be kidding me.

Kacy took his partner's hand and their fingers entwined. "We thought talking to a surrogate would give more personal insight."

"You clearly don't know anything about our side of things." I stared into my bowl as I spoke. "Surrogates are completely separated from the infants at birth. We don't even see them."

"Oh," Gene mused. "But you can feel the infants moving, starting at, what gestation week is it?"

I looked up at him, and I guess my expression caused the smile to vanish from his face. "Yes. I could feel them. The most unnerving sensations I've ever experienced."

Kacy raised his eyebrows. "You didn't like them?"

"Do you think I liked being a vessel used for someone else's convenience?" My voice threatened to escalate to a yell.

Gene appeared surprised. "It's your duty as a negative; I don't see why you should get so emotional about it."

I took a long slow breath so I wouldn't scream at him. "Why was this my duty instead of my choice?" I hissed.

"I'm sorry. It should be, but life has not allowed negatives that luxury."

It was a luxury to live like a real man. I guess he was right. "Anything else?"

"How many surrogacies did you have?" Kacy asked.

I shuddered. "Six. Seven if you count the abortion of a Y negative."

Gene frowned. "That's illegal."

"Maybe not twelve years ago when it happened, and especially not if you paid enough," I spat. The experience had left me with a question that followed me through the years: if my parents had been wealthy, would they have aborted my brothers or me?

"How horrible! We will accept our son either way," Kacy professed. I'd believe it when I saw it. "One more question, then? I've always been curious how much birthing hurts?"

I grabbed my empty bowl and stood. "It hurts a lot."

Being a Y negative wasn't as respected as Dad had tried to tell us it was. It was slavery. Was there any masc that understood that? At least I would never have to worry about going through the experience ever again. I hadn't even hesitated to get sterilized after my last surrogacy.

Dropping my bowl on the counter, I turned toward the hallway and locked eyes with Jess, who was leaning against the wall right outside the lounge. He pursed his lips in an expression that told me he had listened in. I kept his gaze while I walked toward and past him. He almost said something. Almost.

I emerged from my room the next morning to find Gene and Kacy sitting on the couch, some televid running on the display. I passed them and raised my arms in a stretch. Through the repaired kitchen window, the sky was muddy and dark.

"Looks kind of dreary out there," I thought aloud.

"It's gonna rain," Kacy said from the couch. "We're taking today off."

Fair enough. Entering the conference room, I worked through my exercise regimen, savoring the strain, though not what it meant. Not enough cardio, no weights . . . I wasn't trying hard enough. Push-ups until my muscles shook weren't enough. I gave up and stormed into the living quarters.

"What're you up to?" Heath asked from the table. I narrowed my eyes at him.

"Exercising."

He shook his head and gave Jess an exasperated look. Jess shrugged. "Whatever makes you happy."

I stepped past them into the kitchen, ignoring my now-sweaty clothes in favor of nourishment. I spread some preserves on a piece of bread and settled on the opposite side of the table from the men. After a few minutes, Jess made him and Heath a similar meal.

"Well I know what will make me happy on this rainy day," Heath said, downing a glass of fruit juice. "J-seven."

"Damn it, do you have to?" Jess grumbled.

"Don't give me that attitude," Heath snapped. "You act like my dad sometime, you know that?"

"Good." Jess's lips curled into a smirk. Heath growled and finished his meal in silence, and then without warning, he left the table. A question blurted out of me that I shouldn't have had the gall to ask.

"So what's the deal between you two?" I winced the moment I shut my mouth. Jess echoed my motion, and stared at his plate.

"Hard to say." He glanced behind me. "He thinks we can be like them." I assumed he meant the lovers.

In the ensuing silence, I thought I got the sense of what he meant. Namely, that they couldn't. He sat straighter and met my gaze, like he was about to continue. And then Heath returned and bounded to the kitchen table, practically crowing with excitement as he pinched open a small bag of white powder.

"This is good shit, Jess. You'll want to try it." He poured a tiny amount of it onto the dirty table.

"Next week," Jess insisted, his expression unreadable.

After a shake of his head, Heath straightened and snorted his line with a metal tube. He pushed out his chair and grimaced.

"Yeah, good shit," he finally uttered, his face flushed to a brilliant red against his blond hair. He gave Jess a laugh, and lofted the tube into the air. "Who's next?" He caught me looking at him and narrowed his eyes. "Come on, andro. Let's see you go."

I shook my head firmly.

Kacy joined us from the lounge, rubbing his hands together. Heath handed off the tube, and Kacy repeated the process before returning to Gene's side. Heath followed Kacy to the couch, already sighing with unknown amusement. He flopped down next to the couple and loudly asked them what they were watching. As Gene went to respond, Kacy threw his arms around him and started whispering into his ear.

"Hey, I'm talking to you!" Heath cried, but when Kacy stuck out his tongue at him, Jess and I stifled laughter.

"I'm not as into this stuff as he is," Jess said. "I don't like the thought of chemicals changing the way I act." He glanced at my arms and winced. "Not that it's wrong or anything, it's just . . ."

"Don't apologize," I said. "Testosterone makes me look and feel more how I was meant to."

Heath returned to the table, his eyes huge black pupils. He scooted his chair closer to Jess and leaned on him with a pout.

"I want you to experience this with me." He grasped Jess's hair firmly before pulling him into a kiss. I should have looked away, but I didn't. Jess kissed back, but there was reluctance in his hunched shoulders and his palms held open in the space between them.

"It's too early in the morning for this," I mumbled. Heath released Jess and laughed.

"Tell me about it," Jess said, echoing my tone.

Later on in the day, I left my room to find Heath and Kacy maintaining their buzz as they all played random televids. On one end of the couch, Kacy still sat curled up in Gene's arms; on the other, Heath kept a hand on Jess's thigh. Giving me an excited smile, Heath jumped to his feet.

"Just the andro I wanted to see," he exclaimed. "Explain what a pseudo is."

I stopped in my tracks. Was he serious? "Didn't your biology teacher show you a damn anatomy chart?"

"Humor us," Jess said. Damn it, him too?

"Testosterone doesn't just make my hair grow," I started, my cheeks undoubtedly scarlet. "It makes other things grow too."

"But," Heath stifled laughter, "you don't have a dick."

"No, but I bet my pseudo is bigger than whatever you have."

"Ooh, acid burn," Kacy giggled.

"Ember, you've got some balls, saying that to me." Heath passed me and poured another line before leaning forward and inhaling sharply. He shakily ambled toward me, a hand over his nose. "Oh wait. You don't have any."

"Heath—" Jess called out, worry lighting his voice.

"Someone oughta teach you to not speak like that to your superiors." Heath shifted his weight, pulled back his arm, and swung at me, but I dodged his attack. He tried again, grinning manically.

I shot out with a right hook, slamming into Heath's cheek and nose. He twisted and fell to the floor. In his inebriation, he made no effort to break his fall, and then lay there stunned. I yelped, and flexed my fingers.

"The fuck?" he gasped. Kacy snorted.

"Ember, what the damn was that for?" Jess yelled, his expression caustic.

My jaw dropped, and I gestured at the man who was still too high to get to his feet without help. "Didn't you see him try to punch me?"

"So you punched him first," Jess uttered, kneeling at Heath's side. Gene joined him and together they helped Heath up.

The accusation in Jess's tone flustered me. "I'm sorry my reaction is to defend myself. You don't know how many times I've been attacked."

"Just the other day you berated us for being willing to use violence," Gene said, his solemn voice grating on my already wound nerves.

Jess put a hand to Heath's face, bright-red blood now on his fingers. Heath waved his hand away with a loopy smile.

I grimaced, then glared at Gene. "This is not the same. I will not tolerate someone targeting me just because I'm Y negative."

"I don't think Heath was capable of targeting anything," Kacy stated, and Heath laughed.

Jess shot me a hard look, then switched his attention back to Heath. "I don't want to see that kind of behavior. From either of you."

My gut clenched, and I took a deep breath. "Okay." *Unless he hurts me first.*

X X

Heath fidgeted at the conference table, and I knew he desperately wanted to confront me after I had successfully avoided him all morning. His face had swollen less than I'd expected, though he had a satisfying dark-purple bruise on his nose.

"So this trip will take the next few days," Jess said, pointing to our planned stops on a map. I noticed the stations were numbered out of order.

"Where are stations Three and Four?" I asked.

"Three was wiped out in a hurricane before I was born," Jess answered. "We'll get to Four later on in the month. This trip is Five through Seven."

He briefed us on our workload, and then Gene told us a bit about his research in the area. Every time I looked up, I felt Heath's gaze dart off of me.

"Today we'll ready supplies and get a good night's sleep," Jess finished, standing. "We'll leave first thing tomorrow."

With the meeting over, the others left the table, and I studied the map. A red box marked the scavengers, in the foothills of low mountains. So strange, a society outside of society. How did they treat Y negatives?

Finally I stood, and Heath appeared from the living quarters, fire in his eyes. I went to step around him, and he grabbed my arm.

"Let go of me," I said, yanking out of his grasp, but Heath shoved me against the wall, his palms pressed against my shoulders.

"So what exactly do you think you are?" he hissed in a lower register. "An andro or a masc? You even so much as think about hitting me again, I'll—"

"Heath!" Jess shouted, rounding the corner. "Let go of him!"

"I have no idea how no one's taught you your damned place." Heath growled, but I stared down his sneer as the adrenaline triggered by his shove circulated through me. Jess pulled him off of me and dragged him out of earshot across the room. I shook out my arms and hopped in place, trying to quell the shaking. Jess gestured, Heath nodded. Heath stuck his hands in his pockets, shrugged.

Jess left Heath's side and strode past me. "Come on."

To prepare for our trip, we raided our stores for supplies, organizing and packing them in silence. In the kitchen, the clanking of cans and rustling of wrappers suggested someone else was packing food. Jess dropped his stuffed bag by the front door and glanced over at me.

"I'm sorry," he said. "Heath's a . . . a damn piece of shit, if you ask me."

"It's okay," I said. "He's just a typical masc."

Jess exhaled and shook his head. "I promise I won't let him hurt you."

Our eyes met, sending a warm shiver down my spine. My gaze snapped forward, and we resumed packing.

CHAPTER 11

"I know you probably won't believe this," Jess said to me, as the sun crept over the horizon. "But the acid's not to be underestimated. Breathe in the fog and it will kill you."

Gene and Heath piled supplies into the ATV, which included not only what we had packed, but also multiple sets of gas masks and what looked like metal leggings.

"What's with the metal pants?" I asked, and Heath chuckled as he shut the ATV's back hatch.

"You'll see."

Kacy leaned on Headquarters's rusty siding. "You guys won't mind if I do some redecorating while you're gone, yeah?"

Gene gave him a smile. "Like what?"

"You know, tear down some walls, smash some computers, stuff like that." He and Gene laughed. Jess shook his head, though he smiled.

"Not funny," he said. "Come on, guys."

We soon headed southwest. I wasn't pleased about spending another three hours in the ATV, but the time passed quickly. As we neared our destination, the hills gave way to flat land dotted with large, scraggly trees. Then spots of light began popping up on the horizon, revealed to be pools of water as we passed. Only a spiny dark-green grass grew anywhere near these pools. A few minutes after this shift of scenery, Gene sighed.

"Every year I hope by some miracle of nature that the land will have changed."

Jess grunted. "I wish we could remind more people of what's out here. From the way so many act, fighting over the same stupid things, you'd think they've forgotten why we live like we do."

Why do we live like we do? I knew why I did. Did he?

As the minutes crawled by, the puddles and ponds grew frequent enough for the land to seem more water than dirt. The ATV stayed on a road elevated above the water that accumulated around us. Groves of trees dotted the damp landscape here, with dark, shiny leaves shimmering in the breeze.

And there was the tower, and at its foot a small station just like the others. We stopped, and the moment I opened my door, a hot, damp breeze blew through the air conditioning, carrying with it a sound I had never heard: a deafening high-pitched buzz, like a hundred overclocked consoles. It bored into my brain and halted my thoughts.

"What the damn is that?" I managed, joining the others as Jess unlocked Station Five's door.

"The cicadas," Gene explained. "Large black bugs that like to make a lovely racket."

"Lovely?" I echoed. Jess and Gene entered while Heath scrutinized the tower and station exterior. Station Five sat on an elevated patch of land, and in all directions but the road, the ground receded into pools of brown water with muddy shores. Two footbridges extended out from the station over the land, their meandering paths disappearing in the yellow haze. All the while the buzz hadn't stopped, gradually wavering in pitch and intensity, churning my insides.

Its sound set the tone as I helped the others set up a rudimentary camp: we installed the awning on the ATV, and removed the backseat to be a makeshift couch underneath it. The sun had crept up the sky since we left Headquarters, and the atmosphere grew steadily hotter.

Gene settled on the makeshift couch and scanned the horizon before writing on his Common.

Jess dug through a crate. "Ember." He held out a gas mask, which sported goggles and large black canisters that filtered the air. "Add this to your pack, along with neutralizer and water. It's rough going out there."

I complied. Jess retrieved similar supplies for himself and lifted his own pack onto his shoulders. He then gestured for me to follow him.

"We'll be done before sundown," he said to Gene, who nodded and resumed scribbling.

We started on the footbridge leading west. The metal planks creaked under our weight, an unsettling percussion to accompany the incessant whirring. The horizon melted into a mirage as the temperature rose: the water reflecting the sky and making swaths of trees float in the air.

"Why don't we have our guns with us?" I asked.

"Scavengers know better than to take their chances out here." That made sense. My throat already burned from the acidic air and we had just gotten started. "Watch your step and pay attention to which side of the walkway is land and which is water. You fall in, you aren't going to have a fun time."

So I kept my eyes lowered, and my boots passed rusted metal, step after step. Sucking in damp breaths, I noticed the subtle smell of wet earth underneath the bitter stink. That sweet earthy smell reminded me of the greenhouses. Too bad it was still so drowned out.

After a few minutes Jess stopped; the footbridge stretched over a wide body of water whose surface was half-covered with a plant with plump, green-brown leaves.

"I don't like this," he mumbled. "We should have our leg armor on . . ." He thumbed through his Common. "The water didn't sit here last season."

"How deep is it?" My voice croaked from the acid.

"Shouldn't be more than thigh high."

I shuddered, imagining the burning if I fell in. The bugs laughed at us in their constant whine.

Jess exhaled, and stepped forward. "Fuck it. Just be careful." He tested each expanse of metal with a toe before fully resting his weight on it. I placed my path in each spot he touched. In that manner we crossed, incident-free.

We reached the sensor array. It resided at the edge of a pool, and an opportunistic vine had grown over half of its cage, the vine's thin tendrils supporting yellowish leaves and tiny pink flowers. Jess cleared what obscured the array's solar panel but left the plant otherwise intact. After saving a soil sample for Gene, we got to work. The instruments weren't just dirty out here; they were muddy, with condensation all over them and inside them, rusting everywhere. As I replaced casings and soldered parts together, I had to stop every few minutes to neutralize my stinging fingers. But I soon stood, and tried to brush the dirt off my pants, disappointed that it just smeared around thanks to the humidity.

"You're handling this really well," Jess said, his face half-shaded in the brim of his brown hat. The hat looked good on him, especially with the dark beard framing the rest of his face. "You've hardly complained while you've worked, you put up with our attitudes, and you know what the fuck you're doing."

I couldn't help but smile. "Thanks."

"Would you want to come back next season?"

"I would, but you've seen how well Heath and I get along."

Jess hesitated. "Heath acts that way toward everyone. You should have seen him ridiculing the lovers when they got together. You just happen to be the easiest target this season."

I exhaled, and Jess fidgeted, maybe waiting for me to respond.

"But . . . I'm trying not to see you that way," he added.

He started back and I followed, the stinging in my throat turning my breathing ragged, my thoughts dissolved by the incessant droning of the Outskirts. The more I tried to ignore the sound, the more it consumed my consciousness. I had been taught the world was dead outside the cities. But it wasn't dead at all. It was just . . . different.

At one point along the footbridge Jess smiled at me, and I looked down before he could notice me blushing. His kind words had settled into my abdomen, and with them came the aching of my muscles, my body's craving for an injection. Because if I were a masc . . . things would be different. Whatever intent I was reading in Jess's words . . . would be real. So I pretended I couldn't feel my body at all. If I couldn't feel it, then I wouldn't know how wrong it still was. I drifted behind Jess over the water, floating on the heat and the sweat, bobbing to a chorus of life I hadn't known existed.

We stopped at Station Five long enough to fill our canteens and satiate our hunger before heading north on the other footbridge. Reentering the hot, damp environment was more difficult this time. Fatigue plagued me, though merely walking around shouldn't have been this hard.

"I'm not used to this damn weather," I lamented.

"You get used to it eventually."

"Is eventually soon?" I asked, and Jess laughed.

"You sound kinda like my brothers when Dad used to bring them out here. They didn't reach 'eventually' before leaving all of this Outskirts stuff to me."

I looked ahead, sun sparkling off water for miles. "Maybe my eventually is just over the horizon."

"Maybe. I hope so." Jess jumped off of the footbridge, and then I saw why: the metal bridge had snapped in two, dark-brown rust caking the broken edges sticking out of muddy grass. We stepped carefully beside its supports, our boots squelching in the mud.

"So, you had said the other day you were the oldest son in your family," Jess started. Wow, he remembered. "I'm the oldest too. What do your brothers do?"

Now past the broken section, he climbed back up and held out a hand to help me. I chuckled and pulled myself onto the footbridge without it. We talked over the unchanging whir. Tiny insects caught the light as they danced in the air around us. Others with large wings and long, thin bodies skirted the top of the murky water. They seemed too big and heavy to float so delicately on the air, and I told Jess such.

"I have some old-world encyclopedias my dad gave me," he said. "Read them constantly when I was younger. Those are dragonflies. A lot of creatures used to be named after others they resembled, but I never found an entry for dragons."

We reached the second array and the time repairing it passed quickly enough. As the sun became obscured by thin, yellow clouds, we returned to the others. Heath lay sprawled out by the ATV on the removed backseat, shirtless and reading his Common. Gene was several yards away in the water, with the metal leggings protecting him as he waded to his knees. I stepped into the shade of the awning and the lack of relief made me wilt. Jess groaned and dropped his bag by the ATV, then his hat, his jacket, and his shirt. He flopped down next to Heath, leaned back, and put his hands behind his head.

"That's better."

With the two men taking up the backseat, I sat cross-legged in the shade, my Common in my lap. I hadn't read more than a sentence before Jess spoke again. "Aren't you going to relax? It's fucking miserable out here."

"There's nothing relaxing about removing my clothing," I admitted. Did I want to take off my wet shirt so it wouldn't continue to insulate my overheated body? Yeah, but it wasn't worth their curious, and probably cruel, observations. Jess stared at me, a slight frown on his features, like he hadn't actually realized the implications of his question. I returned my attention to my Common.

Gene joined us with a dozen sample jars and a wide grin as the sun began to set. We ate a canned meal warmed on a hot plate. The men talked of previous seasons and previous employees. I only half listened.

"And so Ashel and Paige got into another fight the following day. I honestly can't remember what riled them up so much, but it ended in Ashel storming out into the rain, I kid you not," Gene said, leaning against the ATV. "So I was yelling at him to come back inside, and it's pouring mind you, and he had no jacket on. Hale tried to reason with Paige, telling him to apologize before the rain killed Ashel, but he would have none of that. After half an hour of this, we dragged Ashel back inside. You should have seen him. His face was red as a tomato from the irritation. His shirt had melted into his skin. We had to dissolve it off with neutralizer."

"That's fucking insane. Father never told me about that. When was it?"

"It was my first season, so . . . a decade ago."

"And Hale thinks we're too rowdy together?" Heath challenged, as he put an arm around Jess's shoulder. Jess brushed his hand away. Gene continued the conversation undeterred. For the rest of the night, Jess avoided Heath's touch, and I stole glances at him over the top of my Common, and wondered.

When the world was completely dark, Gene excused himself and settled to sleep in the front seat of the ATV. I soon followed and curled up in the large cargo bay. Sometime later Heath and Jess crawled into the cargo bay as well, Jess's back two inches away from me, a world apart.

After a quick morning of checking out this station's consoles, we packed up our camp and headed to Station Six, an hour to the north. The station resided on the top of a hill, giving an elevated view of waterlogged lands. Patches of trees broke up the expanse, and the horizon disappeared into yellow haze. Footbridges traversed the lands, disappearing into the mist as well.

We settled into our new location, and then resumed our work, except now everyone was one day dirtier, sweatier, and crankier. But as soon as Jess and I were clear of the camp once more, his expression brightened, and our conversation picked up right where it had left off: what was our favorite music.

"I can't believe you and Steph got to go see an Elize concert. He was seriously my favorite singer when I was in primary school."

I laughed. "Just a perk of my father overseeing the concert electronics. I hope it doesn't ruin your childhood to know Elize's vocals are completely pitch-corrected."

"No way!"

By the time we started back toward Station Six, we had drifted back to business. Jess told me random facts about the stations, about data they had collected, research they had inspired. Some of what he said I had read about already, but I let him talk. Did he have any idea how much it meant to me, that he would talk?

"My father used to tell me about a lot of this research when I was a kid. He said this work is for younger men, but I think he just wanted to stay in his acid-free offices."

"Right now, I don't blame him," I said. "My dad works in the greenhouses in Atlanta."

"That's noble work." Jess smiled. "He's helping us survive this miserable existence."

I hummed in affirmation and decided against criticizing his understanding of the word "miserable."

After a few moments of silence, I asked, "So your father's at the offices. What does your dad do?"

"He . . ." Jess cleared his throat. "He died almost two months ago."

"I'm sorry," I muttered.

"He was a lot like Gene," he said. "Exploring, searching, learning."

I nodded. "That's noble work too."

"That's the work I hope to continue. I want to run these stations permanently. I want to have more freedom than being stuck in an office in Kansas City."

"Nothing wrong with that. There are plenty of men who will want to stay in the city."

"Yeah, but my father will make that call."

And not mentioning the scavengers would help his case so much, of course, when his father inevitably found out. But despite my bitter thoughts, something sweeter came out of me. "Don't be afraid to speak your mind on this kind of thing. You want to be doing something with your life that you enjoy." I winced. Damn it, was that flirty? Was I blushing?

"You're right." Jess looked down and ran a hand through his hair, and my insides melted. "Do you enjoy what you do?"

"I understand computers. The circuitry, the electricity, the inputs and outputs, it makes sense. It's probably the only aspect of life that is logical to me."

Jess laughed. "Yeah, people don't make sense at all."

"No, they really don't." I couldn't wait until we got back to the camp for him to take his shirt off again. And for what, so I could keep hating myself?

Sure enough, we arrived at the ATV and Jess stripped. I tried not to look. Heath smirked and insisted I "make myself comfortable." I told him I already was, and buried my face in my Common.

"So how're the signals transferring?" Jess asked, and Heath groaned.

"Took me all day to debug this error I'd never seen before: 742-3? Whatever, I figured it out."

"Good." Jess refilled his thermos with water before gulping some down.

"And your bog-walk?" Heath asked.

"On schedule. Ember's very efficient."

Heath stuck out his jaw. "You're making me look bad, aren't you?"

I hid my smile behind my Common.

A few minutes later, Gene joined us; he was a muddy mess, like he had been rolling around in the muck.

"Gene, what happened?" Heath laughed, helping him out of the metal leggings.

"Got a bit distracted chasing down a species of reptile I had never seen in the wild."

"Ooh, tell me all about it!" Jess exclaimed, following him into Station Six.

Once the sun set, the other men settled under the awning to enjoy the cooling atmosphere as I grew more nervous by the minute. My body ached for my choice addiction. It was bad enough trying to take a piss with no privacy, how would I inject?

After some internal deliberation, I resolved to give them all a much-needed lesson in living as an andro. I felt their eyes on me the whole time I prepared my needle, except for Gene who kept his head in his notes and jars of mud. After injecting, I glanced up.

Jess leaned forward and rested his elbows on his knees. "And that's it?"

"Yeah."

"And then what happens?" Heath asked.

I stared at him coldly. "I live."

I returned my supplies to their fabric bag, eyeing the two doses I had left. The timing of this trip would put me back in Atlanta right after taking the last one.

A few minutes later, Heath again proved predictable. "Is it doing anything yet?"

I kept my focus on my Common. "Maybe."

"Have you ever done anything crazy when it kicks in? My cousin once challenged my brother to a wrestling match. My brother broke his arm."

"Like I'd tell you." That memory was between me and the other three guys.

"Oh yeah? Well, are you up for a go?"

His aggressive tone threatened to set me off, but then I caught Jess subtly shaking his head. He let out a laugh, and shoved Heath playfully. "Man, when was the last time we wrestled?"

Heath's response was to lunge at Jess, and they fell to the ground, their limbs tangling as they grunted. I kept my eyes down, as my body had already begun to burn.

"Fuck, fuck . . . agh . . ." Scuffling, hands slapping skin.

"Ahh! Gotcha!"

I bit my tongue hard and pressed my knees together.

"Hey, Ember, let me show you something," Gene said over the sound of Jess counting out a pin in deep, panting breaths. I joined Gene against the side of the ATV, trying to hide my trembling. On his Common were a few circle graphs, showing the content of previous years' samples.

"You can see what these samples have in common: way too much acid. I've done a lot of comparison—it's not as pronounced in the city as it is out here."

"Why?"

"Some of the men back in Kansas City believe the acid may have been the result of a volcanic eruption. That could produce the volume of sulfuric acid we see, and allow us to guess what happened to the civilization that existed before."

"Is the acid all over the planet?"

"The acid is in the soil, and the atmosphere. Wind kicks sulfuric acid dust into the clouds, thus their yellow tint and acidic rain. Hundreds of years of wind and ocean currents have distributed the acid everywhere. At least, that's the current theory. There is a lot of land out there that has yet to be reexplored."

The vehicle rocked, interrupting our conversation as Jess and Heath tumbled into the awning supports.

"I said no, and I said I was done," Jess snapped.

Heath shoved Jess's shoulder against the ground and growled. "Come on."

"Fucking no."

"Guys, cool down," Gene called. Heath shoved Jess again, then shot to his feet. He faced away from us, his arms crossed. And despite myself, I couldn't look away from them. Jess lay on the ground an extra moment, his breathing still deep. Finally, he climbed to his feet.

"This is too much," he mumbled. Heath approached him hesitantly, and ran the back of his hand down Jess's arm. Jess kept his gaze lowered and didn't react.

"Anyways, Ember. Let me show you how these samples have changed over the past ten years." I tore my gaze from the other men and gave Gene as much of a smile as I could muster.

It was dark, everything pitch-black except for straight up. I lay out beyond the awning, the ATV visible only if I turned my head. Above me was what must have been thousands of stars, all twinkling and beautiful and mysterious. It utterly unnerved me to look at them, unhindered by city lights.

The stars weren't thrown across randomly; instead they formed clusters and patterns. I imagined drawing circuit lines between them, tracing the flow of energy from one star to the next. The universe simplified to code: zero, one, zero, zero, one.

The others had gone to sleep not that long ago. No one had questioned me when I didn't follow them to the ATV. The burning hadn't stopped all evening, through Gene's soft words, through Jess and Heath's fight defusing. Though the world was now dead silent, cooling and dark, a fire still consumed me from within.

My lips parted as I slipped a hand beneath my belt. I still stared ahead at the stars, but for a few minutes, I didn't actually see them. I imagined Jess and Heath's bodies entwined, writhing, while my throat buzzed with my stifled voice. Infinity stretched on indifferently, even after my exertion ended with my head tilting back as my body shuddered.

The burning had cooled to a faint glow when a commotion erupted from the ATV. The stars lurched right as I turned my head. Jess stomped away from the vehicle, his arms around his chest. He settled on the backseat and rocked. I approached him, my heart suddenly hammering.

"Jess?"

"Oh—you're still awake?"

I settled next to him, barely able to make out his features in the darkness. "Yeah. Are you okay?"

Jess switched on an electric lantern, but kept it dim. "Heath is driving me crazy."

The blue light accentuated the angles of his body. His muscles weren't sculpted like so many of the men I had seen in the gyms, but I somehow didn't mind this. Even while slouching he had a grace in the slope of his shoulders, the slightest hints of ribs down his sides.

"I . . ." He stopped. I waited. "He . . ." His second pause shuddered through me. After a few minutes of him staring at the ground, I changed the subject by taking off my shirt. He looked up at the sound of the fabric peeling off my skin. I tried to keep my face calm as he studied me.

"Those are some wicked scars," he finally said. I nodded. With a light laugh, he turned toward me, our knees now touching. His finger traced one of the scars on my chest.

"People always say you can spot an andro from a mile away," he said quietly. His hand slipped down to my waist, and he squeezed me, an almost-caress. "But you don't seem any different."

Our eyes met for a moment, and then he sat back, burying his face in his hands. "This is harder than my problem with Heath." He raised his head and scanned my body again before his eyes darted forward. "Fuck."

If only I knew what was going on in his head. I wanted to reach out to him, but I didn't. I couldn't. "I'm sorry."

"I can't go back in there with him."

"Then don't."

"I can't stay out here."

"Why?"

"Because where else would you be?" He left, and I heard the ATV's hatch open and then shut. For a moment I had no idea what had happened. Was he suggesting that he . . . No. I put my shirt back on and lay down on the backseat. It took a long time to fall asleep with the memory of his fingers on my skin.

CHAPTER 12

My eyes flew open, woken by someone shaking my shoulder. I sucked in a breath painful enough to seize my chest in panic. My vision was fuzzy, vague shapes in shades of morning pink. I coughed, and tried to take another breath, a mere wheeze, my entire mouth, throat, and sinuses burning.

"Jess! Get over here!" The blurry figure was tall, skinny, ah, Gene. He pulled me up. "Can you understand me? Can you see me?"

I nodded, and Gene helped me to my feet. His touch felt distant and numb until I realized all of my exposed skin was stinging.

"What..." I croaked, my speech erupting an itchy fire deep in my throat.

"The fog came in. Did you sleep in the open air?" Gene asked.

Someone stumbled out of the ATV. "Oh shit." It was Jess. "Fucking humidity."

"There's neutralizer vapor in the med kit," Gene urged, leading me inside Station Six. He sat me on a stool, and left.

"Fuck," I managed, rubbing my eyes, which didn't help at all. I cringed and hissed.

Jess joined me, muttering under his breath and rustling through what I assumed was a med kit. Gene returned with a canteen.

"Water'll help, drink."

I did, but the first swallow was torture. I forced down a few more.

Jess ripped open a wrapper. "Lean back." I obeyed, and he draped a damp cloth over my nose and mouth. "Just breathe normally. This is going to burn worse for a moment, but it'll help, I promise."

"Shhhhhiit . . ." My eyes watered from the stinging, which amazingly helped my vision clear. "This is what drowning must feel like."

Gene sighed. "Not in the slightest."

"This is totally my fault," Jess said. "I didn't tell him to go inside, or warn him, or anything."

"It's not always this bad," Gene said. "Especially this time of year. We're lucky the fog was mostly down the hill. If he had been in the thick of it, this would have been much worse."

"Ember, I'm sorry. I'm such an idiot."

I waved a hand, hoping he saw it. "Don't beat yourself up. I'm the dumbass who stayed outside." Now that the burning was starting to subside, the heat of embarrassment replaced it.

"How does it feel now?" Jess put a hand on my shoulder. My gut clenched.

"Better."

"He got corroded alive?" Heath exclaimed from outside, and Jess and Gene caught Heath up on the situation as they left me. Taking one more deep breath, I freed myself, and joined the others. Heath took one look at me and doubled over laughing.

"Fucking tomato red," he crowed. Jess had his face in his hands, but I could make out a smile behind those fingers. *Yeah, yeah, I get it, I fucked up. Give me a break.*

I touched my cheek and winced. It was definitely that bad. At least the rest of me had been covered, though changing out of these damp clothes was in order. I climbed stiffly into the ATV and reemerged a few minutes later in a dry shirt and pants, and by that point the pain was bearable.

Jess handed me granola and mixed fruit. "We still have Station Seven to visit before heading back. Are you up to it?"

I nodded between spoonfuls. "A little acid can't keep me down."

"That's the attitude," Jess said. "But you're wearing a gas mask when we're working, that was enough acid for one day, okay?"

"If I can still work in it."

We loaded the ATV and descended into the fog to head toward Station Seven, Jess proceeding slowly to stay on the road. The thick, yellow mist was unrelenting at first, but soon revealed shadows of bushes and trees as we passed. By the time we reached the small station, it had mostly cleared.

"One of the arrays is right here," Jess explained as we left the ATV. "And there's only one other that we service anymore. The other two were flooded one season and Father didn't think it was worth rebuilding them from scratch."

"This'll be fast, then," I said.

"It would, except the footbridge is wiped out too." Jess lifted up the back hatch of the ATV and hefted the metal leggings.

"Seriously?"

He nodded. "Suit up."

Now this was a fucking workout. My legs were lead and my breathing through a straw. I fought the dizziness as well as I could, treating it like running in slow motion. Timed inhalations, even footing. Jess was just as slow, luckily, and wore a mask too, maybe to make me feel better, I wasn't sure.

The water came up to lower-thigh as we followed the remains of a footbridge. The coldness on my legs unbalanced the heat on my torso as though the elements were only capable of extremes. We waded past long, thin plants that stuck out of the water, puffs of brown at their tops.

"Cattails," Jess commented.

"And what's a cat?" I asked, and Jess laughed and recited for me.

More of those dragonflies buzzed around us, some blue, some red. One had a wingspan almost as wide as my forearm, and it floated on a nonexistent breeze a few feet above me. The mask steamed up with my breath, and for the fifth time I wiped the goggles clean. We passed near a grove of trees, the whirring of the cicadas accompanying us once more.

How could they not teach us about all of this? I had learned that the world was dead, lost under the rust and decay. Drowned in unceasing acid. But here, the brown water swirled with my movement, tiny bugs on its surface scattering. The cattails swayed in the warm breeze. The bugs chirped.

All of this life and I felt even more hollow, cheated by one more layer of man.

"This is an alien world," I said, testing my weight on slippery rocks and thick sediment, pulling my heavy leg through the muck.

"I don't think so." Jess climbed a shallow bank onto the land. I inclined my head; the rusted cage of the array was visible past the grasses. "This is earth, the cities are alien."

He began clearing vines from the array cage. As I finally caught up to him, he let out a strangled screech.

"What—?" I started, struggling to find some unseen assailant through my fogged goggles.

"Fucking damn, get back, get back," he wrapped a hand around my wrist and pulled me behind him.

"What is it?" I tried again.

"Right there, in front of the cage. A snake."

Amidst the soggy grasses lay what looked like a thick, black cable, loosely coiled.

"A what?"

Jess must have realized that he still held my wrist, as he let it go with a mumbled apology. "A reptile. Predator. Could kill a man. This one's old world name is 'cottonmouth.'"

"That thing could kill you?" I steadied my breathing, my trembling limbs.

"Yes. My dad taught me what creatures to be cautious around. This species was at the top of the list. I haven't seen one in years, and never this close."

"Well, can we move it out of the way?"

"Hopefully. I need a stick." Jess stepped a wide berth around the creature and broke a thin branch off the nearest tree. "Stay back, I don't want you to get bit."

I took off my face mask and moved away with my arms crossed. I didn't yet know what to make of this. How was this creature deadly? Jess approached it, pushing the stick slowly into the coiled black cable. And suddenly the word "cable" became a wholly inappropriate description.

The reptile undulated, twisting its body around itself and raising its head. Its movements were eerie. Unnatural. Much worse than the spider back at Headquarters. And as Jess pushed the stick forward, the reptile hissed, exposing a strange white mouth.

"Shit, shit . . ." Jess leaped back with a *clunk* of metal. "Damn it."

I held my breath, preparing to run in these metal leggings if I had to. But the snake stopped writhing, and slipped away through the disturbed grasses.

We stood there, staring at the place the snake had occupied. Jess looked over at me, and when our eyes met, he burst out laughing.

"What?" I asked, his changed mood making me smile.

"That was probably the stupidest thing I've ever done."

"Oh really?" I challenged, and he snorted, kneeling in front of the caged array.

"Okay, you got me. I can think of stupider. And his name's Heath."

I gasped, and he gave me a sidelong glance as he giggled again, and there was a spark in his eyes that got my blood pumping. I . . . No way. I had to be imagining these things.

"At any rate, we're not telling Gene," Jess said. "Or he'll want to come out here and try to find it again."

"That man may be too devoted to his research," I declared, and we chuckled as we got back to work.

But that glance . . . I couldn't get it out of my mind. It did not look platonic. Maybe I was reading my own yearning into his features. Anything made more sense than the desire that trickled through me. I had to be careful, or Jess wouldn't be the only guy doing something stupid.

Twilight surrounded us as we pulled into Headquarters that night, and Jess eased the ATV into the garage as Heath shut the gate. We had started unpacking the ATV when Kacy ran out, and into Gene's arms.

"Damn, am I glad to see you," he uttered, and the men shared a kiss. Kacy pulled away, and his dark expression perked my interest. "We have a problem."

"What do you mean?" Jess asked, pulling his bag onto his shoulder. I grabbed my own bag and joined the others.

"Yesterday, scavengers checked out Headquarters." He paused when the others swore. I stood back and listened, my arms crossed.

"I was finishing up on the roof," Kacy explained. "They circled a few times on off-road buggies, eight men, two to a ride. They circled, and left. Maybe because they saw me."

"Jess, I think Hale needs to know this," Gene suggested, but Jess swore and stormed through the open front door. "Jess!" Gene followed him, and the rest of us followed as well.

"We don't need to bother him with this. The scavengers will obey the treaty. They're snooping. Nothing more." Jess was sitting at the conference table, his rifle laid across it.

"So what happens if they do more than just circle?" Kacy asked.

Heath growled. "Hale will blow the fuckers into orbit, and it'll be less than they deserve."

Wasn't that a bit much? Jess stayed silent, his jaw set as he stripped down his gun and cleaned it. Heath and Gene began unpacking supplies.

"They'll stay away," Jess finally said, snapping the rifle's pieces back into place. "They know one more toe out of line will be the end of them."

"It's a bit more than a toe out of line by this point, don't you think?" Gene asked quietly.

Jess stood. "My stations, my rules, and I say we're fine. We keep going."

He laid the gun by his console. Heath grunted and strode past us and Jess followed him out. I met Gene's worried gaze.

"What would Mr. Cameron do if you told him?"

"Cancel the rest of the session," Gene said. "I wouldn't want to leave this early, either. I'm sure Jess is right, the scavengers won't mess with us again."

Gene and Kacy soon left me alone in the conference room, wondering what the damn just happened. I had anticipated battling the outskirts—like our creature encounters and my raw throat and sinuses attested. But scavengers . . . They hadn't been part of the package, and I didn't like it.

Jess nodded, his arms trembling at his sides. "You hungry?"

Heath laughed. "Yeah."

"Let's have some chili," Gene pitched in. "Gimme five minutes ...eat some up." Gene stood, and gave me a dirty look when he ...ed me.

This isn't my fucking fault . . .

I sat shakily on the couch, and Kacy left as well. The music was still ...ing and I listened to the highs and lows as my head settled back ...ormal. After several minutes, the clinking of silverware beckoned so I served myself and scarfed down a bowl.

When the mascs did their next lines, I didn't join them. They ...on a televid, a romance that made my stomach churn. I stayed at ...kitchen table with my Common out. The televid hadn't been on ...long when Jess settled on Heath's lap. I suppressed a groan as they ...sed feverishly, and with effort, I resumed staring at my Common.

"Hey! Guys!" Gene called. "Remember what you used to tell ...cy and me? Below the belt is bedroom only!" His words ended ...shly. I blushed and kept my eyes down, and Heath chuckled. Then ...s's bedroom door shut, making me jump.

Damn it, I have to get out of here. I pulled on shoes and slammed ...e Headquarters's door behind me. After some stretches, I jogged ...ng the inside of the fence, glancing at the shimmering horizon as ...an. The heat soaked into me, sobering me faster than even those ...ascs. Eventually I stopped and gripped the fence, staring out at the ...mnants of Arkansas, alone in an expanse of dried grasses and ruddy ...es. The low mountains to the north were shrouded in wispy yellow ...ouds, but the clouds, and the mountain's occupants, kept their ...stance.

I ached with disappointment and confusion. Why had I lured ...ss into this attraction toward me? Was I really that desperate? I ...ill had eleven more days out here, stuck with these men and their ...elationships. The time would pass quickly, but I dreaded the next ...me I saw Jess. That was, if he didn't bury this down too.

A rifle's report echoed from the north and I jerked my head in ...hat direction. With a shiver, I went back inside.

Gene and Kacy still sat cuddled on the couch watching televids. ...he other men were still absent.

The next day, the other men were back to normal. Talking and laughing while Gene chopped up the last of our fresh fruit for breakfast. Like the scavengers didn't matter. And then Jess met my gaze, and my gut flip-flopped. So I stared at my hands, rubbed my palms together. Damn it.

"Well, boys. I believe it's time to start the celebrations," Heath announced, eyeing Jess hungrily before scanning the rest of the men.

Jess sighed, and Kacy let out a squeal as he bounded to the living room and turned on some music. Heath laughed deeply, and left us.

Jess scooted his chair closer to mine. "Will you do it with me?" I raised my eyebrows at him.

Heath returned, revealing that his stash wasn't limited to one bag. He snorted quickly, then made a second line, holding out the small tube for Jess. He let out a cheer as Jess took it.

Kacy bounced toward us, and smacked Jess on the back. "Happy Birthday, man. Now do it."

Heath repeated the sentiment, and Jess's doubtful frown suggested his inexperience. He glanced at me again.

"Will you?" He repeated. Why did it matter if I joined in? But still I nodded. He smiled at Heath, and leaned over the drug, then he coughed, sniffled, and wheezed. Heath and Kacy clapped.

"Come on!" Heath urged, pulling Jess into the living room as an upbeat melody increased in volume.

Kacy did his share, and I drummed my fingers on the table. Flames of desire licked through me as I recalled echoes of thumping music and the tingle of skin on skin. The sharp clinking of dishes caught my attention, as Gene cleaned up after us, just like a parent.

"Thank you," I said, and he gave me a gentle nod. "Did your parents teach you to cook?" Jess's laughter cut through the music and tugged at me.

"My father, yes." He smiled. "The secret is in the spices."

"Oh really?"

"I know it's rare, but black pepper is marvelous—"

We were startled from our conversation by Jess shrieking my name. My face heated up at the sight of his wide smile.

"You saaaiiiid you would do it." He had reentered the kitchen and now he propped himself up on the table with a loud smack of his palms on metal.

"I guess it can't be a party unless we all join in, huh?" Gene asked.

"I guess not." I studied Jess's wild eyes and flushed face and fought my imagination. A shiver shot down my spine as I straightened in my chair, my lower abdomen starting to burn. J-seven would make it a blaze, and kill the part of my mind that kept me roped in.

It was my own damn fault that was what I wanted. I poured the white powder, and Jess clapped excitedly. Heath laughed. *Oh, this will not end well . . .* I prepared it, and inhaled deeply. Oh shit, my burned sinuses! "Fuck!" *Note to self, don't snort after breathing acid fog.* I scrunched my nose and wiped watering eyes. Jess grabbed my free hand and led me into the lounge, oblivious to my plight.

"Get back over here." Heath yanked Jess from me and the two men began to dance as I stood, still shrouded in doubt. Gene collapsed onto the couch and laughed at Kacy, who danced by himself with twirling hands and random footwork. Jess sang along to the song with his eyes shut, his hands held loosely above his head. He was hopelessly sexy like that, uninhibited and blissful. Heath kept Jess close with hands squeezing his waist, and I imagined hands all over Jess's body as the awkwardness that kept me stationary melted away.

Tingling erupted in waves across my skin and the loud, bright music eased my hips into a rhythm. A smile bloomed on my mouth like a cherry tree's pink blossoms. My body went hot as the melody moved through me, my apricot cheeks betraying my excitement.

"Damn, Ember, you're not afraid to move." I opened my eyes and caught Jess's gorgeous smile, framed perfectly by his smart beard and sharp jawline . . . but his brief attention on me wandered as Heath gripped Jess's hips, his lips on Jess's neck. Jess tilted his head back, and I fought the weakness in my knees, imagining Heath's hair my color. Yeah, I shouldn't be thinking this. But as Jess twisted in Heath's grasp and their mouths met, I didn't care. I stared at the men, my jaw hanging open.

Then Kacy took my hand and danced by my side. I laughed at the electricity of his skin on mine, my eyes slipping past him to Jess every few moments. The beat kept me moving, Kacy's twiddling fingers in my hand and on my shoulder giving me flashes of wattcreds long spent, of the taste of sweat and oranges.

"Kacy . . ." Gene called from the couch. I had troub[le] him. "Stop it, you're teasing him."

Kacy's loose grip on my limbs suddenly disappea[red] alone. I remembered this abandonment well . . . Years [ago,] right masc and resist my gag reflex and leave smears [on] thighs, but then I'd be alone and confused, my lips puc[kered] sour of someone's lemon paint.

Heath was the first to go back for more, but we all [fol]suit. I took the drug like a masc this time, and Heath['s] shoulder shuddered through me and caught in my throa[t] throwing around our hips and limbs to incoherent beat[s.]

Soon thereafter, Heath excused himself and bumb[led] hall. A door clicked shut. Hands grabbed my hips. I th[ought] Kacy again, but Gene and Kacy were staring wide-eye[d from] the couch. Jess's hand eased to right below my belly bu[tton and] pulled me toward him until my hips pressed against his. [I] flushed once more, but I couldn't feel it over the spinni[ng.] Jess's breath warmed my shoulder as his other hand ran [up] and the pleasure and shock of it tugged me down from m[y]

"You don't . . . feel any different," he breathed.

"You're high, dude. Heath's gonna kill me if he sees th[is.]" frantically at him, rotating in his grip to face him.

"It's a damn good excuse if you ask me." He leaned fo[rward.] Gene and Kacy erupted in a hushed chorus of nos. I lo[oked at] him shooting them an icy scowl, but his tight grip rema[ined as] he kissed me hard, and my eyes fluttered shut as I wrappe[d] around him. Only andros had ever kissed me like this, [so] hungrily. I stifled a moan, tentatively gripping his back.

As abruptly as the kiss started, it ended. He let go of [me] with a shove. Now that, only a masc would do, and I splaye[d] to not fall over. He stormed into the kitchen, and I scanned [for] but he had not yet emerged. I got my bearings and straigh[tened my] shirt, just as Heath appeared and frowned at us.

"No more dancing?" he asked, following Jess.

"When can I have more?" Jess poorly concealed his upse[t.]

"Hey, you always told me to not get too crazy here[. Give it a few] minutes and then we'll float above the clouds one more time.[

"How was it out there?" Gene asked.

"Just as stifling as it is in here."

"Ember . . ." Gene's tone was uneasy. "You and Jess can't—"

"I know," I spat. "You don't have to tell me."

"I'm sorry." Gene rubbed his temple. "It's extremely upsetting to see anything het. It freaked me out when Kacy touched you that way."

I didn't respond, even as Kacy muttered apologies to Gene, and blamed his behavior on his inebriation. "And I mean, come on. Ember looks surprisingly masc."

It was infuriating how my greatest accomplishment could be portrayed as a fault.

CHAPTER 13

These men had no sense of organization. The next morning, I had to go through every cabinet and drawer as I restocked my supplies for the rest of the trips we would make, and I wanted to take everything out, dump it into a huge pile on the conference table, and sort through it all. I pulled open all the drawers in one cabinet for the third time, and finally found the size screws I needed.

With a slam of the drawer, I turned around and noticed Heath look away from me and resume typing at his console. His beard had grown thick since leaving the cities, and he had yet to trim it, giving him a disheveled appearance.

Jess entered the conference room, and hesitated when he saw me, his eyes darting to the floor. Oh good, he at least remembered. But he had to face what happened at some point. We both had to.

My pack ready, I settled at a console and connected to the stations to check on my repairs. Around me, Gene typed away under a display of graphs, Heath scrolled through code, and now Jess was bent over maps at the table. Together, yet miles apart.

The stations took their time answering my queries, and my mind wandered, recalling Jess's grip on me, his fierce stare. I glanced over at him, tapping at his Common, tracing paths with an index finger across maps. Damn it, I wanted him to do it again.

After dinner that evening, I retreated to my room while the others stayed up to watch a televid. Shortly after the men settled down for the night, fighting broke out in the hall. I had never shut my door, so their words echoed clearly.

"Jess . . . what's wrong? Why do you always act like I'm pressuring you?" Heath sounded like he was inside their bedroom. Jess must have been in the hall.

"Are you kidding me? You get defensive the moment I turn anything down. And then everything's my fault; it's always my damn fault."

"I don't do that."

"Don't even try, Heath! You outright blamed me last year!"

And with that, my full attention was on their voices.

"I try to tell myself it wasn't your fault," Heath bit out. "I try to tell myself that I wasn't that close to him, but I haven't forgotten . . . any . . . of it."

I tilted my head to the side. Someone Heath was close to?

"You think I could?" The passion in Jess's voice sounded diluted.

"But you . . . help me forget it all," Heath said, and his words made me uneasy. Or maybe I was reading too much into his strained voice. "Being here, being reminded, I need you."

Oh, no. Heath was playing him, and Jess would probably be lulled right into the trap.

"No. I can't do this anymore. I can't keep lying to you, or to myself."

"What are you saying?" Heath asked, his voice wavering.

"I knew when you asked me out it was because of him. It's my damn fault I let it get beyond that. There's nothing here, not for me." The emotion in Jess's voice was shocking. Was their relationship this rocky? Or had I caused him to snap?

"How could you call what we have nothing?"

"This has been a long time coming and you know it. Get out of my room."

I put a hand to my mouth. And then there was a thud from something getting knocked over.

"Fuck, you selfish piece of shit, you always gotta be right huh? You think you're the victim in this?"

"Get out!"

"Adin was the fucking victim!" Heath shouted. Adin? *Wait, this is about the guy I replaced?*

"I told you to get out!"

"And what, sleep on the couch? I'm not sharing a room with a damn andro."

There was a pause, and my stomach flipped. Fuck, no, I didn't want Heath near me.

"Fine. Fine," Jess uttered.

"What are you doing?" There was rustling. "What . . . what are you—"

"Fuck you." Footsteps approached. Jess pushed my door open, and slammed it shut behind him. He dropped the pile of clothes in his arms, and didn't even glance at me as he flopped onto the other bed, a soft cloud of dust puffing into the air around him as he wrapped his arms across his chest.

The other door banged shut, and there was murmuring from the lovers' room. Jess remained motionless and silent. He breathed deeply, his face flushed and his jaw cocked in frustration. His hands were white-knuckled fists.

Our gazes met, and I wanted to tell him he did the right thing, but then his throat bobbed and he looked down and the moment had passed. He had stood up for himself, his first act of courage I had seen, well, except for possibly our kiss. But what did he mean, choosing to come in here with me? Why was he doing this?

In the ensuing silence, I hesitantly lay in my bed and flipped the light off.

"Ember . . ." Hearing his deep voice in this dark room made me flinch. "Is this okay?"

"Yes."

There was a knock at the door, and I blinked groggily.

"Jess . . . can I talk to you?" It was Gene, and his words reminded me what had happened the night before. I stole a glance at Jess, who inhaled deeply and turned over, his bedsheets a twisted-up mess. Biting my lip gently, I tried not to stare at him, but I couldn't help it.

Gene knocked again. "Jess?"

"Damn it, hold on." Jess scratched his head, freed his legs from the sheets and sat up. He squinted at me. "Good morning." I nodded. With a groan, he shambled to the door, stretching his arms back, leaning his head to each side. He cracked the door open. "Okay, what do you want?"

"What do you think you're doing?" Gene's voice was frantic.

"Sleeping."

"I'm serious, Jess, you can't do this."

"Can't two men sleep in the same room without fucking each other nowadays?" Jess snapped. A wave of surprise ran through me. He called me a man . . .

"You kissed him."

"I was in orbit."

"I don't think that matters."

"Gene, I appreciate your concern but this isn't your damn business."

"I'm sorry," Gene said. "You're quite right. But . . . just be aware I'm not comfortable with any of it."

"Duly noted," Jess muttered, already turned away. The door shut with a click, and his eyes met mine. "This is all insane."

"What happened between you and Heath?" I asked.

He leaned on the door. "The whole world didn't hear us yelling?"

"I heard, but I don't understand. What's this about Adin?"

"Please don't make me get into it right now." He took a few steps toward me, his arms loosely crossed. His cheeks were red and his expression haunted. "I don't know what I'm doing with myself. I . . . broke up with my boyfriend last night."

"Would you really call him that?"

"Yeah." Jess met my gaze again, and shook his head. "I didn't mean to drag you into all this."

With a frown, I studied his lips, his jawline, the strand of dark-brown hair that was long enough to almost touch his eyebrows. "Why did you kiss me?"

"Fuck, I'm sorry. I shouldn't have done that, I was totally out of line—"

"I liked it." I stood, and approached him. He took a few quick breaths, fear in his eyes. I stopped within arm's reach, and echoed his stance by crossing my arms. "So don't say you're sorry."

He stared past me now, still breathing with a hint of irregularity.

"What are you fighting?" The fear that had been in his eyes settled in my stomach.

"It's wrong. It's . . . wrong."

I reached out for him, and he took a step back, his hands held up. "It's wrong!"

I gave up and sat on my bed.

"Fuck." Jess stepped toward the pile of clothes he had left by his bed. "Fuck this nonsense dead." He pulled on pants, and left.

They all ignored me. Every one of them, not a glance, not a word. When they settled for a lunch I hadn't been invited to, I had to serve myself, and ate from the kitchen counter. They spoke to one another like I wasn't even there.

"So you two are really going to be parents," Heath said happily. The lovers sighed and smiled, clasping free hands together.

"It's hard to explain the excitement," Kacy started. "I can't wait to see an ultrasound."

"Have you thought about names?" Jess asked.

"I've always liked Chris," Gene said.

Kacy shoved him playfully. "No way. None of those old names. Let's name him Exon, or Histone, or . . ."

"No." Gene smiled.

"My brother's name is Valence . . ." I added hesitantly. Some of them glanced at me and just as quickly looked away.

"Neutrino." Kacy laughed at Gene's exasperated expression.

"I'm not naming our son after a decay product." The others snickered. I finished my plate and left them.

My mind swirled so severely with confusion about Jess that remote-checking sensors was a thankful respite—so of course I finished sooner than I had expected. With the extra time, I ran around Headquarters a few dozen times. The cloud cover had grown, though it didn't look thick enough to rain. The temperature had not cooled at all. After my run, I settled beside the conference table and performed as much of my workout regimen as I could. The men walked around me. I would have preferred their shunning a few weeks ago. But now . . .

As I worked my muscles, they shook with the strain; this weakness made me sick. I did push-ups until I was exhausted, thankful for the lack of full-length mirrors out here. When I got back home I'd be working double-time to return to how I had been.

Finally I gave up exercising for the day, washed the sweat off of me, and shut myself in my room. If they could ignore me, I could ignore them too. The plan worked fine until someone knocked lightly on my door, and then didn't wait for me to respond before opening it.

"You missed dinner," Jess said, sitting on his bed and sticking one of the data cards into his Common.

"I'll eat when I want to."

After a few minutes, he spoke again. "This tension is ridiculous. Everyone knows what's going on but doesn't say a word about it. I know I'm not helping that, but I don't know how to."

"What do you want me to do about it?"

"I'm just talking, damn it. Trying to get some of this stress out."

Climbing to my feet, I stepped to the edge of his bed. "Keep talking."

"I don't know what to do." He wouldn't meet my gaze. "I'm not sure how much I cared for Heath. He's been a friend for a few years, yeah, but after sleeping with him . . ."

When I propped a knee on his bed, he touched his fingertips to my thigh.

"And who knows what's going on in my head?" He sucked in a breath. "You're raised a certain way, you know? You learn not all men are born the same."

Leaning forward until I could place my hand by Jess's waist, I brought my other knee to rest between his legs. "You learn that not all men can be whatever they want to be. There are rules," I said.

"The rules are screaming inside me," Jess said, his face pale and his eyes anywhere but on me.

"The rules aren't a part of you."

His hand moved to my waist, and slipped under my shirt and gripped my skin. I closed my eyes and enjoyed the sensation, and then his other hand touched the back of my neck and I was pulled toward him until our lips met. Again I was reminded how mascs usually didn't kiss andros like this. He kissed me like an equal, instead of obliging my perversion before shoving my face below his navel.

I let out a muffled moan and pressed my body against his. He broke the kiss and pushed my shoulders gently, so I eased off of him, my halted desire clenched in my abdomen. He sat up, breathing deeply, and kept his eyes down.

"Sorry. This is very difficult."

Difficult to stop, at least on my end. I sat back and ran a hand through my hair. Gave him a moment to look back up at me. He didn't, so I stood and left.

While I ate leftover pasta alone in the dark kitchen, I attempted to parse the emotions flowing through me. But I could not separate my desire from his curiosity. This was going to go further before he'd separate that curiosity from reality. And when he did . . . *At least he appears to be one for mercy instead of violence.*

When I returned to my room, Jess eyed me briefly from above his Common. Maybe he watched as I shed my pants and shirt and settled down for the night, throwing thin sheets over my head, but I didn't look up to find out.

Sooner than I was expecting, the other bed creaked as Jess stood. I studied the blue weave of the cloth in front of my face as the rustling of fabric reached my ears. The light clicked off.

And then Jess got in bed with me. My chest tightened with excitement, and my heart began thudding as he pressed against my back, his knees tucked up so the contact flowed all the way to our feet. One of his hands rested on my waist. His moist breath warmed the back of my neck.

Shit! Don't move! I struggled to swallow. *Is he really doing this?*

We lay there in silence for a long time, and I savored every nuance of his contact. The warmth of his body, the hair on his legs and chest . . . Could I feel his heart beating?

"Is this still okay?" His voice was sharp so close to my ears.

"Yes . . . Why are you—" Doubt collapsed my throat.

"I'm trying to understand why everyone says this is wrong." His whispers eased occasionally into the deep resonance of his voice. The sound reverberated through me.

"Have you figured it out?" I asked, and he squeezed my hip.

"No."

CHAPTER 14

"We'll be gone almost four days," Gene explained, rummaging through his bag of supplies one more time.

"Good, you'll return in time for the last two stations," Jess said.

"And you're going south?" I asked as we helped them load the ATV.

"Southeast to a river," Gene elaborated. "There's a sparse forest around those parts, lots of places to collect samples from. The stations down there were destroyed by a hurricane before even my time."

"I hope we see one of those rabbit things again," Kacy said as he climbed into the ATV's passenger seat.

"Bring one back if you do!" Heath called, waving as they drove through the gate. Jess shut it behind them, and regarded Heath and me uncertainly.

"Just the three of us for a while."

Heath glared at us both, the pleasant disposition he had shown the lovers completely gone. "Stay the fuck away from me and we'll all survive this." He stomped back toward Headquarters.

"Not surprised," Jess mumbled to me.

We wandered back inside and Jess regarded the calendar on display in the conference room. Completed items were crossed out; some arrows pointed to projects moved around. We were on schedule, and now the drive home would be too soon.

Oh, how spending all night in someone's arms could change my outlook. I blushed at the memory, and Jess cracked a smile at me as he turned from the calendar.

"Well I have some reports to write up today."

I sat a few consoles away from him and started drafting reports that summarized my progress, my least favorite part of any corporate gig. For a while we worked in silence.

After no more than an hour, Heath bounded toward Jess with a reddened face, a Common in his hand. He threw the device down next to Jess's keyboard.

"I'm not doing it!" he yelled, crossing his arms. Jess picked up the Common, thumbed through it, and grimaced.

"Bad timing on this, but it's your job to do it."

"I don't give a fuck. At all. I'm not fucking doing it, I'm fucking done with all of this shit." Heath yanked the Common from Jess's hand and stormed off. A door slammed.

I chuckled at Heath's behavior. It was unsurprising to see a masc act like such a brat. And after all his talk of me getting my work done? This was satisfying. "What's the problem?"

"Father's code boys just released an upgrade to the server software; they want it upgraded and fully tested before we leave." He shrugged.

"I'll do it."

Jess nodded, and headed toward the hall.

"Ember's gonna handle that upgrade. You just get the rest of your shit done and I'll ask nothing more of you. Agreed?"

I couldn't hear Heath's response. Jess returned and gave me a quick rundown of the upgrade, and I started in on that without much of a problem.

Jess tried to get Heath to have dinner with us, but the door stayed shut. I searched the cabinets, and grabbed some green beans, potatoes, and an onion; I had the potatoes cooking in the radiator when Jess joined me.

"We have a chef in Gene's absence?" he asked.

I smiled, preparing the beans and onions to be sautéed. "My dad works in the greenhouses, so when I was growing up, we always had fresh food. I helped him cook often."

"My dad was usually the one who cooked," Jess said, his gaze withdrawn.

After we ate, Jess wandered into the living room. "Would you want to watch a televid?"

He scrolled through a directory on the console, clicked on one, and then the title screen showed as it started playing.

"'*Restless Summer*,'" he read, flopping onto the couch. I raised an eyebrow at him, as this was another of those horrible romances. He patted the couch next to him. I reluctantly settled, and he wrapped an arm around my shoulders.

I scooted out of his grasp. "What are you doing?"

"It's okay," he urged. "Really, it's okay."

I exhaled and leaned back, and then his arm draped over me. Why was he acting like I was a masc? Didn't he understand I was different . . . didn't he understand what he was doing . . .

As if he were reading my thoughts, he whispered, "This is how you want to be treated, right?"

Yes, it was, and here it was finally happening. I trembled, my heart hammering as my thoughts rushed frantically nowhere. His thumb rubbed my shoulder, each tiny movement shooting electricity through me. I tried to focus on the televid but couldn't. Resting my head on his chest, I closed my eyes. The sound of his breathing, so intimate and calm, hinted at what could be, and for once, I dared myself to believe it.

Jess laughed at something in the televid and squeezed my shoulder, and riding the wave of excitement his touch caused, I tilted my head up and kissed the stubble on his jaw. He blinked, and then pulled me up to kiss me fully.

Before I could make sense of what I was doing, I had straddled him, and he didn't resist. The slickness of his mouth sent shivers down my spine.

And of course, this was when Heath left Jess's room. He made a gagging sound, and I scrambled off of Jess.

"You are sick," Heath spat. "You are fucking sick!"

"Do you have a problem with this?" Jess challenged.

"Yes! What the fuck do you think you're doing? When . . . when in your whole life have you ever felt het? Where is this coming from? It's like I don't even know you!"

"I'm just figuring shit out."

"And that means shoving your tongue down an andro's throat? What's next, your dick? 'Oh, I'm still figuring shit out, I'm not het!'"

Jess had stood up. I stayed on the couch, my arms around my knees and my breathing slowing, thankful to not be the focus of their anger this time.

"You're just mad at me for leaving you!" Jess yelled.

"Not anymore. I don't want to have anything to do with you if you're het. It's fucking disgusting."

"There's . . . nothing different about this!" Jess threw his arms out, a frown deep in his features but his eyes wide, almost scared.

Heath laughed darkly, and regarded me. "He hasn't experienced it yet, huh?" He returned his gaze to Jess, and my skin crawled as he spoke. "You never had any negative siblings. You never had any negative friends either growing up, right?"

"So?"

"You'll find out, soon enough." He sneered. "Have fun experimenting, or whatever you think you're doing. Stay away from me. Both of you."

So Heath would remind us of reality. I should have figured. He strode past us to the kitchen, and Jess followed.

"You don't get it! Come on, you're being ridiculous!"

Heath completely ignored him.

Jess came back and collapsed next to me, his head in his hands. We kept space between us until Heath retreated to Jess's room. The televid's credits rolled a few minutes later.

"I'm sorry about all this," he said.

"I hope you're not surprised."

Jess glanced at me, almost pouting past his furrowed brow. "Heath's right about one thing: I don't really understand all of this. But he's treating you like shit, just like he usually does to andros, just like my friends did back in school . . . And for what reason? Who cares about your genes?"

"He just treated you like shit, not me," I pointed out.

Jess shook his head. "All that? He's not getting his way and can't stand it. No, I mean him talking about you like you're . . ." He grasped at the air. "A thing. Unequal. I don't know. I had never been able to figure out what was wrong. Not before I met you."

I stared at him wide-eyed.

He sighed. "Everything I've ever known about negatives has unraveled. It's still falling apart."

My jaw trembled, my eyes and nose itching with imminent tears. How could any masc say what he had? Even if he had no idea what he was saying . . . even if Heath was right, Jess was still trying harder than any masc I had ever known. He wrapped his arm around me, and I rested my head on his shoulder. I rubbed the fabric of his shirt between my fingers, savoring his closeness.

Jess lay next to me, on his back with his arms over his head. The dim light from under the bedroom door suggested it was morning. His chest rose and fell, and I dared to run my hand across it.

He inhaled, and his eyes fluttered open. "Good morning."

A smile twisted my lips as my core warmed. What would be the harm if I took the initiative? "May I?" I twiddled my fingers above his navel. He echoed my smile, and gave a subtle nod. With a shiver, I slipped my hand below the elastic of his boxers. I had spent so little time around mascs who weren't already excited, that his soft flesh was strange. I reveled in every texture and change as he grew hot and hard from my touch.

He buried his face in the crook of my neck, his beard tickling my throat, and I rubbed him lazily. For a few minutes I enjoyed him in a way I'd never been able to enjoy a masc before: casually, intimately, his warm breath on my skin as my hand moved.

Far too soon, he looked up at me and caressed my cheek. "All right, my turn."

I withdrew my hand as he gave me a soft kiss. His hand ran across my abdomen, and I trembled, anticipation erupting between my legs.

"Crazy," he muttered, fingers tracing my stretch marks, inching downward. I settled on my back and watched him, my breathing already deep.

When he reached the point where he would have expected something different, he hesitated. His fingertips brushed over my pseudo, and I stifled a moan as my legs instinctually widened. Jess took a sharp breath and withdrew his hand to my navel.

"Okay . . . damn."

I chuckled. "Go on."

So he did, exploring me with shaking fingers as I succumbed to the ecstasy of his light touch. But then he pulled his hand away and sat up. My eyes fluttered open; he had gone pale.

"What?" I snapped, more angrily than I should have.

"How . . . does this . . ."

"Haven't you ever seen a Y negative down there?"

"No."

As I removed my boxers, the lingering pleasure eroded, crumbling into cold reality. Jess pushed one of my knees away from the other, and studied me.

"You look like you were mutilated."

I bit my tongue hard. "Get out of my bed!"

He was shaking as he stood, and he grabbed a fist full of his hair and opened his mouth to speak. I stared him down, and that stupid mouth shut.

"Just . . . leave me alone!" I spat. "And know what you're getting into next time you fuck with someone's desires."

His expression grew angry as he pulled on clothes and left. I buried my face in my pillow, as that familiar disgust at myself surfaced in full force. For a moment he'd had me believing he could like me despite what I was . . . For a few minutes he'd treated me like a real man . . . But now I was a subhuman freak again. Inhaling sharply, I got a nose full of his scent, alluring and maddening. I scrambled out of the bed, tears wetting my face, and looked down at my naked form. Mutilated—I was mutilated. By nature, by chance, by bad fucking luck. I gripped my abdomen like I used to when I was younger and images of bright-red blood dripping down my legs flashed through my mind. Memories of the pain, the fire inside of me, burning, consuming. Those tumors consuming me so they could live. And everything they took I could never get back; everything he promised had been as real as my ability to call myself a man.

My knees gave out, and I sat on the floor. I screamed. Neither man bothered to see what was wrong.

CHAPTER 15

An hour later, Jess called from beyond the shut door.

"Get out here, it's time to get some work done."

I yanked the door open, and walked past him without a glance. After downing a glass of fruit juice, I finally regarded him.

"Get your gun." His emotionless tone dug into my chest.

My gun over my shoulder, I followed him to the garage, and he took the cover off a quad, a much rustier version of the type of dirt bike I had only seen in televids. He swung his leg over it and drove it to the gate, then looked up at me expectantly. It was all business, his gaze. And it hurt in a way I hadn't expected.

I opened and shut the gate for him, then eyed the quad, reluctant to climb on. "We can't walk to Station Four? You said it was close."

"It's seven miles."

I sat behind him, grumbling. While I was still figuring out where to put my feet, he sped off, and with a yelp, I grabbed his waist.

We kicked up dust as we drove, and the rifle bounced on my back, its presence strangely comforting. Hot, wet wind whipped by, and beneath my hands, Jess's muscles flexed as we traversed the uneven terrain. My body yearned to be closer, but I denied it the satisfaction.

We soon reached Station Four. Hardly a shed, it was just big enough for the consoles that relayed sensor data. Jess inspected its tower and the array that sat right next to it in the grass while I started on the consoles. Beside us, a grove of thin trees swayed in the breeze, and the now-familiar buzzing serenaded us.

Really, an hour-long wait for this update to apply and for the system to reboot? What the damn did Heath do all day? Sitting outside, I swung the rifle around to my lap, popped out the magazine and moved the bolt through its motions, listening to the clank of metal on metal. The yellow, overcast sky made the Outskirts feel smaller, suffocating; a deep breath burned my still-scratchy throat. The wind blew dust in my eyes, so I turned away, and watched the thin trees quiver. Maybe this was a farm, long ago. Imagining the orchards made my stomach rumble.

Jess was pacing incessantly. His boots hitting the gravel set a somber beat, not quite following the whoosh of the wind brushing metal, the chirp of the cicadas. Was he thinking about what happened this morning? Was he asking himself why he even tried to get close to me?

Because I was. He got further than any masc had ever bothered going. Fuck, I had liked it. I loathed myself for admitting it, after how it had fallen apart.

"How long'll the consoles take?"

"About fifty more minutes."

"Fuck." Jess held his gun loosely with one hand, the barrel swinging past his calves. He squinted, and sat by my side. *Miles of nothing and you sit right next to me.*

"I bet Heath's not gonna get any more work done before we leave," he said.

At least a minute of silence ticked by.

"Um. I . . ." He put a hand on my thigh, but I scooted away from him.

"Stay away from me."

"Can you give me a fucking break?" he countered. "I have no idea why you expected me to handle it differently."

I withheld my next verbal barrage.

"And it didn't . . ." His cheeks flushed, and he stared forward. "Stop my . . . attraction . . . to you."

I blinked away dust as I regarded him.

Finally, he sighed. "But I'm gonna need some time to figure stuff out."

I turned my face from the wind, and the scraggly trees still trembled. "Okay."

Jess put his hand on my thigh again, and rubbed the fabric of my pants with his thumb. I rested my hand on his and our fingers entwined. I savored the feeling, despite the sound of my heart hammering in my ears. His hand shuddered underneath mine, then he withdrew.

"Let's get the arrays repaired while we wait," he announced.

After this long at the job, we were quite the efficient team. The array just off the packed-in dirt took minutes; the one on the other side of the trees took barely longer.

"Check it out," Jess exclaimed as we walked back to Station Four. I followed his outstretched hand to the foot of a tree. "Don't worry, this one's harmless," he added.

A brown-green creature about two feet long climbed across a rock. Its movement was slow, controlled; an ancient being out of time and place. I stood mesmerized.

"See the black and white stripes at his neck? That's a collared lizard."

"How do you know all of these things?"

Jess sighed, and a soft smile graced his features. "My dad taught me."

"I'm glad he taught you," I mumbled. "Someone needs to remember."

We returned to Station Four, with ten minutes still to go on the console. So I hefted my rifle, and picked a bush halfway to the horizon.

"Hey, Jess. See that bush out there? Next to the big rock."

I aimed, and it was only after the report echoed around us that I realized Jess had told me to stop.

He winced. "Fuck, don't attract attention to us right now."

I lowered the rifle. "If we see anyone coming, we'll run."

"But we're still vulnerable if we're running away on a quad."

Okay, he had a point. In the utter silence following my shot, I squinted at the dirt, still gripping the rifle, thinking about his hand in mine. And then another shot echoed.

My eyes met Jess's, and my stomach dropped.

"Time to go," he said, slamming Station Four's door closed and fumbling with his keys.

"The console?"

"We'll have to figure out a remote connection to finish the upgrades." Now I could hear men yelling. We swore simultaneously.

Jess climbed onto the quad, and I jumped on behind him, and he pulled my hand across his waist. He sped off, and I buried my face in his shoulder and held on. I stole glances behind us as he drove, but there was nothing but our dust trail settling back into the deceptive stillness of the Outskirts.

It wasn't until the Headquarters's gate was shut and the quad's engine was off that we could gauge if we had been followed. Rustling, the hum of equipment inside Headquarters, of the water purifier.

Jess let out a breath, and squeezed my hand. "That was too close."

Way too close.

"But we're safe in here," he finished.

I squeezed back, and tried to believe him.

After several hours of installation the next day, the last-minute software update passed its final stress test, concluding my last major job at Headquarters. As evening descended, each moment brought me closer to my injection. The difficulty of waiting added to the question of what I would do once I hit my high. Anxiety pulsed through me. Apparently it was blatant enough for Jess to notice.

"What's shaking you?"

I put down a plate with a clatter and averted my eyes. "That time of the week."

He grinned. "Can I watch again?"

I blushed. "Yeah."

Not even an hour later, here he was, sitting on the edge of the bed with me as the needle pierced my skin. Afterward, I put away my supplies with shaking hands.

"You take this very seriously." He went to touch the tiny red dot on my arm and my free hand stopped him. His fingers entwined with mine. "You take this seriously too."

"Yeah, I do."

He eased me horizontal with the push of a hand, and we kissed, his hips pressed against mine. His body's glorious warmth seeped into me.

When he paused for a breath, I whispered into his cheek. "You've figured stuff out, I take it?"

"Mm-hmm." His lips curled into a smile. "I wanna ride your high."

I shuddered beneath him.

Hesitantly, we kissed again, exploring each other with fingertips and palms; I rubbed my cheek against his beard as he kissed my neck. Never had anyone . . . Was this what mascs did . . .? He ran his fingers along the stretch marks on my abdomen, up across my chest, his touch so delicate yet so electric that my back arched and my breath caught in my throat.

With a chuckle, Jess yanked at the tie of my pants. He eased the knot loose, hooked his fingers around the crisscrossing laces, and pulled. "Do you—do you know what the best way is to go about this?"

I smirked at him and shimmied my pants down. "I have some ideas, yeah."

Now that I was moving, confidence flowed through me. I stripped, and Jess did the same.

"Get on your back." I had always wanted to say that to a masc.

He lay back, shoulders broadened with muscle he didn't have to fight for, brown hair dusting between his nipples and trailing off to his navel, hip bones that sloped down to accentuate his erection— I stopped myself from merely staring, and crawled on top. His hands slipped around my waist, and I kissed him.

"Now what?" he asked, his deep voice making my elbows buckle.

My fingertips danced down his torso until I grabbed him, hard and warm in my palm. *I can't believe this is happening.* We inhaled simultaneously when I lowered my hips enough for me to push him inside, igniting a thrill of pleasure within me that hinted at the fulfillment of half a lifetime of fantasy.

He let out his breath in a moan, but my throat caught as a sharp pain accompanied the blooms of ecstasy. Oh, he was bigger than a toy. My arms shook, and as I started a rhythm, the hurt and the gratification came out in my cries.

Jess moaned again and gripped my hips, amazement on his face, despite his closed eyes. That enjoyment . . . that should have been all I felt, not this dichotomous intensity. I was supposed to be confident, sexy. Everything he was so he wouldn't remember I was different. That's how it had always gone in my head. The pleasure was there, but wasn't enough. Soon I collapsed onto his chest, and he wrapped his arms around me.

"I can hardly tell the difference." He squeezed me. I raised my head to look at him, and his joy faded. "What's wrong?"

My voice broke as I spoke. "It's so . . . tight." I shifted my hips and grimaced, tears spotting his chest. "Can . . . we try something else?"

"Yeah," he whispered, running a thumb across my damp cheek. "It hurts?"

I nodded. "I still like it."

He smiled. "I like it too. But do you want to stop?"

"No."

I stifled a cry as I collapsed next to him, disappointment panging through me. When I spread my legs, he settled between them and kissed me again, his tenderness refocusing me. The electricity of his lips against mine was almost too much to stand; it felt so good.

When he finally broke the kiss, he caressed my thigh, sending a shiver up my spine. "I don't know where," he mumbled.

With a chuckle, I helped him. "Right here."

"Oh—oh . . ."

He moved with much more finesse than me, making my vocal chords vibrate with every push. The pain pulled me under, but his moaned words, and the whoosh of his breathing past my ear, captivated me enough for the pleasure to grow. I clung to it through the waves of burning, and in turn I clung to him.

I had spent so long searching for a masc who was willing to fuck me, but this was so much more than that. As I breathed with Jess, moved with him, I realized I had never felt so close to a person. For a few beautiful moments I didn't remember that there was something wrong with me. I felt not just like his equal, but like a human being.

A few minutes later he slowed to a stop. I shook in his arms. "This is kinda overwhelming," he whispered. "I don't think I can . . ."

"That's all right." I whimpered as we separated, and he settled beside me.

"But it was great."

I rubbed away my tears and smiled, completely unable to think of anything good to say. So I crawled down the bed a few feet and buried my face between his legs. His orgasm came as easily as I had expected, and after returning to his side, I rested my head on his shoulder and enjoyed the bitter taste in my mouth.

"Wow," he uttered, tightening his grip around my waist. The havoc he had wrought inside of me ached sharply. Frankly, I didn't mind at all.

CHAPTER 16

J ess and I entered the conference room the next morning as the patter of rain began above us. He crossed a few tasks off of our schedule, leaving just one more station and a couple days of clean up. And then . . . I couldn't think about it.

"Station Nine is easy." His tone was subdued. "But it's the closest to the scavengers. There's a reason I usually save it for last."

"Do you think they'll bother us again?"

Jess's expression darkened. "Not if they know what's best for them."

I set my jaw, and changed the subject. "Um, I've finished my work, what else can I help out with?"

"You can go through our electronics and remove anything that's outdated. We'll bring them back to town and sell or scrap them."

I nodded and opened the nearest cabinet.

"That's really it, as long as Heath does his share."

"He will," I said, pulling out boxes. The hard drive in my hand was from two years ago and already obsolete. That's why I didn't keep too much stock on hand at my apartment—people wanted the newest and the best, even if that wasn't what they needed. I piled up the old parts.

Jess put a hand on my shoulder, and kissed my cheek. "Let me know if you need anything." I let the wave of excitement he'd stimulated flow through me, and couldn't help but smile as I got back to work.

Later in the day, Heath finally emerged from Jess's room. He approached Jess with crossed arms.

"So what shit do you want me to do today?"

Jess made a point to finish what he was doing before regarding him. "How's that stats update going?"

Heath stepped to his desk and grumbled as he booted up his console. I resumed my own work, though I felt his sharp stare cut me a few times. It wasn't long before his emotions got the better of him.

"Jess, how do you live with yourself?" He stuck a hand on his hip. I raised my gaze but Jess didn't seem fazed.

"I don't have any problem living with myself," Jess replied. "But I'm sorry I had a hard time living with you."

"You're afraid of commitment." Heath tapped at his keyboard. "That's why you couldn't take me, that's why you fucked the one person on the planet you could never commit to."

His words hit me like an ATV. My stomach lurched, but Jess just continued scrolling through text on his screen. *Please stand up to Heath's lie*—but it wasn't a lie. I shuddered, my soreness losing its pleasant undertone.

Rain rapped on the shut solar panels in the ensuing silence. Heath wore a smug expression; he knew he had identified the problem perfectly.

"Fuck this," I spat, leaving my post. I brushed past Jess.

He reached out to me. "What's the matter?"

"Fuck you," I hissed, heading down the hall.

"Ember?" Jess called. Heath laughed. I shut my door, and sat on the edge of my bed. Even if I wasn't surprised by this, it still hurt. Someone knocked.

"Go away."

"Heath's a jerk and you know it." Jess talked through the door. When I didn't reply, he let himself in and settled next to me. "Responding to him would have just made it worse." He wrapped an arm around me, and I shrugged it off.

"He was right."

Jess propped his arms on his bent knees and sighed. That was a yes, then. "You know what I think about what Heath said?"

He touched the side of my face and pulled me into a kiss. *You're ignoring the problem, Jess . . .* but after a few moments of relishing in his contact, I was breathless and pinned underneath him. The weight and warmth of his body grounded me, the tickle of his beard on my lips and his fingertips caressing my neck, steadying. Okay, we were both ignoring the problem. There was no future. No us. Couldn't we just not care?

The rain increased in intensity as the day wore on. Gene and Kacy returned earlier than planned, due to concern for the ATV's battery life. They greeted us cheerfully enough, though Gene appeared to pick up on the tension between us. He narrowed his eyes at Jess.

"Any action from our neighbors?" Kacy asked. Jess shook his head.

"Did you guys find any creatures?" Heath spoke over the rumble of distant thunder.

"Seven species of insects and three species of arachnids. We've seen most of them before, but one of them is new to me. I can't wait to look it up." Gene looked around. "You didn't put Headquarters in standby?"

"Not yet," Jess replied. "Waiting for a weather report this evening from Atlanta."

"Maybe we should reduce pull on the batteries just in case."

"Standby?" I asked.

"If we can't open the solar panels for more than a few days we'll run out of power." Jess typed at a console briefly. "Our energy cells are at seventy-five percent right now. So standby shuts off all noncritical systems and allows sensor data to transfer only every few hours. It can last for a few weeks like that, if it needs to. We've just never had to do it with people here."

"Do you think it'll come to that?" Kacy asked.

"Regardless of when we finish here, we can't leave until the sun comes back out."

"Because of the ATV's battery?" I questioned. Jess nodded.

"In all likelihood we won't have to worry about that. This isn't the season for large storms," Gene said, removing soil samples and equipment from his bag. "So what happened while we were gone?" His tone was nonchalant, but Jess stuttered anyway.

"We . . . uh, we updated the servers, took care of Station Four. Um, Heath, did you ever complete that—"

"Fucking yes," Heath cut in. "Get off my back about it, I finish my damn work."

"Okay. Sure." Jess stared at the floor, his thumbs in his pockets. "Still fighting?"

"You aren't gonna tell him, huh?" Heath hissed at Jess. He brushed past him roughly, and from down the hall he called, "I didn't know andros could still scream like that!"

A door shut, and I jumped. Kacy gasped. I buried my face in my hands, trembling with embarrassment and anger.

Gene shook his head. "What does he mean?"

Kacy elbowed his partner, pointed at Jess and I, and raised an eyebrow. Gene frowned for a moment, and then gaped at Jess. "What the fuck do you think you're doing?"

"It's none of your damn business!" Jess declared, as another roll of thunder sounded over the rain, louder this time.

"But you're going to ruin your life! What would Hale think? You're so young, don't throw out your reputation like this."

"Why should you care what I do? I'm not your son; I'm not your responsibility."

"I'm just trying to keep you from making a wrong decision. You know Tori wouldn't have wanted—"

"Don't you dare bring my dad into this! You have no idea what he would have wanted."

Gene sighed, and I wondered why the fights Jess had about me never included me. I approached Jess, and he grasped my outstretched hand and held it firmly.

Gene's eyes widened, and he turned away from us. "I can't even look at you." The disgust was blatant in his tone.

"This isn't about my father, or my dad," Jess started, his voice low. "This is about you. You're arguing so adamantly because you can't handle it."

"Can you?" Gene countered, regarding his partner though he was clearly talking to Jess. "Can you really handle the implications of your actions?"

"I don't care." Jess embraced me, and whispered into my shoulder, "I don't fucking care."

Gene strode from the conference room, his gaze still averted. "Kacy, I can't deal with this," he called.

Kacy stared at us wide-eyed. "I'm sorry, but this is pretty fucked up." He left too.

Jess clung to me, his breathing irregular. "Everyone hates me. Why? Because I like you? I seriously can't even do that?"

I slipped my hands around his waist and exhaled into the crook of his neck. I'd always thought that the andro would be the vulnerable one if a het couple was attacked. However, here I was the cause, and Jess was the one suffering. Still, hearing him profess his feelings, even in this context, was something I had never known I wanted to hear.

That night, I lay awake listening to the rain, and the random low crackling of thunder. The weather report had come in, predicting at least three more days of a storm. The news hadn't helped our sour moods, and when the world darkened, Jess had dropped Headquarters into standby and we had to use the light of our Commons to guide us.

Jess stirred and gripped my thigh. His fingers relaxed again, and I rubbed the back of his hand.

I knew damn well that this was over the moment we started driving home. It was for the best. Like they said, he didn't know what he was getting into. I didn't want to make him live an existence riddled with the intolerance that andros had to accept as normal. He wasn't tough enough to take the abuse. I had grown up with it, I had lived through the words and the fists, but he could hardly handle Heath's attitude.

Granted, Heath had been a friend, a lover even. I didn't have a comparison, though I imagined Niche suddenly threatening me with bodily harm if I ever talked to him again. Just the thought made me uncomfortable. Maybe Jess did have something worth being upset about.

I nestled against him and enjoyed his body heat as I lost track of time. Sometime later I woke to him kissing my neck. He rolled me onto my back and loved me like I had shown him. This time I got to watch what happened when his body shuddered, instead of taste it. I still felt it though . . . and it felt good.

As morning approached and dawned, we delayed starting the day as long as possible. I resisted the urge to miss what I still had as the light stayed gray and the rain grew louder. After a few more minutes, a crash of thunder roused us fully.

"It'll be a soggy mess out there," he said, releasing his grip on me. He dressed, and I soon did the same. We left the bedroom together, and Jess knocked on the other bedroom doors.

"Guys, I'm gonna turn the power back on so we can make some breakfast, then it's going off again, okay?" There were grumbles, then the muffled sound of movement. "Make sure you charge your Commons while it's on." He opened a circuit breaker on the wall and flipped a few switches. The conference room emitted a chorus of starting chimes as the consoles powered on. I plugged in my Common at my desk, and the others wandered into the kitchen. Then Jess gasped.

"Fuck . . . Ember? Grab our guns."

"What are you griping about now?" Heath mumbled.

I took a few cautious steps toward Headquarters's front door. "What?"

"Get our fucking guns!" Jess hissed.

Heath swore, then I heard the scraping of metal on metal, chairs or the table being shoved.

"Jess. Jess . . ." I whispered, lifting my gun from the wall and slinging it over my shoulder. I picked up Jess's. "Why?"

"We have company. I saw them out the window. Hopped the fence," Jess explained, his voice strained.

"Bastards think they can take us, huh?" Heath stepped toward me, and I handed him his gun.

"Calm down, everyone. Please," Gene tried.

"Five . . . no, seven scavengers. Armed. They're standing near the fence. A leader is talking to them." I heard Jess slide down the kitchen wall. "Fuck, I think one saw me."

The adrenaline already pumping into my system kicked up a notch. This was seriously happening? In the middle of a storm? Jess strode toward me and took his rifle. Our eyes met, and the gravity in his scared me.

"Let's get together . . ." I grabbed the last two rifles, not caring when they clattered against each other. "Let's hole up in one of the bedrooms . . ."

Lightning flashed through the windows, blinding me temporarily.

"Fuck no, I'm not gonna hide and let them take everything!" Heath hissed as the thunder arrived, rumbling angrily.

"Not after Adin," Jess professed, standing by Heath's side. Understanding clicked in my mind and my jaw dropped. Then the door in front of me buckled with a loud thud, and I jumped back. Gene took the other guns from me and the air filled with the clicking of magazines and bolts.

Someone yelled and pounded at the door again.

"Go away!" Jess bellowed. "We'll shoot!"

"We'll shoot back!" one of them hollered. Then they fired at the door's locking mechanism. I yelped and backed up, and Jess flipped the conference room's table on its side, sending maps fluttering to the floor. Kacy swore as we ducked behind the metal tabletop. With one more crash, the door was down.

A man leaned past the doorway briefly, then retreated into the cover of the doorframe. His face was suntanned and pockmarked, his hair and beard cut unevenly. I had gotten a glimpse of bent, rusted metal protecting his shoulder.

"Do not take one step inside this building!" Jess shouted, keeping his gun pointed at the doorway. "Or you will violate the treaty with Kansas City!"

"Give us your batteries, your water filters," a man grunted from outside the doorway, an unfamiliar accent slurring his speech. "And all your food."

"No!" Jess declared. "Leave, now!"

The man laughed and fired his rifle at the ceiling. There was a sharp *thwang* as the bullet embedded in the metal sheet. Each sound shuddered through me, my heart thudding in ringing ears.

"I don't want to shoot them," Jess whispered to Heath, his voice strained.

"You're not gonna have a fucking choice," Heath bit back. I kept my rifle aimed at the doorway. Maybe the table would be enough to protect us.

"If you don't give us what we want," the man threatened, "we'll feed you bullets."

"You show your ugly face past that doorframe and it's coming off!" Heath retaliated.

"This is impossible . . . What do we do?" Gene pleaded.

"Hold steady," Jess told him. "Just— Fuckin' damn, I don't know."

I stole a glance to my left to see Jess's face flushed and his hands shaking.

"What's it gonna be?" another scavenger shouted. "We ain't gonna stand out here in the rain all day."

"It ain't much off your back," the first man added in. "I bet you're Cameron's boy, eh? Born and raised off creds stolen from good people."

"What?" Jess exclaimed.

"Anything we take, you won't even miss."

"Oh, my father will notice," Jess growled. "Believe me, you don't want to mess with him!"

Heath had a moment to voice his approval before the first scavenger lunged through the doorway. Gene peered over the top of the table just as the scavenger fired in a quick, smooth motion, spraying Gene's life across the floor.

Gene crumpled to the ground. Kacy screamed, dropped his gun, and lunged for his partner. Heath fired at the scavenger, who then went down. I stole a glance at the bloody mess now forming the right side of Gene's face, and gagged.

"Fucking damn!" Jess managed. "Everyone please, don't do this! Don't shoot!"

Yet as he ducked next to me, he and Heath readied their weapons all the same. I blinked away tears. I'd just seen a man die. His face blown off, right in front of me. A stray bullet imploded a console screen, and I numbly watched the pieces tumble across the desk.

No! I can't shut down. Either I help here, or I die here.

I had kept my head low when Gene fell. Peering over the table, I aimed at one of the men now advancing through the doorway. I went to squeeze the trigger and something erupted in my chest and—

Pain shredded through me, and the blackness swallowed me up.

PART 4
JESS

xx

CHAPTER 17

A pair of shots rang out from the scavengers, and a strangled cry cut through Kacy's screaming as Ember dropped to his knees.

Seeing him fall was a stab in the gut; it ripped at me in a way that stole my breath and slowed down time. As Ember brought a shaking hand to his chest and then slumped to the ground, my mind raced through memories of the last few days with him. *This could be it, it could be over.* Then the screaming and the gunfire caught up with me. *No! Not yet.* I sucked in a breath and leveled my weapon.

My first shot hit a scavenger in the gut. My second missed a man to his left as one of their shots grazed my shoulder and filled my senses with fire. Beside me, Heath had gone ballistic, yelling and shooting as fast as he could pull his bolt. The men who remained outside the door were still aiming at us, and Kacy continued to wail.

"Get the fuck out of here!" Heath yelled before he bounded over the table, and I chanced a look. The last men were gone. I jumped after him and stopped at the doorframe. Heath was out in the rain, bellowing at the remaining scavengers as they scrambled up the fence. He shot one of them, and the man screamed and fell. Heath went to fire again but the rifle clicked uselessly. He threw his gun at the ground and swore.

"It's over, get the fuck out of the rain," I pleaded, stepping toward him. Engines started up, and the last two scavengers retreated on quads.

"Gene . . . fucking Gene!" Heath ran past me back inside; rainwater stung my skin as I scrambled under cover as well. Heath and Kacy were with Gene, so I went to Ember.

He lay on his side, his breathing shallow. A red stain on his shirt was growing visibly. I took him in my arms, and he clutched at me. His eyes were vacant—I wasn't sure if he was actually conscious. Thunder boomed as if the sound was bubbling out of a dream.

"Ember . . . can you hear me?" No response. I ripped open his shirt. The wound was high on his chest on the left side, possibly high enough to have missed the important stuff. Pulling off a strip of fabric, I balled it up and pushed it into the wound. Ember cried out, but he still wasn't behind those wide eyes. Heath and Kacy looked up at Ember's shout, and I met Kacy's devastated expression. He couldn't even say it; he just broke down in tears and collapsed onto Gene's chest.

"He's fucking dead," Heath said for him.

"Why?" Kacy screamed, the sound fading to a pained wail. He tugged at Gene's bloody shirt, his jaw trembling. "Gene . . . who's gonna raise our son with me?"

"Kacy . . . Kacy . . ." Heath tried to pull him from Gene's body. Kacy screeched, and fought his grasp.

"Let him be for a second, and get me the damn emergency kit!" I yelled. Heath ran out the front door. Kacy held his partner and rocked. Still, I pressed the fabric against Ember's chest. Gene's death didn't feel real. I laughed at the absurdity of it all, tears cleaning the acid from my cheeks.

Heath returned and popped open the red case. "This is pointless."

"Give me the bandages," I cried. Heath tossed a roll to me, and I wrapped Ember's shoulder until the fabric stayed in place.

"It's fucking pouring out there. You know what? I'm calling Hale."

I sucked in a breath and the screaming desire to handle this on my own came crashing to a halt at the sight of Ember's bloody chest. "Fuck it, Heath. Call him."

"Finally listening to reason." Heath got to his feet and approached a console.

I ran my fingers through Ember's hair, feeling my pride get stuck in my throat. "Ember . . . we're gonna figure this out. I'm not gonna have you die here."

Heath typed at the console and swore. Reluctantly, I laid Ember on the floor as gently as I could.

"Something wrong?"

"It won't connect," he admitted. "The power's on, the com-tower's functional, but it won't fucking connect."

"What do you mean?"

"What do you think I mean? Look at it yourself!" Heath shoved the keyboard toward me and stood before punching the side of a cabinet hard enough to leave a dent. I consulted the console, my fingers shaking so badly I could hardly type. The connection log showed failed connections since we had turned the power on this morning. Some setting was wrong . . . or some part was wrecked from the storm . . . or the update was faulty? Fuck, I didn't know.

"You gotta be kidding me," I muttered.

"This is fucking fantastic! We can't even send for help! We have to fix the damn connection first! What if we need something we don't have?"

"Then we'll . . . uh . . ." I couldn't think. "We'll drive back to the city."

"After the storm clears. You do realize he'll be dead as Adin by then, right?"

"This isn't Adin again; he's not as bad as Adin was!" I defended.

Heath grabbed my shoulder. "It'll be five days, at least. Are you listening to me? Five fucking days before we're in Kansas City. You think he'll last that long?"

From near the front door came a soft voice. "Please . . ."

"We forgot one," Heath hissed, picking up Ember's gun.

"Please, we have a doctor!" the scavenger cried. His wet hair was plastered to his face and neck, his expression a grimace. I grasped Heath's arm before he could raise the barrel.

"With the other scavengers?" I asked. The scavenger nodded his head jerkily, holding his abdomen. He must have been dragging himself to the door, because blood stained a line across the floor.

"I can show you," he said in a high, negative voice. He scrunched his eyes shut. "I can convince them to see your friend."

"You killed Gene!" Heath hissed. "Murdered because you're all too stubborn to handle a little authority!"

The scavenger let out a sob, and met my eyes with a face twisted in pain. "Please . . . it wasn't supposed to go like this . . . threaten, but not kill. I tried to warn him . . ."

Heath shook off my grip. "Enough of this shit."

"Damn it, Heath—" I shuddered as the rifle went off and blood splattered. "Fucking damn it!" I wrapped my arms around my chest.

"Hale will bomb the scavengers to the ground, and it won't be enough." Heath returned to Kacy's side. "But we'll get them all, you hear me?" Kacy nodded, his hands white-knuckled fists grasping Gene's bloody shirt.

Ember had said, only two weeks ago, that our violence was barbaric. We were idiots, turning differences into shootings. Heath was full of fire, burning for revenge. But me? I was hollow and scared.

And the scavengers lived forty miles away. That was an hour and a half, maybe more, in this weather. I checked on Ember as lightning flashed. His blood had soaked through the bandages.

"Fuck this." Thunder rumbled over my muttering. I found Ember's jacket on his desk chair, and struggled to dress him. He moaned when I moved his arm on his injured side but I pulled the jacket onto him anyway.

"The fuck are you doing?" Heath demanded.

"Getting him ready to move."

"Where?"

"To the fucking ATV!" I wrapped an arm around Ember's waist and hefted him onto a chair. He was the body builder; would I be strong enough to get him to the ATV? Beside me, Kacy now sat still and silent, Gene's hand clasped in his own. I could hardly look at him.

"You're so damn stupid, Jess. Stupid as shit! The ATV's battery will run out before you get there and Ember will die and then you'll be in the middle of fucking nowhere—"

"I gotta try!"

"—and we won't be able to come for you for days, man, fucking days—"

I grabbed my backpack, and stormed into the kitchen. I filled it with all the food I could; all the while Heath's barrage didn't stop. He grabbed at my arms, my waist, screamed in my ears.

"They'll kill you when you get there!" he pleaded. "I lost Adin, I lost Gene, I can't lose you! I can't lose you, not after what we had—"

"And I can't lose him!" I hissed, lifting the backpack to my shoulders. I pushed past Heath and out into pouring rain. My exposed skin erupted in stinging. I went to the garage and threw the backpack in the ATV's backseat.

Heath had followed me. "I won't let you do this! I won't!" He blocked my way out of the garage. I shoved him against the ATV.

"Get. The. Fuck. Out of my way."

I strode past him. Lightning barraged my senses and distracted me from the translucent stream of red rainwater flowing from the scavenger by the fence.

"You bastard!" he called, coming after me. "You didn't try half this hard when they shot Adin last year! We just took him back to Headquarters and watched him bleed to death!"

We were back inside now. "What'd you want me to do? He was shot here!" I pounded my chest over my heart. "He died in less than an hour! Ember has a damn chance!"

"You didn't give a shit how much I cared for Adin," Heath protested. "And then you lied . . . lied to your father and Adin's family—gonna fucking lie your way out of this one?"

"I don't fucking know." Exhaustion crept up on me, the adrenaline gone from my system, leaving my muscles all shaky. Taking a few deep breaths, I willed Heath's pleading to blur into the patter of the rain as I crouched in front of Ember. He sat slumped in the chair, now clearly unconscious. Trying to summon what strength I had, I wrapped an arm around his waist and pushed his torso over my shoulder. Hesitantly, I stood.

"Jess!" Heath shouted, as I stepped carefully across the bloody floor.

"Just stop it, Heath."

I paused at the sound of Kacy's wavering voice.

"Let him go." Kacy's face was flushed and wet from crying, but something in his tone seemed to command Heath's obedience.

"Why are you siding with him?" Heath asked.

"If you had cared for Adin at all, if you care for Jess, you'll let him do this."

I resumed carrying my burden outside. Once Ember was in the passenger seat, I covered him with a blanket. With a kiss on his cheek, I tried to swallow my fear.

What had the scavengers wanted? Electronics, something like that? I wasn't about to ask Heath or Kacy. My backpack of food would have to be enough for now.

Thunder rumbled monstrously loud, and it was so strange that I could only hear it and not feel the world shaking with its might. I climbed into the ATV and started the engine.

"We'll just have to hope, Ember."

While I backed out of the garage, Heath stood in the Headquarters's doorway. I rolled down the window and met his distraught eyes.

"Is he worth it?" Heath asked. "Is he worth risking your life for? You've known him for a damn month."

"That's all it took," I replied, and left him standing there.

Something about saying it made it true. This truth rattled around my gut as the ATV shook on its suspension. The rain on the windshield blurred my view, and lightning occasionally blinded me. Facing the vast expanse of the Outskirts, the low mountains ahead obscured with cloud, the fight in me evaporated, leaving just this truth and the crumbles of my resolve. I was risking my life for a man I had known for a month. And no other choice would have been right.

As the minutes passed, the acid on my face and scalp began to sting tremendously, and the shot that grazed my arm had left a wound that throbbed as well, especially wet with acid. I fumbled around my seat for a tube of neutralizer, and rubbed some into my cheeks. When the pain spiked, I grit my teeth. But then it was gone altogether. My arm couldn't be helped right now, and that was okay.

"We're fucked, aren't we?" I said to the unconscious man beside me. "But I'm damn trying, and that's all you could have expected from me. I'm truly, grossly sorry."

There was no response. I kept driving.

"I guess you deserve the truth."

After driving for almost an hour, I didn't care that he couldn't hear me. Nothing broke the unchanging landscape but flashes of white and the surreal booming—I had to talk or I'd go crazy.

"I lied to you about the scavengers. You knew that part. I've been lying to Father about the scavengers for years. I guess it started as me not wanting him to tell me it was too dangerous out here, tell me I couldn't work out here. I kept telling myself that the treaty was enough to hold them back. Childish thinking, I know that now. The scavengers grew completely out of control last year. We saw the same damned warning signs we saw this year. Evidence they were snooping around Headquarters when we weren't there. Standing out there, watching us. Waiting. Whatever the fuck they do in the middle of fucking nowhere, an hour's drive away from their camp."

I sighed. The storm sighed back.

"So last year, it rained on and off the first week, just enough to get us behind on our schedule and discourage us from working hard to catch up. Things got pushed back. We spent too much time cooped up inside. Before I knew it, Heath and Adin were sleeping together. I couldn't tell him it was a bad idea, 'cause Gene and Kacy had gotten together a few years prior. And of course Heath didn't know at the time that I liked him. So the two of them would get high. They'd duck in their bedroom, then come out an hour later and pretend to get work done. It drove me crazy.

"Adin was shot during our last week, when we had finally gone out to Station Four. I was doing my damn job fixing arrays and then Heath and Adin started yelling. I thought they were fighting, so I ignored it. Then I heard gunshots. Adin had seen the scavenger watching us, had started yelling at him. Shot at him. So the scavenger retaliated.

"We drove Adin back to Headquarters. Got blood all over the ATV. Took me hours to clean it out so Father wouldn't notice. Adin . . ." My voice wavered. It was a hard thing to remember, the first time I'd seen someone die. "He stopped breathing ten minutes after we got back. Heath didn't cry, or anything like that. He was just cold. Distant for a while. Then he started acting like he was fine. Helped me think of a cover story so we wouldn't have to tell anyone what happened. Told Adin's folks that he bid us farewell when the trip was over; we didn't know why he never showed up at home. Guys our age like taking things independently, that's what you did, yeah?

"But I think Heath blamed himself. And then what did he start doing when we were home again? He started blaming me. If only I'd enforced the schedule, it wouldn't have happened. A few months later, I was still trying to put all that shit behind me when he got high off his ass and hugged me and told me he missed Adin. I wish I'd have had the strength to stop him then. Damn it, I didn't like his mood, I didn't like him pulling that guilt shit on me, but I couldn't help myself."

I blinked off more lightning and groaned, scanning the increasing number of trees. "I've gone so off track I can't remember what I was trying to say."

Ember whined weakly. I shivered as a knot in my gut loosened. *You're still with me.* He had turned his head, his hair matted with what I hoped was sweat instead of rain. His eyes were still shut tight.

"Hang in there," I said. "We'll get you healed, and then . . . I dunno. I— Damn it, I don't know how to say this, even when you can't hear me." I laughed nervously. "You're the fifth guy I've been with, by the way. And yeah, you're different. I know. I think that's why I've been drawn to you."

Even with the rain, vehicle tracks cut through the dirt, the road sloping gently upward. If these tracks weren't heading toward their camp, we would be completely fucked. I grimaced at the low battery light on the dashboard.

"So let's look ahead. What if we don't get our asses shot the moment we enter their camp? What if they save you? Maybe Father doesn't kill me for all of this? But then you go back to Atlanta and I never see you again. Do I want that? You know, I don't think I do."

I sighed, gripping the steering wheel. "So what do I want? Gene— he always heard me out and reasoned with me, but he saw me with you and freaked. He . . ." I had known Gene for almost ten years. I had spent not only countless hours with him at the stations, but also back in Kansas City. And he was gone. Dead. "Fuck . . . Okay, can't think about that. But I mean, is this the sort of reaction I should expect from everyone I know? Is that what I'd have to look forward to if I tried to pursue a relationship with you?"

It sounded as ridiculous as I thought it would. Then I glanced at Ember, and my gut lurched with concern for his well-being. I cared so deeply that it confused me.

"I don't know what's going on in my head. You're a good man. And yeah, I'm gonna call you one. I've really enjoyed getting to know these pieces of your life over the past few weeks. But seeing you get shot . . . It fucking changed me. I want to say something to you that I've only ever said to one other guy. I told my first boyfriend I loved him. But when you're seventeen, you don't know what love is, do you? When it ended, I stopped dishing the phrase out. Did I not care for my other exes as much, or did I not want to get my heart broken like that again?"

The road eased right around a grove of twisted trees, revealing the beginning of the scavenger's camp, if I could call it that. There was a sign on the side of the road, a mishmash of abandoned billboards cut up to spell out the phrase:

The Outskirts are freedom.

Immediately past this, outlines of buildings resolved past the scraggly trees. Not shacks, or tents, or homeless men living in damn caves, but whole buildings. I slowed the ATV.

"Whatever happens here . . . I want you to know you aren't facing this trouble alone. So you're an andro. I don't think I care. We're in this together."

A pair of men approached the ATV with guns drawn. They wore pieces of other billboards for armor, remnants of white paint still clinging to the rusted metal. My hands shook on the steering wheel as I brought the ATV to a stop amidst the booming thunder.

"Get out of the vehicle! Keep your hands up!" their muffled voices called.

I shut off the ATV and raised my hands. Ember faced me again, a pain I had never fathomed twisting his features. He couldn't hear me, but I wouldn't get another chance.

"I love you."

Then I opened the ATV's door and held my palms up as I stepped into the rain.

"My friend is injured, I heard you have a doctor—"

One of the scavengers shoved his gun barrel against my shoulder, pushing me into the side of the ATV. "Shut up and don't move!"

The other scavenger patted me down. "He's unarmed."

"Who are you? Where did you hear we had a doctor?" the scavenger snapped.

"Jess Cameron. Some of your men—"

"Cameron?" the other scavenger gasped. He pointed the gun at my throat. "Gimme one good reason not to, boy."

I blanched. "I brought some food for you . . . I can bring more—I'll get you whatever supplies you need, just please, he needs a doctor."

"Where are they?" the first scavenger demanded. His face was blistered and scarred from the acidic rain. Under the awning of the closest building, people were standing out of the rain, watching.

"Who?"

"Our men!"

"My friend was shot." Lightning lit up the world, and I got a view down the road. There were about six buildings, stained brown with rust. The rain soaked into me, and again my skin stung.

"So they're dead, then."

"Some of them ran. I didn't see them anywhere on my way here. I'm fucking sorry for this shit. But I'm willing to help you out if you'll damn help me."

The scavengers exchanged glances. "We can't make that decision."

"He's fucking dying!"

The first scavenger growled. "Then come on."

"I'm not leaving him here."

A man strode toward us through the rain. He had a large rifle slung across his back, and wore a thick, dark-blue jacket that went to his knees. His face was shielded from the rain with a wide-brimmed hat.

"Stand down, Sterling," the man said. The two scavengers stood at attention as thunder rumbled. The man regarded me. "You're Cameron's son?" I nodded. A hint of a smile appeared on his pockmarked face. "Name's Riley. I look after this settlement. I heard you tell my men you'd outright give us whatever we needed."

"If you'll save my friend. He was injured and another of mine killed when your men tried to raid us."

"Didn't your father ever tell you not to play with guns? You shoot us, we shoot back."

I narrowed my eyes, hatred welling within me, but the reason I had come here was too important to give in to his distraction.

"Are you going to help me or not?"

The man smiled fully. "Sterling? Take Cameron's injured to Harris."

The scavenger opened the passenger door. "Can you walk?" I looked back to see Ember nod. Fucking damn, how long had he been awake? Ember went to sit up, and screamed. I flinched, wanting to go and help him, but Riley stood in my way. And I wasn't about to just walk around the guy.

The scavenger wrapped Ember's good arm around his shoulder, and helped him to his feet. They began walking, and Ember glanced back at me. In this overcast light his blue eyes were gray. Another step made him grimace and turn his head forward.

"Follow me, Cameron," Riley said. "Let's get out of the rain."

CHAPTER 18

The scavengers lived up to their name. I saw seats from ATVs used as chairs, their torn upholstery mended with scraps of worn clothes. Tables were sheets of scrap metal propped up on filing cabinets or car batteries or unidentifiable hunks of metal, all dirty and rusty. The scavengers didn't have electricity inside the walls, but instead had hanging fluorescent lamps with cords that disappeared through drilled holes. The console on Riley's desk was hobbled together using such varied parts that Ember would be impressed by the scavengers' ingenuity. Damn it, I couldn't stop thinking about him.

"After this storm, we'll have CamCo bring us solar energy cells, water filters, and a portable welder." Riley removed his jacket and hat, revealing medium-blond hair that lay scraggly on his shoulders. His shirt was reinforced with the fabric of a different color, but the rain had already started to eat through both layers. "And you agree to get us two crates of canned food a month. But what more can you offer? We are intimately aware of how much your father has at his disposal."

"What do you want from me?"

Thunder rolled clearly, unmuffled despite our shelter. Riley fiddled with his rifle, which he had laid across his desk. "Do you understand why we're out here? People like your father make us sick. He feeds off the gullible and the blind."

I stared at him. "What the damn are you talking about?"

"He's been sucking creds from good people for years. Don't you know anything about corporate greed?"

"You're lying."

"Where do you think he gets the wattcreds to do his research? The Democratic Union? They're just as dependent on the corporate sector, with its promises of comfort. Promises that you all can live the old-world life. Your father sells those promises, drains millions in taxes to fund his research and his own pockets. But that life is dead. The promises are lies. There is no comfort in the cities for us."

I didn't want to believe him. I'd thought Father's work was honest. Focused, but honest. But I had always had the sense that my family never struggled like some families did.

"Even if you're right," I started, "his research is still valuable."

"It's pointless," Riley spat. "The planet is just as useless as it's been for centuries."

"That's not true. Acid levels drop a statistically significant amount each year. The plant and animal life are diversifying."

"You spout your father's shit like a good little boy, huh?"

"It's not shit; it's real research done by dozens of educated men!"

"What good does it do you? You still shroud yourselves in metal and eat food grown under glass. You're still struggling, and you seek to bury that struggle under jargon, and ignore it with entertainment."

"We're just trying to live our lives," I argued. "Maybe we don't want to be constantly reminded of how shitty everything is."

"And that's why you choose ignorance. We don't." The thunder cracked in emphasis.

"What's your point in telling me this? In trying to ruin my father's reputation for me?"

"We can manage more than just supplies and food from your father's millions."

"He doesn't have millions," I countered. Riley smiled, and my stomach flipped at what his claims could mean. Even if Riley couldn't really prove them. I wouldn't put it past Father to hide something like this from me. The rain picked up outside, changing the ambient *whoosh*ing to a rushing, patterned hiss.

"You hear that?" Riley asked. "It's only going to get worse. I keep my men inside in storms like this. So we will have plenty of time to work this out before we can act on our decisions."

"And in the meantime?"

"You live as we live."

After leaving Riley, I was escorted by two of his men to a building across the street. I wiped the rain from my face onto my sleeve, but it was no use, as my sleeve was wet too. My clothes were damp enough to sting, providing an annoying discomfort. I scanned the road for my ATV so I could get the tube of neutralizer from under my seat, and my gut dropped as I realized the ATV was nowhere on the road. My hands flew to my pockets—yeah, I really was that stupid. I'd left my keys in the slot. *Don't tell me we're on our own to find a way home . . .*

They left me in the building's entryway, next to scavengers huddled outside the reach of the rain. I stepped into the gloomy interior. A few men sat around a low table made of a cracked solar panel, their rifles laid across it. They stared at me; they could probably tell that I was different just by my appearance. Their skin had rain scars. Their clothes were mismatched and worn. My origin was obvious.

"Where is the doctor?" I asked.

One of the men pointed down a hall. "Harris is up those stairs." They kept their eyes on me until I moved on.

Ember was in a side room, lying on his back on a small cot, the needles in both of his arms attached to suspended bags of clear liquid. He was unconscious again, and there were smears of blood on his neck and cheek. The blanket draped over him was stained and threadbare. His soiled clothes and bandages were piled by the side of the cot.

"I just finished with him," a high voice said. A shorter man stepped up to me. His hair was shaved short and his clothes were too big. The shape of his body seemed odd. Then I got it, he was a negative. Not visibly pregnant, but clearly not injecting.

"Is he okay?"

The negative sighed. "Yes. He lost a lot of blood. I had to glue his shoulder blade and collarbone back together, so he has to remain unconscious until the bones set."

"How long?"

"At least a week." He frowned. "I thought he was masc until I changed his clothing. You forget, when you're out here, what Y negatives do to themselves."

"I don't understand."

He rolled his eyes. "You wouldn't. A masc from the cities? You drive Y negatives to become andros. You cause this mutilation." He gestured at Ember.

His accusation stung as badly as the rain, but I shrugged it off as well as I could, and gazed at Ember's unconscious form longingly. A week? We'd have to be here a week regardless of the weather? As if on cue, thunder rumbled in the distance.

"Thank you, Harris," I blundered.

"Call me Marin."

"I'm Jess."

"Word's spread through the whole settlement who you are," he mumbled. "But you're welcome."

"I wouldn't have expected a scavenger to be capable of helping him."

"No surprise there," he bit out. "I'm an assistant nurse."

"Why'd you leave the cities?"

"I was sick of mascs telling me what I was capable of. I wanted to be a doctor, but they'd never let me qualify as one." He scowled at the floor. "So I stole over thirty thousand wattcreds in supplies and an emergency vehicle, and ran. The cities think the scavengers would kill someone like me and take everything I had stolen. But they welcomed me. Bullet wounds and acid burns happen often. I learned fast."

"How long have you been out here?"

"Almost three years."

"And you intend to stay?"

He nodded. "I'm a part of the community, instead of feeling like an outsider. Instead of being pressured to mutilate myself." He scowled at Ember.

"I like how he looks. In fact, I rather . . . um." I blushed. "I'm sorry. I know it's weird."

Marin looked back up at me, his gaze intense. "Love is love. It doesn't matter what's below his belt."

I couldn't respond. This negative was more opinionated and unafraid than any I had ever known. Damn, Heath would have beat the shit out of him. And I would have been insulted by his behavior a month ago. Now . . .

Marin turned to leave.

"Wait, could you . . ." I removed my jacket and showed him my wounded arm. He hummed and grabbed a jar from a table by Ember's cot. He poured some of its contents on my wound, and I stifled a curse.

"What is that?"

"Concentrated rain water." He wrapped a bandage around my arm. "Sterilizes the wound."

"Huh." I rolled my sleeve down, then Marin nodded at me and left. I knelt by Ember, the quiet rumble of thunder still discomforting me. "I'm not completely sure what we've gotten ourselves into," I said to him. But we weren't shot, and he wasn't dead. That was two what-ifs down.

Hunger eventually drove me to leave Ember's side. The darkening gloom out the glassless windows suggested the approaching night; what had Heath and Kacy spent today doing? Cleaning up? I couldn't even consider what they would do with Gene's body until they could properly take care of it. Damn, Gene's life had ended far too soon . . . Just like Dad's. It wasn't fair.

The front room stood empty. Outside, men darted this way and that across the street, while the rain fell steadily, if not too heavy. Most men traveled toward a building on the other side and down from me, so pulling my jacket over my head, I followed. Adrenaline quickened my breath as the rain wet my hands, as my boots splashed. I ducked under an awning at my destination and wiped my hands on my pants. It didn't stop the stinging.

Voices hit my ears over the patter of rain, and entering the building I discovered it was full of scavengers, most standing in a long line. The line started at a counter where a team handed out bowls and glasses. The scent of onion and celery fought the bitter stink of acid. This was my only choice for food? Many scavengers met my gaze as I looked around, most of whom narrowed their eyes until I turned away.

I got in line as a group of older children ran inside, their clothing soaked and their expressions wild, but happy. Didn't they care about the acid? Maybe growing up out here made them immune to the pain.

Around me, the men talked. I fixed my stare on my boots.

"Jan's gotta reel his son in before he gets stabbed in his sleep."

"I keep telling him to stay away from that boy, but you can't stop a teen."

"He won't listen to his uncle neither?"

Kids weren't much different than in the cities, huh?

"Riley's got problems if he thinks the downstream gang'll join us. They're all city-runners."

"Just because your family's been out here for longer'n dirt doesn't mean you're better than those of us that left the cities."

"Yes, it damn well does! My family built this house. We have a say who lives here."

I frowned at that last exchange. Some scavengers had been out here for generations? How had they survived that long?

"We'll have to hit the warehouse on Burnet South again, we're almost out of cans."

"I heard the Cameron boy brought us some."

"Only enough for a day."

"So the raid was a bust, then?"

"I don't know; then why is he here?"

"Maybe he's joined us."

I held my tongue at that. Beside those men, another one whispered, "He's right there, you idiots."

Their exchanges grew too low for me to hear.

The line moved slower than I expected, and lanterns were the only light by the time a thin-faced scavenger handed me a scoop of condensed soup, small slices of flatbread, a glass of cloudy white supplement. I gulped the supplement, my first drink since that morning, and almost gagged at the taste. Damn sobering, knowing that's how these men survived when here I had forgotten how bad plain supplement tasted.

The rain had let up by the time I headed back to Ember. A group of men talked and laughed in Ember's building, most of their clothes hung up on the wall to dry. Among them were a few negatives. Their lumpy chests unnerved me—they looked so different unaltered. I climbed the stairs and Ember lay just as I had left him. After pushing another cot in the room up to his, I settled by his side. This had been far too long of a day. But if there was anything I was thankful for, it was that the day ended with him and me still together, at least for now.

I entwined my fingers with his, and he reflexively squeezed.

The next morning, the rain fell as hard as it ever got. I stared out the front door, muggy wind swirling moisture into my face. The world was dark gray and quiet, interspersed with flashes of bright white, crashes of sound. The trees hung sadly, their shiny leaves quivering under the acid's assault.

Ember rested in the building across from me. Fifty feet away but a universe apart, with him lost in whatever dreams his condition allowed. I yearned for his laugh and his smile so badly that the gloom blurred with tears. I didn't get it. What was wrong with me?

"What are you staring at, Cameron?" a man leered, the ripped pants he wore sporting visible dye patters, hallmark of a designer a few years back. I focused on my feet. He laughed. "We finally have a prisoner of war. I hear Riley's gonna ransom you for millions."

I couldn't help but frown. The rumors had sure escalated from yesterday. However, I didn't want a confrontation from disagreeing with them.

The scavenger kicked my shin. "You still think you're better than us. I can see it in your pretty, clean face."

I couldn't respond; after so little food and with my whole body aching and itching from acid, my energy wasn't there. The scavenger joined others in the next room, and their conversation floated my way, mixed with laughter or yelling. They must be playing card games; I could hear the calls of challenges and bets.

A few minutes later, a pair of negatives walked by, their hands entwined. They stopped before the game room and kissed deeply. Despite the differences being much more obvious among the scavengers, I still had trouble recognizing them in the same faded, baggy shirts and worn pants as everyone else. Did they seem more equal out here than in the cities? I missed Ember, watching them talk softly. They wrapped hands around each other's waist, and walked on.

How would I last a week here waiting for Ember to wake up? This isolation stung as badly as acid.

"Cameron."

A young man with a brimmed hat obscuring his eyes had idled halfway up the staircase. I turned away from the door and regarded him.

"Get over here," he called.

"What d'ya want?"

"I wanna talk. Name's Sam."

I kept my gaze on him as I climbed a few steps, then hesitated.

"You're not in trouble, Cameron. Just wanna talk."

"All right."

He led me to a room upstairs, where men lounged on cots and the floor. Many of them snickered when they saw me. Some of them were shirtless, with acid scars across their shoulders and for one of them, down his chest and back as well.

"Sit down, right here, damn it, Jackie, move." He pushed me down onto the cot between two of the men.

"He looks like a billboard," one of them said. "No scars or sunburn. All fat off real food."

"Quit it, Jackie," Sam said harshly. The others laughed. "We gotta know what happened to our men yesterday."

"Riley won't tell us," another added.

I inhaled slowly. They had a right to know, but they were going to beat the shit out of me when they found out.

"They broke into our research center. Shot the lock, kicked down the door. Killed one of my best friends right in front of me. Do you really blame us . . . for . . . ?"

For a moment they were so quiet that I could hear the rain. The sound filled me with nausea. Then reactions started.

"Fuck."

"You fucking bastard."

Sam glared at the men. "We already knew they were dead. Don't act so waterlogged."

"Did you kill any of them?" one asked. I knew he meant me personally.

"When rifles are firing all around you, would you hesitate to pull the trigger?" I asked, my eyes down. "It's so fucked up."

One of the men at the back of the room uttered a string of swears as he lunged at me. Sam tackled him, shoving him into one of the others.

"You would have done the same thing," Sam hissed at him. "All of you would have."

Tense silence surrounded us as many of them fidgeted, keeping their eyes on me.

Sam regarded the group. "We're just tryin' to survive. Some people die, others don't."

"He probably shot your man," a negative said.

"Don't fucking say it." Sam's voice was harsh.

"I'm sorry," I tried.

"Sorry doesn't bring him back."

"Was your man the negative?" I asked. Sam nodded, and my throat squeezed when I tried to continue. Here was another man, not that different from me, making the same decision I had. Suffering, like I almost had the day before. "He saved my boyfriend. He was a good man."

Sam regarded me with hardened eyes. "Get out of here, Cameron."

CHAPTER 19

Riley wanted to talk to me again the following day, and he wanted me bad enough to get a pair of men to help me to his office. The rain had let up enough in the night for travel to be possible, but we still became soaked. I shed my jacket once we got inside, groaning at my stinging skin.

"I'm gonna get scars from this shit, aren't I?"

"Here." Riley was standing at the base of the stairs, and he lobbed my tube of neutralizer from the ATV at me. I caught it. "Slather on your vanity."

"Whatever." I stopped the pain, and Riley scowled at me with blatant disgust.

"The sting of nature is a part of living out here." He led me down a hall. "Your scars are a testament to your endurance."

We entered a sort of conference room, lit faintly from a small window. A dozen men stared me down, each as scruffy and pockmarked as Riley. Some of them sat at a table made from a sheet of roofing and bent rebar.

"I've been talking to my men about our agreement," Riley started. "We have some amendments."

"You're just as corrupt as businesses in the city, you realize that?" I said. Many of the men laughed.

"You got it all wrong, son," one of them said. A jagged scar ran from his eye to his ear. "They hurt others to make themselves richer."

"And we hurt others to survive," Riley finished.

I was getting tired of the shit coming out of Riley's mouth. "What the fuck do you want?"

"We want the materials to build our own greenhouse."

"I can't get that for you without my father knowing."

"We want him to know."

I shook my head. This was rapidly spiraling out of control. "You really don't want that. Kansas City has been withholding action against you, and that kind of threat would give them justification to act."

A broad-shouldered man growled. "He's spouting jargon at us."

"Jargon with merit," Riley said, waving a hand. "Cameron, you don't have to explain Kansas City's little treaty. We are not going to them with this. Just your father's organization."

Helplessness trickled into fear inside me, and everyone could probably see it. "What's my role in this?"

"You will be our spokesperson. You're going to convince Mr. Cameron to give us what we want, or we will kill you, and all your friends back at the station."

How could I manage such a feat, when I couldn't even convince Father to buy me my own car? But I wasn't about to say that. I just nodded, and he slapped me on the back.

"Looks like your father did teach you right." And the men laughed.

Dumbfounded, I left them. Somehow, an act of desperation, an act of love, was going to destroy Father's reputation and my future, or cause the death of too many good men. I wanted to believe it was still worth it. But the dread in my gut begged otherwise.

"Hey, Ember." I sat beside him, and took his limp hand in mine. "Everything's all fucked up."

He was still pale, his hair matted against his forehead, his brow furrowing occasionally. The bags attached to his arms were mostly empty.

"Everyone hates me. Is this what you go through? I'm a city kid, I'm Hale Cameron's son, and that's all it takes for most of these guys. You're an andro. That's all it takes, huh?"

I sighed and rubbed his fingers. "They're not gonna let us go when you wake up. I know, I know. What the fuck, right? All the what-ifs have changed on me, and now I'm asking what if the scavengers go through with what they're planning? What happens to us then? I didn't mean for things to go like this. I feel so damn sorry for you, I can't stand it."

Was it strange that I got comfort from talking to him? I studied the dirt under his fingernails and traced the lines on his palm.

"Those scavengers that shot you . . . I'm thinking about them a lot, now that I'm surrounded by men they knew. I ended their lives, right there on the metal floor. Was there no other choice? Did we really think they were savages? They're smarter than Kansas City ever gives them credit for. They're us, choosing a different path. We easily could have been on opposite sides if our lives went differently."

A rustling caught my attention; Marin was leaning on the doorframe.

"How long have you been there?"

"Couple minutes."

"I'm sorry." I let go of Ember's hand and got to my feet.

Marin shook his head. "I don't mean to interrupt your conversation."

"Might as well be talking to a wall."

"Part of him can still hear you." Marin wiped the sweat off Ember's face with a cloth. "He's unconscious, not dead."

While the negative tended Ember in silence, I wondered how different our relationship would be when he woke up. Would he hate me too?

Marin had collected his supplies to leave when someone knocked on the doorframe gently. It was a pregnant negative, his abdomen larger than I had ever seen. Marin smiled at him, and embraced him awkwardly around his bulge.

"How are you feeling?" Marin asked.

"Achy, but well. It won't be long now." The negative patted his stomach, and I stared at it. How did they manage surrogacies out here?

"Two more weeks," Marin confirmed. He grasped the negative's hands. "Are you still scared?"

The negative gave a weak smile. "You'll be there. His father will be there. I trust you both."

They embraced again, and the negative left.

"Why is he scared?" I asked. Marin's gaze held a hint of disdain.

"How much do you know about childbirth? With my limited supplies, emergencies could be difficult to handle."

I didn't know much, and I wasn't about to admit that. "Are his fathers—?"

"One father," he corrected. "No science out here to make a chimera from two mascs' genes."

"Oh." Natural conception? I hadn't known it was still possible.

"Do you know what the old-world word for a Y-negative parent is?"

I shook my head.

"Mother."

Another day passed. I forced down supplement, and then cleansed the taste from my mouth with bread. As horrible as it was, I would readily admit the meal was filling. I munched on the slice of bread while beyond the awning, scavengers cleaned debris and mud from the road. The clouds were still thick and dark, but the rain had eased to a drizzle. Heavy boots *thunk*ed on metal, approaching me.

"What do you think you're doin, Cameron?" Riley asked.

"Waiting for my friend to get better."

Riley chuckled and stepped out past the awning. "Men, you want another hand?" They nodded. He regarded me. "Get out there."

Thus began my service to the scavengers. I shoveled acid-drenched muck and pounded paths level. I dragged broken tree limbs, the scratchy bark cutting my skin and inviting in the sharp sting of muddy acid. I held my tongue when the pain made me wince. The men around me worked like they didn't notice; I didn't want to give them any more excuses to target me.

I joined Ember that night exhausted, my body all sore muscles and skin aflame. And then in the morning, I dragged myself to my feet and prepared to do it all over again.

Outside, a sky like gleaming metal allowed the scavengers to open solar panels to suck energy through the clouds. I finished my bland breakfast and traveled toward dozens of men idling in the streets. The hum of electric engines echoed past cheers, and calls of farewell and good luck.

Riley's men were equipping many others with guns. Five men piled into my ATV, and started the engine.

"Hey!" I called, stepping toward them. "Who said you can use that?"

"Riley did. Got a problem with it?" one of them said, waving a gun out the passenger window.

"Yes!"

An older man standing on the sidelines with me, his skin wrinkled and scarred, grasped my shoulder firmly. "It was a donation to our cause, Cameron."

"Fuck you guys," I muttered, as the ATV drove off. "That's it, I'm fucked. They're gonna get killed, and the ATV'll get blown up, and that'll be that!" I kicked an awning support.

"What's this city boy whining about?" someone asked.

Riley in his big hat caught my eye as he sent off another team of scavengers. He beckoned me with a wave.

"You want to prove your worth as a real man?"

I stopped in front of him and fought to keep my anger from changing into anxiety. "What do you think you're getting at, using my ATV? What are these men leaving for?"

"Raids. Your vehicle will still run fine with bullet holes in it." He smiled. "Do you want to join my men or not?"

And get in another firefight? And kill again? "No. I will never shoot another man again, not for protection, not for food, not for anything."

Riley peered at me. "That's a stupid thing to say out here, son." He drew a small pistol from his jacket and pointed the short barrel at my chest.

"You kill me, you can't ransom me," I said through gritted teeth.

"Everything you brought here is now mine," Riley said coldly. "Including you, your ATV, and your negative."

I narrowed my eyes, but remained silent. With a hum, he lowered the gun, and it disappeared underneath his jacket.

"And I don't need the negative for your ransom," he added. "You're to pull your fair share of the duties here. If I say you join a raid, you join it."

"I won't kill anyone."

"You won't have to." He held out a key from my own set. It was the one to the warehouse by the Memphis Bridge, a warehouse that rarely had any visitors. "You, Kearney, and Russell will take the truck and load it with as much metal as you can. Get going now and you'll be back in time to share the spoils when the other raiders return."

I exhaled sharply and took the key from his hand. He called the names of the scavengers I would travel with, and they emerged from inside. One of them was Sam, the other was one of his friends. Sam regarded me with disgust.

Riley repeated our assignment to Sam, then nodded in farewell.

"This way, city boy." Sam strode past me and down the road. His friend threw a rifle over his back and jogged after him. I followed, glancing up at the window of Ember's room. *I'll be right back.*

I hope.

CHAPTER 20

"He made us take him on purpose," Sam complained.

We drove in a truck a few feet longer than the ATV, its bay the perfect size for standard metal sheets. Its rusted sides would have made Kacy cringe.

Sam's friend, a shorter man named Chelsea, shrugged. "Does he even know how to handle himself in a raid?"

I was disturbed that they would talk about me as though I couldn't hear them, even though I was brushing shoulders with Chelsea. "We're going to a storage warehouse that's manned for only a few hours every other week. We won't have to 'handle' anything."

"How do you know?" Chelsea asked.

"Because I've used it dozens of times over the past few years. We pick up supplies that are dropped off there for the stations."

"Don't mention those damn places near me," Sam grumbled. His inquisitive disposition of the other day had clearly evaporated.

We hit the main road eventually, and followed it east. The truck splashed through the muddy tracks, and there was the lone tree that marked the road toward Headquarters. I looked away, my gut clenching. *Gene is dead. Ember is shot. I've ruined so many lives.*

Damn it, I couldn't think about that. But it wasn't even over yet. Now that the rain had stopped, Riley had likely contacted Father and made his ridiculous demands. Wait— How did he communicate with Kansas City? Hmm, it wouldn't hurt to ask.

"Can your . . . uh . . . village contact Kansas City?"

Chelsea snorted and didn't look at me.

"We wouldn't do that," Sam replied. "Don't want anything to do with them."

But you scavengers are totally dependent on their trade of goods to survive. In my hours spent around their camp, I couldn't recall a communications array, or tower, but keeping my head down and trying to stay alive had been a higher priority. How else could Riley communicate?

The road made a gradual turn north, and soon the warehouse was visible, with the bridge just past it. I straightened in my seat, straining to see any vehicles, but there were none. Sam stopped in front of the warehouse, and climbed out of the truck.

I opened the warehouse door for him.

"Shit, look at all this!" he exclaimed, as a few small lights flickered on. Stacks of new metal sheets lined the walls, crates of other supplies climbed halfway to the ceiling in the back. I stepped to the larger doors, and pushed them open.

"Let's get this the damn over with."

By the time we were almost done loading, exhaustion tugged at me, and the ache of hunger that I had habituated to the past several days reached a peak that was much more difficult to ignore. How did these men keep this up? I guess if my life depended on it, I'd keep pushing too.

After the repetitive *clang* of metal on metal as we piled up the sheets, the crackling of tires on gravel caught my attention. I craned my head.

"Fuck, there's a semitruck passing through. Guys, get behind the truck, they'll know you're scavengers. Let me deal with them if they stop."

"Cameron . . . you check in the mirror lately?" Sam grunted.

I shrugged off his comment and pretended to riffle through equipment as the truck driver slowed to a stop beside me. His boots hit the rocky ground with a crunch.

"Need any help, son?" he asked with a deep, friendly voice. But once he saw me clearly, he took a step back, his eyes wide.

"You're . . ." He zipped open his jacket and fumbled with an inside pocket.

"Cameron! Down!" Sam yelled. I ducked. A rifle boomed. I swore and jumped out of the truck's cabin, my body shuddering. The truck driver lay sprawled in the dirt. I slammed the truck's door behind me, and confronted Sam in the warehouse's entrance.

"What the fuck! What the fuck!"

"Got 'im." Sam threw his rifle over his shoulder. "Now get your city ass back here and help us finish loading." He peered into the dark warehouse. "Chelsea! Get the trucker's keys. You can drive a semi, eh?"

"Why did you shoot him!"

"'Cause now his stuff's ours?" Sam dismissed.

I couldn't stop shaking as I helped the men finish loading the truck. The semi had a mostly empty trailer, just some few pieces of furniture and crates of clothing. The scavengers voiced disappointment, and I hid my disgust. They chose to head back, crowing with the success of the day. Chelsea drove the semi, and I went to join Sam in the truck. Recalling the truck driver's reaction with a flip of my gut, I adjusted the truck's side mirror so I could see myself.

"What the fuck have I become . . ." My clothes were as soiled and ripped as theirs. My hair had grown long in the past month, and it curled in random tangles of sweat and dirt. My beard had grown in full and scruffy. I looked just like them. I looked . . . Tearing my eyes from my reflection, I climbed into the truck's cabin.

As we drove, I kept my head in my hands, thinking about that poor truck driver, who'd been thrown into the back of the semi so they could destroy the evidence. Nausea added to my rumbling gut. How could they handle killing like that?

Sam punched my shoulder hard. I stifled a curse and lowered my hands, the sun's bright light blinding me.

"Maybe you're biding your time, Cameron, maybe you've got one of Riley's holds on you." Sam drove in a world of shiny yellow-white and dull brown, a world devoid of shadows. "But we don't forget why we're out here. We turned our backs on city life, and city men. You're one of us, or one of them. And I'm damn sure you'll never be one of us. You're city through and through."

He was right.

I figured if I kept my head down, kept my eyes on my plate, no one would even remember I was still here. Sam and Chelsea had abandoned me upon our return for the same group of men I had seen them with before. I preferred the cold shoulder to any painful alternative.

The men yelled, laughed, stuffed their mouths full of stolen food. I had retreated to a corner of the crowded dining hall with a plate, and after a mere two days living off supplement, the food tasted fantastic. I didn't care that it was stolen. I was just glad it was now mine.

Men next to me burst out laughing. One of them, his left hand wrapped in a bandage, gestured excitedly with his right as he recounted his day. His audience listened with smiling faces as the scavenger described the innocent man he'd shot, and the spoils he'd collected.

Suddenly, two men near the middle of the room started throwing punches at each other. The conversations hushed for a moment before people broke out in cheers for one man or the other. The scuffle turned bloody when one of them, a brown-haired man wearing a dark-blue tank with tattered seams, landed a fist on his opponent's jaw. A spray of blood streaked across an onlooker's shirt. Some of the surrounding men clapped.

"Break it up!" Heads craned toward the booming voice: Riley came from the entryway and approached the two men. He grabbed the brown-haired man and shoved him in the opposite direction. His opponent brought a hand to his mouth; he shook visibly.

"What's the reason for this?" Riley asked.

"He says. . . since he killed a man for these spoils, they're his more'n mine," the man said through bloody teeth.

"You killed a man for these, eh?" Riley asked the other. The man puffed out his chest. Someone behind me hollered his name: Shay. Riley scanned the men. "Who else killed a man for us? So we can live as we live?"

Almost every man raised his hand.

"Not so damn special, Shay. If you're part of our community, you fight for us. Not with your brothers. You understand me?"

Shay nodded, though the cocking of his jaw suggested discontent. Riley slapped him on the shoulder, and the tension among the scavengers dissipated. Murmuring started, and as Riley beckoned the injured man to follow him, the men resumed their conversations.

"You look awful shaken up, huh, city boy?" a man sneered, approaching me. "Get dirt on your pretty clothes?"

Seriously, can't you guys leave me alone? I brought another forkful of beans to my mouth. The man squatted in front of me and grabbed my wrist.

"Don't see why you should get to eat our spoils. You didn't fight."

"I got you people a truckload of metal."

"'You people,'" the man repeated. He smiled, revealing yellowed teeth.

"If you can single me out, I can do the same." I tried to twist my wrist from his grasp, but he held tight.

"Smart-ass city boy." The man glanced past me, then shoved my wrist away as he stood. I shook out my hand and noticed Riley passing through the crowd again. His whole speech had been politics and hypocrisy. I didn't want to have anything to do with it, but with the possibility of being stuck here, I didn't have a choice.

Several vehicles drove out into the early morning sun the next day, and I watched Riley idle under an awning, talking to some of his men. Hopefully, he would be out away from his office today. I needed to know how he contacted the modern world. A quick walk to the end of the street and back had shown no visible communication tower, but there were other ways to network. If I could get to his console, I might find my answer.

Not much later, Riley started toward the community house and disappeared inside. I counted to a hundred and wished Ember could help me crack into his console. There were some men chatting a few houses up, but they didn't look out at me as I crossed the street.

Approaching the office's back porch, I tried to peer through its windows, but the building was too dark inside to see anything. I'd take my chance with the open door, then. Men were talking loudly in a room off to the right, but a wall obscured their sight of me. I veered left at the first doorway, and cut around past an empty lounge to the office's staircase.

My boots clomped against the metal stairs as I ascended. I winced, but thought better of trying to lighten my footsteps too much. It would rouse more suspicion than me ascending normally.

On the second floor, someone was walking around in a side room. It was the one next to Riley's from what I could remember. I reached out for his office door, and turned the knob—no locks in a hastily constructed place like this. Carefully, I pushed the door open.

There was thankfully no one here. The console on Riley's makeshift desk had a monitor like the kind in mounted home displays, which ended in a frame with shoddily melted weld-lines. The console's tower was a mess of metal parts and various colored wires. I tapped the screen, resulting in yellow and blue light flickering to life. There was no status bar along the top indicating network connection speed like in the consoles I was used to. Obviously, this wouldn't be that easy.

I scanned program names. A word processor . . . statistical software . . . calendar program . . . something called "Mark Utility" . . . nothing that insinuated network connection. Selecting the search field activated the screen's virtual keyboard: a light display on the desk. Well, this was an unusual feature. Ember would know more about it than me though. I typed "network preferences," and tapped Enter. Ah, there was the program I wanted.

"'Ready . . . network ready' . . . but does that mean on or not?" The system was for home use instead of business, so the technical stuff was buried behind a simplified screen. I noticed a small dialogue box labeled "modes of connection." I tapped it.

It read, "last connection: satellite, 2868.6.22:7.34."

"Satellite? You gotta be kidding." Where was the receiver? And what day was that? The twenty-second? I frowned. Satellites were old-world technology. I didn't even know we had any.

So he hadn't contacted Kansas City yet, but he could. I tapped on the connection history. It was at consistent two-week intervals. Okay, then how much time was left? I opened a calendar application. It would connect in five days. So I would have to—

The hair on the back of my neck stood straight up. Something was horribly wrong. I tore my eyes from the console, and a young man with a shaved head leaned in the doorway, smiling at me.

"Fuck."

"That sounds about right." He sauntered forward. "Get away from that."

"I'll get out of here," I offered, rounding the desk.

He shook his head. "City boy on the boss's computer? Naw, that's worth a little something. You're gonna follow me."

I didn't move. "Worth a little what? I don't have to take shit from you. The 'boss' wouldn't be keen on that."

"What's the worst the boss'd do to me if I hurt ya?" he asked. "Kill me? We're all dead men out here anyway."

"Stay away from me." I went to push past him, but he shoved me against the open door and his knee kicked up, hitting me hard. The world spun, and before I knew it I was kneeling on the floor. My vision flickered with bright lights of intense pain.

"Fuckin' damn . . ." I stifled a moan and a surge of nausea as I collapsed against a wall. Laughter echoed, and I strained to look up at my assailant.

"Come on, Cameron." He pulled me downstairs, and shoved me out the front door.

For a few moments, I lay on the porch and focused on fluffy yellow clouds above me as the pain throbbed. I didn't know how these men managed to work together to build this attempt at a society if they were constantly at each other's throats.

They could keep their freedom. The moment Ember woke up, we'd run.

When I was able to walk without pain and dizziness, I returned to him. My hunger would have to wait a bit longer. Sitting sounded a lot more appealing. I joined him on the cots, and grasped his limp hand.

"I'm tired, Ember." I brushed his hair off his forehead. It had grown noticeably since I had picked him up in Atlanta. "I'm tired of this shit, I'm tired of this food, I'm tired of one-sided conversations. Not your fault, I know, but damn, I want to go home and have a shower and a salad and a shave."

I sighed, and listened to the murmur of life filtering through the hallways. The higher pitched voice of a negative caught my attention from the next room. I regarded Ember again. "You're not going to like it here when you wake up. Or maybe it'll feel just like home."

The soreness and fatigue pulsed through me, followed with a hiccup of anxiety that shivered down my spine. I rubbed his palm with my thumb. This isn't how I expected the season to end. Not this sort of unpredictability. At the stations, even with my father so far away, I knew I could always count on him, but out here . . . the unpredictable wild sprouted wilder men.

There was a soft knock on the doorframe. Marin gave me a grin, and took a minute to look Ember over.

"I like seeing you in here with him," he said. "I'm cutting down his anesthetics. He should wake up sometime tomorrow."

I smiled and squeezed Ember's hand. "He's doing okay, then."

Marin nodded. "His bones will be healed but his muscles will need weeks of therapy."

"He's a gym freak, so I'm sure he'll be fine."

Marin's disposition sobered. "We'll see." He removed the needle from Ember's arm, and he cleaned and bandaged where the needle had been. Ember exhaled and turned his head, and Marin's tone filtered uneasily through me. No, he'd get back on his feet in no time. But whether or not we'd get out of here . . .

Soon, Marin left us. Taking Ember's hand again, I studied his face.

"I get you back tomorrow. I get to see your blue eyes again."

I kissed him, and his breath was shallow but warm on my skin.

PART 5
EMBER

XX

CHAPTER 21

My clouded vision resolved into an unfamiliar metal ceiling. Suspended bags of liquid caught my eye to either side of me, and I traced a tube from one of them to my wrist. I lifted my head, my muscles responding with stiffness and pain. The room spun, and I laid my head back down. I strained to remember what had happened to me, but my mind remained fuzzy gray. A chance movement of my left arm erupted a sharp pain in my shoulder and chest—

The report of the rifle. Kacy screaming. Jess holding me. His frantic voice. Talking... pleading, crying.

"Fuck." My voice was incredibly scratchy. Okay, so was I in a hospital? There was no light in this room, but fluorescents out in the hall. Quite a shitty hospital, if it was one.

"You awake?" someone asked. I grunted in response. A middle-aged man, his face lined with dirt and covered with acid scars, leaned over me. The man pursed his cracked lips, and left me. If I didn't know any better, I'd say he was a damn scavenger.

"What kind of hospital is this?"

A few moments later, a different man stepped through the doorway.

"Good afternoon, Ember," he said, and my stomach tightened— he was Y negative. His face was just as dirty as the other man's, though less scarred. His shoulders were narrow, his faded patterned shirt too big for him. He scrutinized me like a doctor. I knew that look well.

"What's going on?"

"You were shot. I operated on you. How do you feel?"

I hated that damn question. "Like shit."

He nodded. "I'm sorry. I only have so much to work with out here."

"Out here?"

"You don't remember where you are?"

I stared at him blankly.

Another man rounded the corner and stopped a few paces away from me. "Ember."

I studied his shaggy dark hair and thick beard, and it took a full second of looking him over before I recognized him. "Jess? What the fuck happened to you?"

He smiled. "The Outskirts happened to me. To all of us."

I blinked.

"I brought you some bread." Jess looked at the Y negative. "Will that be okay for him?"

He nodded. "If he feels up to eating."

I felt extremely nauseous, though I wasn't sure why. "I can eat."

"I'll sit you up." The Y negative reached toward me, and I pushed his hands away.

"I can sit my damn self up." But the moment I tried to put weight on my palms, my arms gave out and pain flared. I yelped in surprise. The Y negative gripped me firmly and propped me up on a thin pillow, all while I stuttered, "What . . . Why . . . can't I . . ."

Jess settled on a cot by mine and took my hand. I yanked it from his grasp. "What the fuck is going on here?"

The Y negative sighed. "You were shot in the chest. I've kept you under since Jess brought you here, but your bones should be healed enough for you to start getting your strength back."

"Where the fuck is here?" I glared at Jess.

"With the scavengers."

"What the fuck!" My breathing quickened, and the Y negative took my hands.

"You're safe here. You're okay."

"Jess . . ." My astonishment brought tears to my eyes. "Why are we with the scavengers?"

The Y negative released his grip on me, and Jess rubbed my forearm and spoke carefully. "You were going to die. We couldn't contact the cities. I had no other choice."

"Going to die?" Tears slipped down my cheeks and a tremor swept through me.

"You will be fine, Ember. You're recovering right on schedule," the Y negative insisted. "In another week you should be able to walk again."

My throat seized. "Another—?"

"We've been here a week," Jess said.

His words kicked me in the gut, and the room spun. "Did you inject me?"

"Did I— Oh, uh, no?"

"What do you mean no?" I yelled, my hoarse voice sounding sickly high-pitched to me, even though it hadn't changed.

"I . . . I didn't think of it," Jess mumbled.

"Fuck! How late am I? What the fuck day is it?"

"I don't know . . . the second?"

Three days late? Three fucking days? No wonder I felt so nauseous. I struggled to sit up straighter and my limbs shook so bad they were useless.

Jess shook his head. "Please, you were dying and I was running out of time—"

"Fuck you!" I shrieked. How could he do this to me? Here another week, another few days after that before we'd be in civilization, two fucking weeks late, fucking damn bastard fucking—

"You piece-of-shit andro!" the Y negative bit out. "Here this poor guy spends a whole week by your side while you heal, and your ungrateful ass can't do anything but scream at him because he forgot about your stupid addiction?"

Jess gasped; I simply stared the Y negative down.

"It's not an addiction, it's my whole fucking life, you freak. Looks to me like you've never shot up a day of your life. You don't fucking understand."

"You're an idiot," he retorted. "An ungrateful fucking idiot. You don't have any idea what's actually in those vials, do you?"

"The fuck are you talking about?"

"It's not just testosterone." His expression remained a twisted scowl. "I worked at a hospital for years; I saw patients who spiked all the fucking time. Almost all of the vials off the streets are laced with J-thirty-two. Makes you high when you take it? Makes you ill when you don't? Keeps you fucking addicted."

"You liar," I hissed.

"So you're late. You feel nauseous? Muscle tremors? Withdrawal symptoms. You think natural testosterone would cause that?"

My frown turned into a grimace; my jaw trembled.

"Ember— I'm sorry—" Jess pleaded.

"Get away from me."

The Y negative gripped Jess's arm, then helped him to his feet. "A few more days and the withdrawal will be over. Maybe he'll see clearly then."

The men left me and the panic pressed in and suffocated. How could Jess do this to me? My body tensed, and the flexing of my muscles was so painful I cried. My gut continued to churn; I was late I was late I was late . . .

The nausea reached a peak, and I couldn't even turn my head before I gagged. I spent several minutes dry heaving until there was bile burning my mouth, the spasms of my muscles terrifyingly painful. Someone rolled me onto my side, and my body curled up, and the heaving didn't stop. I couldn't open my eyes. My mouth stung. He rubbed my back, and I let out a sob.

"What do I do?" I croaked.

The Y negative sighed. "You live."

I didn't see Jess during the rest of the day. The Y negative brought me a plate of bread and a glass of supplement, but didn't speak. The movement of his natural body sickened me. How could he live like that? How could he stand it? For a while I lost track of time, and woke with a scratchy blanket tucked neatly around me. Scavengers passed by the open doorway, and I scrutinized their appearances with disgust. The man who had first noticed my consciousness idled on another cot in the room with bandages around one leg, and the occasional scavenger greeted him from the hallway.

The Y negative joined us after some time. He handed me a bowl of canned vegetable soup.

"It's not warm," he said. I brought the soup to my lips with shaking hands. He studied me with that medical look. "Are you in any pain?"

"I hate doctor questions," I said.

After a moment of silence, he spoke. "How many did you have?"

"Six. You?"

"Five."

I drank down broth. "Why the scavengers?"

"They don't judge your genes. Only your class."

"Where's Jess?"

The Y negative raised an eyebrow at me, and took my empty bowl. He left me without answering.

In my boredom I started working what muscles I had left. The first time I raised my arms over my head I cried out from the pain in my shoulder, but I clenched my jaw, and kept going. I soon became fatigued, and after losing myself to sleep for a few hours, I picked up where I had left off. The Y negative brought me dinner and berated me for the overexertion. I didn't give a shit. By the next morning, I could sit myself up, albeit after a bit of struggling and suppressing groans.

I needed to become independent again damn quickly. Being stuck in this cot reminded me too much of being a surrogate.

Now successfully sitting up, I pushed the blanket off of my body. Just a moment of looking at what had become of me was enough. I stared ahead and bit back tears. It would take a full year to regain the muscle I had lost since getting in that ATV a month prior. My revulsion kicked the nausea back into gear. Bringing my knees to my chin, my legs trembled with the effort.

You're a damn scrawny Y negative again. I held my thin legs and felt the throbbing pain of my shoulder, the ache of my muscles. Somewhere inside hurt too, a hollow ache I couldn't quite place.

There was a soft knock on the doorframe, and I looked up to see Jess leaning against it. He wrapped his arms across his chest and waited.

He was scruffy, the dirt caked in his hair and on the extremities of his clothes. His gaze was lowered, and he ground the toe of his boot into the floor.

"I'm four days late. I've never been this late in five years."

His face scrunched up, but he kept his eyes down.

"I feel sick," I lamented. "I'm in pain. My shoulder hurts like shit."

"You're damned alive."

That sobered me. "I'm alive."

Jess joined me on the cot and put his hand on my good shoulder. My gut fluttered with enjoyment from his warmth, but I couldn't get myself to reach for him. He had ruined my identity. That wasn't something I could just let go.

"Is there anything I can do for you?"

"I'm hungry."

Jess nodded, a smile visible through his thick beard. "The line's long this time of day. I may be an hour."

He slipped out of the room, and my whole body ached with confused appreciation. I used the emotions coursing through me to straighten and bend my trembling legs. By the time Jess returned, I couldn't move them at all.

He settled by my side again, and I suppressed a sob.

"Please kill me," I whispered.

"Don't say that," he said softly, handing me some bread.

"I can't live like this."

"It's temporary." He held out a glass.

After I drank its chalky contents, he took the glass from my hands. I took a deep breath, which hurt.

"I'm so sorry," he said, and a crack in his voice got my attention enough for me to take in the concern tightening his face, his hands wringing in his lap. My vision blurred with tears. Everything hurt and ached and a fear I didn't understand gripped me so hard that I grasped for Jess, and when he held me tightly I sobbed into his chest.

"I'm so scared," I managed, holding on to his filthy shirt. "I don't know what's going to happen to me . . . I don't know if I'm going to lose myself . . . I don't want to stop, I don't want to change . . ."

"Okay, let's try standing . . ." My voice rang slightly in the quiet room as I planted my feet on the cold metal floor. I pushed off from the bed, and stood in a half crouch, spasms of pain shooting down my back and across my shoulders. Soon my legs buckled and I collapsed onto the cot.

"You are incredibly stubborn," the Y negative announced, approaching me. Jess had told me his name was Marin. "Can I check your surgery site?"

I shrugged my right shoulder, and Marin unbuttoned my shirt and studied me. He touched my chest and back, and I hissed.

"You're lucky." He covered me again. "You didn't get any infection. I wouldn't have been able to do anything for you then. We would have had to petition Riley to send you to a city." He shuddered.

"Who's Riley?"

"Our mayor, you can say. He helps keep everyone under control out here. I'm sure the men would have all shot themselves dead by now if it weren't for him."

"Are there other Y negatives?"

"Yeah, we even have many natural born children," he said, pride in his voice.

I frowned. "Are some of you het?"

"Some, yes. Those that grew up in the cities don't take too kindly to it, but the others don't mind."

Even among scavengers, more of the same. I should have figured.

"I have something for you," Marin said, producing folded-up fabric. "It's a sling. I want you to wear it for at least six weeks."

I scoffed. "I don't think so."

His expression became stern. "You wear this or your recovery will be twice as long and much more painful."

He opened up the fabric, a thick black canvas that appeared to have been a pair of pants. With a sigh, I waved him on, and he lifted my arm into the sling and wrapped a strap up over my good shoulder to clasp in the front. A shooting pain that had been traveling in waves down my arm instantly eased up.

"Thank you," I grumbled, and he nodded.

Time to try standing again. I pushed myself up, splayed my free arm, and Marin motioned for me to stop. When I straightened my back, pain throbbed through me and the room spun. *Fucking damn it, can I do anything?* He grabbed my arm, and I leaned against him until the dizziness passed.

"I told you, you aren't ready for this yet," he said, and I used my grip on him to settle onto the cot. For a skinny little Y negative, he was surprisingly strong.

"I can't wait until I'm ready. I have to get home."

He averted his gaze. "I said you'd be up in a week . . . I never said anything about you going home."

CHAPTER 22

Jess fed me and Marin cared for me, but a few days passed before I succeeded in hobbling across the room. My strength returned more quickly after that, and another day later, Jess took to being my crutch as he showed me around the scavengers' mini city.

He pointed out their innovations. Basins collected rainwater from sloped roofs; solar panels were multiple pieces fused together and held up with axles from vehicles and covered with windshields. The kitchen had a mixture of repurposed scientific equipment and utensils made of sculpted scrap metal. They did what they could with what little they had, making them more like the men that reestablished our world than anyone living in the cities.

But many things about them remained disappointingly the same. While Jess showed me one of the more crowded lounges, a masc shouldered Jess hard as he passed, and when Jess's grasp on me shook, I couldn't keep my balance. I landed on my hip, thankfully breaking my fall with my right arm. The masc laughed and joined a nearby group.

"Fucking jerk." Jess clasped my outstretched hand and pulled me to my feet. I winced at the motion and the new pain in my hip.

"I gotta sit down," I said. He led me to a chair made of bent metal that resided near a table whose top was a dead solar panel. Jess rubbed my right shoulder, and I tried to enjoy it.

"This your boyfriend Harris's been taking care of?" a man said, and a thrill tickled my chest. "Is he okay?"

"Would you be okay if you were shot?" Jess asked. The man grunted. Jess had been calling me his boyfriend?

The man punched my forearm gently. "The Outskirts'll try to get ya. Keep strong." I nodded at him, and he left us.

Jess leaned toward me. "You think you can stand now?"

I stared at the solar panel's hexagonal cells. "I'm your boyfriend?"

He cracked a smile. "You want the title?"

I bobbed my head. He inclined my chin and kissed me.

"I got a couple more things to show you if you're up to standing," he said. I smiled, and reached out to him.

Jess led me to the back porch of the building, and beyond that, the treed land sloped downhill to the right. The mountain the scavengers had settled under was visible only as the appearance of taller trees out to the left. The sky was burnt yellow with clouds alight from an imminent sunset.

"So I think Headquarters is that way, by the looks of the sun." He pointed ahead, and then glanced behind us. "Okay, I don't think anyone will hear us out here. I couldn't chance talking to you with Marin or any of the others within earshot."

I frowned. "Go on."

"Riley wants to ransom me to my father, even though I told him how horribly he would retaliate. He wants to blackmail Father into giving up supplies so these damn hypocrites can live more like the people they hate. And he's threatened to kill all of us if things don't go his way."

I blinked, and tried to keep my breathing calm. "So what does that mean?"

"Well . . . I'm not sure how much he's bluffing. As far as I can tell he only gets an occasional connection to the cities. There's no tower. His console talked about a satellite."

I laughed. "Very old computers had satellite connectivity but it was discontinued for that reason. We launched five satellites, modeled them after the old world. They all either broke down, or completely deviated from geosynchronous orbit."

"How come I had no idea?"

"It was over a hundred years ago."

"Oh."

"Does the console look that old?" I scanned the land, the sunset advancing the whole world toward yellow-orange.

Jess looked over his shoulder. "Someone's watching us." He put an arm around me.

"Kiss me," I whispered. "To ward off suspicion." I blushed and felt like I was in one of those lame romance televids. Jess hummed affirmatively and complied with my request. A few moments passed before we pulled away from each other, and all the while the ache in my chest didn't feel as strong.

"Yeah it did look that old." He kissed my cheek. I ran my fingers through his shaggy hair. It was greasy and sticky, but I bet mine was too.

"How often does it get a connection?" I asked. He kissed me again.

"Roughly every two weeks." He fiddled with the bottom of my shirt, and I leaned onto his chest and wrapped my good arm around him.

"Which gives us how long?" I spoke into his shirt.

"A day or two, but I don't want to let him make his call."

"Oh?"

"No. I want us to get in there, send a distress call to my father, and sabotage the console."

"Who is this Jess, standing up for himself?"

"Someone who doesn't want to die out here." He kissed my forehead.

His plan was suicidal, of course, and I should have said so. But instead I held him, my face buried in the crook of his neck against rough fabric and dirty skin, breathing in the dirt and the sweat and the acid and feeling calm deep inside. There was something about being in his arms . . . something that made nothing else matter.

By the time we had returned to Marin's building and settled on a vacant couch in the front room, Jess had made up his mind to scope out Riley's house that evening for us to "attack." He left, and longing coursed through me.

This morning had been the first time I had slept in his arms for almost two weeks, even though for me it had hardly felt like two days. It had been lovely, and I didn't want those times to stop. My previous fury with him seemed like a bad dream. I wished my surroundings and damaged body were a bad dream too. Because I desperately wanted to wake up.

Eventually, Jess returned, flopping down beside me. "Fuck, Ember. We're gonna have to do something special here."

"What?"

He squeezed my waist and whispered in my ear. "Riley's got guys in his office. They're not touching anything. Just standing there. So . . . I have an idea, and yes, it's dangerous."

I raised an eyebrow at him. "Go on."

"Last week, a brawl started, and everyone showed and rooted for a winner, until Riley broke it up. So I'm gonna start a fight. Those guys in Riley's room will probably run over to check it out."

"Dangerous indeed." But it might be worth it, if it worked.

He entwined his fingers in mine. "I don't think we have the time for me to think of something better."

He was probably right, but I could imagine the blood flying too clearly. "So I guess this means I need to do the dirty work."

He nodded.

"When?"

"Are you up to it now?"

I took a deep breath and nodded. Jess motioned to help me stand—I refused and stood myself. It hurt, but I couldn't care. Our gaze lingered for several moments, and he kissed me.

"Good luck," he whispered. I returned the sentiment, and started on my slow trek toward the front porch. Jess strode past me, and sprinted toward the community building. *Not so fast, Jess . . .*

I was halfway across the street when hollering broke out. Echoes of the bursting pain of being attacked ran through me, settling into an ache in my chest. It should have been me; I could handle myself in a fight. Well, I used to be able to. Now, we hadn't a choice but to have him handle it in my stead.

Struggling to keep my gait as normal as possible, I advanced slowly. Men trickled into the streets to investigate the commotion. There was an outburst of cheers from Jess's location, and my gut twisted. A few men bounded out of Riley's building, laughing and wondering aloud who it was this time.

I stepped onto the porch when they were out of sight. Hopefully Jess had been right, and they'd all be curious. My shoulder throbbed from the effort of climbing the stairs, even though my legs were doing the hard work. I gritted my teeth and pushed onward.

Cheering echoed distantly, but the house remained silent. I didn't hear anyone around me, though they could have been idling out of sight. I reached the top landing, and glanced down the hall ... nothing.

An eruption of applause sent a chill down my spine. That could mean it was already over. I shuffled toward an open door at the end of the hall. The room was empty, so I walked right in.

The console in question was a masterpiece of mismatched components. A Litany 7B hard drive, an Askeron 200, a F22-B8 coolant fan, a wall display from a house, a mess of wires. Whoever had built it was a genius for getting it all to work, and an idiot at the same time—it would take me a second to permanently disable this contraption.

I tapped the screen, and a keyboard projection lit up. Stifling a chuckle, I opened the applications folder, and chose "command prompt."

A window opened on the screen, and the familiar slash-colon flashed expectantly.

```
      'md_cnct'
:     satellite JC07:35B2 CnectView 2.0
:     last connect 2868.6.22:7.34
:     host no connection
      'ip_host'
:     host ip 124.162.47.25
      'ping 124.162.47.25'
:     ping 124.162.47.25
:     packet received 1273 ms
```

It's in range ...

Someone yelled, a big booming voice whose muffled words held an air of command. That would be Riley.

```
        'cnct_host 124.162.47.25'
:
:
:       host connected
        'ping 182.75.14.98'
```

This was the ip of Headquarters's console I usually used.

```
:       ping 182.75.14.98
:
:
```

I waited a few seconds but nothing happened. Jess had said they couldn't connect . . . it still couldn't, or I wasn't through to anything at all.

```
        'ping 112.213.25.01'
:       ping 112.213.25.01
:       packet received 2417 ms
```

I stifled a cheer—I could get through to CamCo's main server in Kansas City.

```
        'ip_self'
:       self ip 109.3.128.35
```

Scavengers were returning to their posts with garbled words and clunking boots. Fuck, I had to type faster, which was made all the more difficult by my left arm pinned in the sling.

```
        'cnct_server transmsg camcord.kc'
:       transmsg camcord.kc connection established
        'snd_msg from 109.3.128.35 to hale.cameron@camcord.kc
:       transmsg camcord.kc ok
```

Men ascended the stairs. I caught snippets of conversation: "Stupid Cameron kid . . . bloody mess," and I shuddered.

'snd_msg data father headquarters attacked help .'
:   transmsg camcord.kc data sent

"Hey! The fuck are you doing?"

I yelped and stood up straight, a sharp pain tearing through my shoulder. One of the men approached me as I stifled a cry.

"Who are you?" he demanded, slamming a dirt-encrusted palm onto the desk. Glancing down at the console, I reached forward, and ripped off the coolant fan.

"You little piece of shit," the one in the doorway hissed. I stared at them hard, the fan still spinning in my hand. They were blocking my only way out. I took a few steps back.

"Get Riley," the first man said to the other before returning a sharp gaze to me. "You move an inch and I'm killing you."

We stood frozen. After thirty seconds, the console's screen flickered off, then the keyboard dimmed. Finally, as the fan I held slowed to a stop, a hiss and a pop escaped the console, followed by a cloud of smoke. I grinned.

The man flexed his arms, then lunged at me from across the desk. I sidestepped, and seeing the doorway was now vacant, I pressed my bad arm to my chest, and sprinted.

The human body has an uncanny ability to disregard pain when pumped with adrenaline. My first few strides were agony, but by the time I was halfway down the stairs, everything was numb. I stumbled through the building and across the entryway, past men turning to stop me. Then I burst through the front door, right into the chest of a tall, broad-shouldered scavenger.

I ran into him with my right shoulder, but my momentum sent me tumbling off the porch and landing left-arm first onto the soil. I shrieked as the pain exploded like dozens of knives through my chest and shoulder. Now on my back in the dirt, I got a glimpse of tree branches and pale-yellow clouds before something slammed against my gut and the world went black.

CHAPTER 23

No, no . . . Fuck . . . I'm done with being in pain . . .

I reluctantly opened my eyes. My abdomen, my shoulder, my arms: their agony smoldered. It was very dark. No windows, but light peeked in from a crack underneath a door. The hard metal floor was uncomfortable against my back. I tried to sit up, but it was too much and a cry escaped me. There was a whine in return, and I lifted my head. It was too dark to see clearly, but something was lying on the other side of the room. Rolling onto my right arm, my left shoulder still screamed. I crawled across the small room, my abdomen shuddering with every muscle contraction.

"Jess? Jess?" I touched his arm.

He groaned and rolled onto his back. I winced at the sight of his face—damn it, this was pretty bad. Even in this light, I could tell his right eye was swollen shut. His lips and nose left trails of blood across his cheek, soaked into his beard.

"Jess . . ." I laid my head on his chest, and he grasped me weakly. My throat tightened as tears stung my eyes. Soon, I lost track of time.

"I think that went okay, yeah?" Jess asked.

I shook my head into his dirty shirt. "Not really." I lay curled between his legs and arms as he sat propped against a wall. It had probably been a few hours, but he still couldn't open his right eye, and my shoulder hurt so bad I couldn't move. But we were at least alive.

"We succeeded in our goals," he said in rebuttal.

"You're a wreck, message filters may block what I sent, they may be able to fix the console . . ."

"You did what you could. Now we do what we can."

"It fucking hurts so much, Jess . . . and I'm hungry. Aren't you fucking hungry?"

He kissed my forehead, and I quieted to fight off another wave of tears. I had been crying ever since we both regained consciousness. The discomfort and the panic had wound up my nerves and constricted my throat so much I could do nothing else. Some man I was.

"Just do what you can. Which right now is to remain calm, and ride this out. My father'll come. Tomorrow evening, or the next morning."

"How are you so relaxed?"

"I've been stressed nonstop for almost two weeks now. I don't think there's any stress left in me." He chuckled. I didn't find it funny.

"I have to piss."

"Can't help you there." He must have smiled because I could hear the crackling of the dried blood in his beard. I couldn't help but echo it a bit myself.

"How did we get ourselves into this mess?"

He shrugged, and rubbed my back. "Sometimes shitty things happen to good people."

"Maybe we're not good people."

"What, 'cause you're a negative and I'm het for you?"

I looked up at him, though his features were still obscured by darkness. It meant so much to me that he was here. That I wasn't suffering alone. I smiled, even if he couldn't see it. "So I was just born bad and you're bad by choice?"

He laughed. "Don't you go twisting my jokes around. Maybe I'm—"

The door flew open and slammed against the wall, and we were blinded by late-afternoon sunlight. Jess grasped me like he was trying to shield me. I buried my face in his chest.

"What do you want from us!" he shouted. "We didn't do anything!"

"Shut up, boy." A man spat. "What did you think you were doing with my console?"

"I didn't touch your console!"

"I know you didn't."

A rough hand grabbed me, my pain flaring with its grip.

"Don't you fucking dare touch Ember! Get away from us!"

"Jess, don't squeeze so tight!" I gasped, and he loosened his grip, allowing the scavenger to pull me from his side. When the man let go I fell to the ground. I hadn't the strength or the pain tolerance to hold myself up.

"Get up, you shit." A boot kicked my leg. I cried out, and then the man grabbed my hurt shoulder and shoved me into a sitting position against one of the room's walls. I couldn't breathe, I couldn't see; it was agony.

"I want you to admit it," he hissed, inches from my face. Riley, I presumed. I glanced at Jess for guidance, but now that we weren't in the dark, his bruised face and the dried blood caked on his shirt and in his hair appalled me.

"What more do you want from us?" Jess challenged.

"He's going to admit what he did." Riley smiled at him, a smile that from my vantage point had no pleasantness in it. "I prefer confessions before executions."

He beckoned someone in the doorway, and then an armed scavenger pulled his rifle's bolt. The metallic clanking made my body tense.

"No, no, please, damn it . . ." I managed.

"You fucking bastard!" Jess shouted, climbing shakily to his feet.

Riley turned his sick grin on me. "Speak, negative."

"Ember . . ." Jess clutched his side.

"I was trying to call for help," I admitted, trembling. "But I panicked, and broke off the first component I could reach. I was just trying to turn the console off . . . so you wouldn't see what I was doing. It was an accident!" The tears still flowing down my face aided my performance. Jess thankfully kept quiet.

Riley glared at me for several agonizing seconds before standing. "Disappointing. City boys are such idiots. You will remain here until Hale strikes a deal with me, or you starve to death. Whatever comes first."

He strode from the room, and the door slammed behind him. Darkness descended, pitch-black and suffocating, and I hissed as I repositioned my arm in the sling. Someone touched my shoulder and I flinched.

"You know it's me, damn it."

I reached for Jess. "I'm sorry . . . I was so scared."

"You . . . that was perfect. You were perfect," he said in a low voice, pulling me into his arms. "I would never have thought of that."

"I'm just trying to keep us alive."

"I think you did."

Night had possibly fallen by this point; I couldn't tell. My tears had dried, and we were too hungry and uncomfortable to attempt rest, so we sought to make the most of our imprisonment. We talked, our topics flitting over subjects, and when I mentioned missing a high school dance because I was in the hospital, Jess squeezed my hands.

"What is childbirth like?"

Though Kacy had asked me the same question, Jess's intent was different. He wanted to know to better know me.

"Imagine waves of acid attacking you from the inside. The waves get stronger and stronger until all you can do is scream and push."

"I don't think I can even imagine that," he admitted. "How old were you?"

"At my first birth, barely seventeen."

He hissed out a breath. "Then . . . the infant went to his parents, and you just recovered, and . . ."

"Waited for the next one," I finished. "I didn't really care. I couldn't care. I just wanted it to be over."

"So you had to detach yourself from it all."

"I think a Y negative would go crazy if he didn't."

For a few moments we were silent. Jess rubbed my arms, and I enjoyed his skin slipping against mine. "The worst things I had to deal with at that age were the end-of-quarter exams," he said.

"How different our lives were because of our genes."

"It's . . . Yeah. It's completely unfair. Our genes aren't even our choice."

"None of it is," I whispered.

"But after your surrogacies, your life is your own, right?"

"It doesn't end when you're done. Sure, our time is our own. But our jobs and housing are limited, and that's just the start."

"Your jobs?"

"Of course. We're expected to do all the low-education service jobs so mascs don't have to. Have you ever seen a Y negative at your office?"

Jess hissed out a breath. "Damn, you're right. There are no negatives at CamCo. And there was only one negative at college."

I huffed. "Can't have a masc job, live a masc life, when you're not a masc."

"Living a masc life isn't quite that simple." I gave him a sidelong glance, and he kissed my temple. "Seriously. What you go through against people like Heath? Fighting to be recognized for your masculinity? We all have to fight, too."

"That's complete shit!"

"Hear me out," he insisted. I shifted uncomfortably in his arms. "Everything a man ever does is judged. If you don't follow the norm, act just like the other mascs, you can't be one of them."

I hesitated. "But . . . you have the Y genes. You're one of them from birth."

"It doesn't matter. You get scrutinized, ridiculed, and harassed all the same. And if you breathe one hint of compassion or friendliness toward andros, it comes down tenfold. Mascs hurt andros, they hurt each other . . . and they hurt each other because their older siblings or their parents hurt them. It's a cycle that keeps repeating, and I don't want to be part of it anymore. And . . . I know once I start down this path with you, there's no going back. And I don't care."

His voice died, and the shock of the raw emotion in it challenged my instinctive skepticism. "So you . . . with an andro . . ."

Jess stifled a sob, and squeezed me. Was this why it had been so difficult? Why it was always so difficult?

"You chose me?"

"I . . . Ember, I love you."

Echoes of a half memory filtered through my recollection—he'd said this to me before. His words trickled through me, and calmed me. That I was worth more to him . . . and he would say . . . Could this be real? I touched his cheek, a ghostly outline in this darkness, and he pressed my hand against his face, the coarse hair and brilliant warmth a shock to my deprived senses.

Then we leaned into a kiss. My back and shoulder throbbed, I was starving, we were trapped, but none of it fucking mattered. Every moment of this thrill, this elation . . . negated the rest.

A few hours, or maybe half a day, slipped by in a painful daze. I wasn't hungry anymore. I was thirsty, and something inside me had begun pleading. I was lost to it for a time, and then Jess's voice brought me back.

"Ember . . . Ember, wake up! Something's happening."

I struggled to open my eyes, and when I did, the world was still black. I grunted.

"People are fighting. I heard gunshots." Jess's excited whisper was close to my ears now, helping me wake.

"Probably scavengers quarreling with each other." Then I heard it too, reports echoing close enough to be within the scavengers' town.

"Keep them secure!" Riley shouted from outside our room. "You, stay right here! Shoot anyone coming up those stairs who isn't me, you got that?"

The conversation became too muffled to hear, and Jess released his grip on me.

"He's here! It worked, it worked—it fucking worked!" He pulled himself to his feet. "Father!" he screamed. "We're in here!"

"Shut up, the scavenger will shoot you!" I struggled to sit up enough to wrap my good arm around my knees.

"Father! Hale Cameron! It's Jess! I'm here!"

Someone banged on our door. "Keep it the fuck down!" a man hollered. Jess was not deterred, and I sat, helpless to stop him.

"Father! Over here! Father!"

"I said keep it down!"

Jess ignored him. There was another slew of gunshots outside. They were undoubtedly closer.

"Father!" Jess yelled, his voice going hoarse. Then the guard slammed the door open, his rifle leveled. Jess had been standing just to the side of the door, and he barreled into the man's side, sending them both to the ground. He ripped the gun from the guard's arms and swung the butt of the rifle into his abdomen. He yelped and curled up, and Jess stood, pulling the rifle's strap over his shoulder.

"Come on; we gotta run." He stepped toward me and reached out a hand.

He helped me to my feet. My shoulder pulsed, and I gritted my teeth, but when Jess moved forward, I followed.

Halfway down the stairs, we came into view of scavengers lined up at the windows, rifles aimed outside. Men in the street yelled, gathering. Jess kept descending, but I hesitated.

"They might shoot us if they see us."

"Then we'll go around back."

We reached the bottom of the stairs and then cut through the ground floor unnoticed. Stepping out into the sun, I marveled at its muggy glory as Jess helped me along.

We stopped when we saw the cars in the road. Shiny, clean, solar panels gleaming. Kansas City logos prominent on their sides. Jess gave me a wild smile, but didn't run forward.

"We gotta wait until we actually see my father. I don't think anyone else would recognize me like this." He rubbed his beard. I wasn't sure if even his father would recognize his son within this scruffy, injured man.

Kansas City peacekeepers stood with rifles drawn, using vehicles as cover. A few scavengers lay in the road. The first of likely many casualties for this rescue mission. That is, if it were a rescue mission at all. It could simply be an extermination.

"There he is!" Jess whispered to me, gesturing to the far side of the Kansas City lineup. Then Riley and over a dozen men fired into the air on the other end of the street.

"Cameron! Before you fire you should know there are over a hundred rifles aimed at your head!" Riley called. Many of the scavengers crowed.

"What do you think you're doing, Riley?" Jess's father called back. His voice was deep and strong. Quite unlike Jess's. "You're violating the peace treaty you have with the cities! We are fully justified to take action against you."

"This isn't about the cities, Cameron. This is between you and me. How long have we been quarreling over this land? Near on twenty-five years?"

Jess coughed, shooting me a wide-eyed look. "He's known all along?"

"Where's my son, Riley?"

"You tell your men to put away their weapons and show me what I asked for, and I'll take you to him."

"If you think for one moment I'm going to trade my son for a truck of supplies, you are gravely mistaken. That is not how I do business."

"He needs to know where you are, now," I whispered to Jess. He nodded, but didn't move.

"Then why are you here?" Riley asked.

"I didn't believe your messenger ten days ago, but the distress call from my son convinced me."

Jess took the opportunity to step out into the sun.

"Father!"

"Shoot him!" Riley shouted, and Jess ducked and ran forward. Damn it, I couldn't follow at that pace. So I stayed back, even as gunfire filled the air.

"Jess!" The reports tore through my senses and froze me to the spot. He dashed behind a car, and as the peacekeepers retaliated, Mr. Cameron darted between the vehicles to his son. They embraced. Jess pointed in my direction, but his father wrapped an arm around his shoulders and pulled him away. Horror shuddered through me. *No, don't leave me here!*

"Hale!" Riley yelled. Mr. Cameron shouted at some of the peacekeepers, though I couldn't hear them over the gunfire. Jess tore himself from his father's arms, came back toward me. But when Mr. Cameron raised an arm, and the peacekeepers stopped firing, the scavengers—and Jess—hesitated.

"Hale, this doesn't have to be a bloodbath! Give me what I asked and my men won't slaughter yours. I'll even leave your damn stations alone."

"I got what I came here for." Mr. Cameron lowered his arm to his chest in a clenched fist, and from the farthest vehicles, fist-sized black objects were fired into the air. They soared through open windows in the second stories of the buildings. Then they detonated.

The shock wave hurled me to the ground, and the world spun and darkened. My shoulder throbbed and smoke surrounded me, but still I crawled with one arm, my ears ringing so loudly that everything else was muffled nonsense. I had to get to Jess . . . any of the peacekeepers would write me off as an injured scavenger and gun me down.

Someone grabbed my waist, hefted me over his shoulder. I screamed, tried to kick my legs. Everything hurt too much to fight.

Then gunfire exploded a few feet away.

Whoever was holding me began jogging, and I hung helplessly. Trying to lift my head to look around resulted in nothing but a burst of pain and swirling colors. I watched the back of my captor's legs, the ground. Bare earth changed to packed-in dirt. The booming of guns was eerily faint.

Suddenly, I was upright in the backseat of a peacekeeper car, and looking up at the face of one of the peacekeepers. With a nod, he left me and returned to the action. I peered out the windows to find Jess standing next to his father, both of them with guns drawn. They were using another vehicle as cover. Past them, the wide hats of scavengers dotted the beat-up houses, in doorways and windows and the alleyways in between. Smoke dissipated from the bombed buildings, which still stood but now sagged precariously, like a full-scale version of a child's diorama.

In the middle of the road, several men lay dead, the dirt stained red around their bodies. *All of this destruction, it can't be happening . . .*

Jess lowered his weapon, and put a hand on his father's shoulder. They seemed to argue. I couldn't read Mr. Cameron's expression from here, but when he motioned to his men, the peacekeepers pulled bolts and aimed. Suddenly, everyone ducked. There was a burst of fire and light as two more buildings went up in smoke.

Men fled the wrecked buildings and ran through the smoke. If Riley was trying to maintain order, I couldn't see him from here. The screams of scavengers and peacekeepers alike resolved as the ringing in my ears quieted. There was yelling, more gunfire. All the while a sense of horror numbed me. I'd thought devastation like this only happened in televids. This was real, and horrible, and I couldn't look away.

An eruption of cheers came from the peacekeepers. I made out the phrase "We got the leader" from a man who ran by my open door. Then Jess got into the car and collapsed next to me. He was crying.

"He doesn't care about them—even though there's a pregnant man in one of those buildings, half a dozen children? He doesn't care!"

I couldn't say anything. Another explosion rattled us. A peacekeeper climbed into the front seat and started up the engine.

"All of those people . . . Yeah most of them were jerks, but fucking shit, I didn't want to see them dead."

"It's like you said . . ." I muttered, wrapping my good arm over the bad and gripping the sling. "They shouldn't have messed with Mr. Cameron."

CHAPTER 24

Jess was eerily silent for the next hour. I didn't press him, and focused on calming my nerves and relaxing my muscles. The peacekeeper offered us food and water, and the sustenance killed the hunger but awakened dread within me. The longer we sat, the more the shock wore off and my shoulder throbbed and I was able to think about what came next. Groves of trees flew by, and I squeezed Jess's hand.

"I want to go home."

"You'll head home tonight."

"Then that's it?"

Jess inhaled, and his grip on my hand slackened as he kept his gaze out his window. I waited for him to say something, my gut tight. The muscles in his face and neck twitched randomly, be it in pain or frustration, I wasn't sure. His silence made me sick.

The longer the silence lasted, the sicker I felt. Eventually I let go of his hand and suffered through the harsh loneliness. *Get used to it . . . we're back in reality.*

"We're here," Jess said flatly. The com-tower had appeared on the horizon. Anger grew within me at the Headquarters's pointlessness. I wanted to be rid of this place. What had I gained from being here? It would all mean nothing once I went home.

I swallowed the lump in my throat as our car entered the gates. Other peacekeeper ATVs soon joined us as we slowed to a stop outside the garage.

"Help me out," I said to Jess, and in a moment, he opened my door for me. When our eyes met he hesitated. He wrapped an arm gently around me and helped me to my feet.

I leaned into him, whining.

"That bad?" he asked. I huffed in response.

"Jess! Damn it, Jess!" Heath approached, his cheeks red, and he embraced Jess despite Jess's arm around me. "Fuck, I'm so damn relieved you weren't killed out there!" He pursed his lips at me. "And you even saved him."

"Yeah, I did," Jess conceded.

"Jess. Come on." Mr. Cameron stood waiting in the doorway. Finally seeing him up close, I saw that he and Jess shared the same strong jaw line and shaped eyebrows. He was starting to gray at his temples, and through the insanity we had endured he'd worn a button-up shirt and slacks. A spray of blood decorated his pant legs.

Jess and I followed him inside, where the battle damage had been repaired: the door had a new lock, and the ceiling was fixed. The bodies and blood were gone. Kacy sat at the conference table with dark circles under his eyes. It had clearly been a hard two weeks.

Once we were all inside, including a dozen peacekeepers, Mr. Cameron sat at the conference table and opened attack on a new target.

"Explain yourself," he demanded. Jess kept a tight grip around my waist. "Let go of that andro and answer me."

Jess helped me travel the few steps to the closest conference chair. I settled into it, letting myself wince and hiccup with the pain of moving.

He shrugged. "Well, I—"

"Do you think this is a vacation when you come out here? That you and your boys can just have fun?"

Jess sucked in a breath. "No. Our work was done. We documented all of it. You must have seen that."

"Then why the damn were you provoking the scavengers?"

"Provo— They fucking attacked us! They killed—"

"Kacy and Heath already filled me in on all of that," Mr. Cameron snapped. "But you should have told me when you first got here and saw the break-in, when you saw the scavengers within a mile of any station. You should have alerted me immediately when one of my employees was killed! Instead I watch the computers for ten days wondering at your silence. Finally you call, and I learn from your subordinates what happened. Your negligence astounds me!"

"What did you expect us to do with communications down? We couldn't call for help! Ember was going to die; I didn't have a fucking choice!"

"You had a damn choice. You should have repaired the damn servers and contacted emergency services immediately!"

"It was fucking pouring; do you remember? We would have had to wait three days for the rain to stop before we could go out there! Three days! He would have been dead in three hours!" Jess countered.

"So you risked your life, my ATV, and the keys to every storehouse between Kansas City and Atlanta?" Mr. Cameron threw Jess's key chain onto the conference table. It slid to a stop in front of me. "Millions of wattcreds in supplies could have been stolen. The other stations could have been attacked and destroyed."

Jess sniffled loudly. "This was so much bigger than supplies, than the stations, this was someone's life. After losing Gene? Fuck, I couldn't imagine losing Ember. I couldn't fucking imagine."

"You do understand the repercussions of your recklessness, right?" Mr. Cameron hissed. "Never again. You are never permitted in these stations again."

"Father!"

Mr. Cameron turned away from Jess. "I appreciate everything you've done for me, Kacy. Would you like me to send you home with your partner's remains?"

"Fucking damn, Father!"

Kacy nodded, and Mr. Cameron gestured to a peacekeeper and told the man to ready a vehicle. As the peacekeeper left, Kacy pulled himself to his feet. "I'm already packed."

"You can't cut me off from this research; I've been working out here my whole life!"

"Mr. Dawson, you can travel back to Atlanta with Kacy. Bill your medical expenses to me," Mr. Cameron said as he stood and retrieved his keys.

Kacy touched my shoulder. "I'll pack your things for you, okay?" Then he disappeared down the hallway.

"No, no, wait, you can't leave me. Not now." Jess pulled a chair next to mine and embraced me. Part of me wanted to reach out to him, but the rest was numb. Numbness won, and I sat limp in his arms.

"What the damn is wrong with you?" Mr. Cameron cried.

Jess shook his head and kissed my cheek, and I squeezed my eyes shut to push down a sudden swell of tears. His father gasped, and stepping forward, he grabbed Jess's arm and went to drag him away. Jess clung to me, but when I cried out, he let go.

Mr. Cameron pulled him up to look at him eye to eye. "This explains everything." Then he slapped his son hard. Jess recoiled and held his cheek. "Tori would be so disappointed."

Jess flinched again, and took a labored breath. "Dad used to tell me to believe in what I felt. I believe in this. I love him."

My heart spasmed in what might have been reciprocation, but then Mr. Cameron's expression broke something in me. He was gaping at his son with more than disgust—it was horror, as if Jess had gone insane.

I couldn't let Jess do this. We . . . Us? We always knew it was impossible. It . . . it was already over. He had to give up before the damage was permanent. And so I locked up the love I had for Jess, and pushed it down into a dark hole in my gut.

"Don't you dare disgrace your dad's memory with that nonsense," Mr. Cameron hissed.

Kacy reemerged from the living quarters with a few bags in his hands, and a peacekeeper helped him carry them outside. Jess shook his head and settled back by my side. He took my hand in his, and I couldn't help but shudder. How easy it was for my mind to revert back to how things were before.

"It's not nonsense. I'm still trying to figure it all out, but I I'm—"

"Jess, get away from him."

Jess narrowed his eyes and did not move.

"Ember . . ." Kacy called from the door. "I can't be here any longer. I want to go."

I agreed with him; I had to, for Jess's sake. So I slipped my hand out of his, and went to stand, but Jess pulled me into a hard kiss instead. His father shrieked something at him that I didn't have the heart to process.

His kiss was all wrong, his mustache scratching my lips and his arms around me suffocating. I pushed him away, and when he struggled for me, I screeched. "Let me go!"

Jess's jaw dropped as I stood of my own accord. I limped toward Kacy, crying on the inside, willing my face to not reveal the turmoil. Mr. Cameron's restarted verbal barrage was like the buzzing of the cicadas, grating noise in the background.

"Ember!" Jess cried. "Don't leave me!"

I paused, and looked up to find Heath taking in the scene with furrowed brows. *Go to him,* I mouthed. And with a subtle nod, he did. I followed Kacy outside, wishing I believed that this was for the best.

I didn't look back.

The hours ticked by unbearably slowly. The peacekeeper driving us kept silent. Kacy sniffled and wiped his face, fixated out the window—I couldn't really understand what he was going through, heading home without his other half. My three weeks couldn't compare to his multiple years, but my gut still lurched when I thought of Jess. With me and gone again. Everything had happened so fast I couldn't yet process it all. And what I could process didn't distract me from the pain in my shoulder.

We passed over the bridge without stopping, bumping over the warped metal sheets. We crossed the remnants of old-world cities, grassy plains. The sun beat down. Amber haze shifted the sky green.

I thought of my last vial, sitting in my bags in the back of the car. I wanted to inject, but the itch, the bodily desire for it, wasn't there. What that meant eluded me. I was too tired to reason, too drained to give Marin's claim of contamination any thought. What did it matter anyway? Especially since given the circumstances, I should have died back there.

But here I was. The moments after I was shot had been an excruciating blur, and then all of a sudden I'd been opening my eyes to a sore body, a fatigued hunger. How close had I come? If I had died . . . there would have been the blur, and then nothing. That truth made the throbbing pain more intense. My memories, my life, were both utterly precious and completely meaningless at the same time. The dichotomy hurt my head.

I only realized I was crying when Kacy put a hand on my knee, and I looked up at him through wet, sticky eyelashes.

"Are you okay?"

"I'm in a lot of pain." I didn't know if I wanted to talk to him about all this life and death shit.

"It's amazing you survived."

I nodded and gazed out the window. Should I have died out there? Why did Jess risk everything to save me? How could five weeks have brought him to say he loved me?

He was gone from my life, now.

Tears slipped down my cheeks and my breath wheezed past my constricted throat. Kacy took my hand, and I wasn't sure if he understood it wasn't just my injury making me upset, but knowing he was there and that it had happened and I had survived—helped? No, it didn't help at all.

The moment we stopped for the evening, I took off the sling and injected. What did Marin know? He had no proof—the men he saw spiking could have been on J-seven. *He just hated that I'm an andro.*

In the warm twilight, we sat on the dirt, leaning against the car's tires. I stuffed myself with canned soup that Kacy had thankfully thought of packing, and he told me stories about Gene. This made me think of Jess, as the familiar burning ate at the pain. My head spun, and though Kacy was sitting right beside me, I couldn't understand anything he was saying. I hummed a song in my head, and wanted to dance. I felt absurd. I missed Jess. I hated that I already missed him.

"What's wrong?" Kacy asked.

I shrugged and stood carefully. Everything was still sore, so I tried stretching my arms. I stifled my cries, the pain mingling with the increasing arousal.

"If that hurts, maybe you shouldn't be doing it."

"Whatever." I reached up to the moon, then yelled and curled my injured arm to my chest. The peacekeeper, lounging in the driver's seat, glanced at us from over his Common.

"Ember, you should sit back down," Kacy insisted.

"And you should suck pseudo." I started jogging around the car in slow, small circles. Kacy tried to convince me to stop, but I ignored him and held both arms to my chest. He grabbed me on one of my passes, and I shot him a glare as I stopped.

"You're gonna hurt yourself further. Please stop and sit down. Let's just go to sleep for the night."

"Can't stop." My head still spun. "Must get back in shape. Now. Where's those protein bars? I saw them in someone's bag."

"Don't be ridiculous!"

I tried to shake out of his grasp. "My shoulder, my shoulder—"

He let go. I jogged again. The agony and the desire coursed through me, the burning fueling my fire to get back on track immediately. Kacy came after me, and grabbed me again and didn't let go until he had pushed me into the car. Once I was seated, the throbbing ache filled me head to toe. Kacy joined me and shut the door.

"What the damn is wrong with you?"

I couldn't respond as my back seized up and my shoulder pulsed, causing tears to blur my vision again.

You're hopeless, I thought. *Useless. Horribly ugly. Skinny little Y negative, broken, pathetic attempt at an andro. Not even half of a half-man. You never deserved Jess's attention. You used him, tricked him, ruined him . . .*

The accusations and the hatred swirled until I lost consciousness.

Once the morning offered enough light, we drove on in awkward silence. I was reminded of my last time on these roads, suffocated by the judgment of strangers.

The Outskirts had judged me and shot me down, a Y negative who had already done his duty for mankind, who sucked vital food and water and air without contributing anything. My bitterness was thick in the air today, tainting my tongue like a sip of acid water.

At least another night's rest seemed to have done my body a bit of good, as moving was more tolerable. Unable to do much while stuck in the backseat with my arm in its sling, I performed hand exercises, and wondered how long I would have to wait before lifting weights again. Even when Kacy tried to talk to me, I remained buried in my mind, so he talked to the peacekeeper instead. Meanwhile, I planned my gym trips for the next six months, categorizing what exercises I should be able to do by what week.

Of course, gym trips weren't all I had to look forward to in Atlanta. I'd be back at my desk, tinkering with electronics, fighting the competition war. Putting on that fake smile. Even worse than that, I'd go through my day at the gym, the grocery store, watching the men walk by, this time knowing what it felt like to be with a masc. Remembering his fingertips, his rough beard, his voice.

I ended it; I pushed him away . . . It's over; he's gone.

By the time we passed greenhouses, the sun had set. The headlights reflected back off their glass, and I shuddered.

"Take the first exit," Kacy directed. "Down that road there'll be a hospital."

"I don't need it. I just want to go home."

Kacy exhaled, and drummed his fingers on his leg. "Fine. I want to get home too."

Every city light and billboard and sound was surreal and terrifying. A part of me yearned for the plains. The stars. We came to a stop, and Kacy walked around the car to help me out.

"Doesn't hurt to walk anymore." I got to my feet on my own.

"But I can still carry your bags."

He patiently let me lead as I climbed the stairs, using my good arm to help me up. We stopped at my door, and I spent a few minutes fumbling around my bags for my keys.

Niche looked up as I stepped inside. His eyes went wide, and he put down his half-eaten dinner and came forward.

"What . . . happened to you?" He scanned me. "I didn't think they'd treat you that bad."

"It's not quite what it looks like."

Kacy brought my bags inside. I held out my hand, and he shook it.

"I guess that's that," he said.

I nodded. "Good luck. With your son, that is."

Kacy stared at the ground for a moment, then turned and left. I shut the door behind him.

"You look awful," Niche said, his arms crossing. "Why are you wearing a sling?"

I exhaled, sitting at my desk. "I was shot. Held prisoner by wild men in the Outskirts."

Niche's jaw dropped, and I started my story from the beginning. I left out what happened between Jess and I—even saying his name was a punch in the gut, there was no way I could tell Niche.

I couldn't bear to relive it. Not yet.

CHAPTER 25

was dreading this, but I had to do it. After slipping into the bathroom and flipping on the light, I shed my clothing.

"Who the fuck are you?"

I stared at a Y negative, his ribs and hips sticking out over slightly loose skin. It looked like he had once attempted to work out—his arms sported rudimentary muscles. His left collarbone had a strange wound, a brown-and-pink starburst, the skin around it still yellowed from the bruising. That would turn into a horrible scar. I turned around, and twisted my neck to see his back. There were thin pink lines on this side of the wound, tracing prominent shoulder blades.

I released my breath in a controlled hiss, the shock and the foreignness lingering, and then looked away. I didn't know who this person was. Where was I? Where had I gone?

After showering for the first time in two weeks, I shaved my head and the rogue hairs off my jaw. I donned clean clothes and ran my hands over my scalp, enjoyed the prickly sensation on my palms. A glance at the calendar told me I had been eight days late with my injection, meaning I'd shoot up on a different day now. After years of the same routine, this was another painful reminder of how my life had changed.

No longer having an excuse not to, I listened to my voice mail. Advertisement, parents wondering how I was doing, potential client—I wrote down his number—advertisement, advertisement, parents again? I listened to their whole message this time, a call from three weeks prior. "Haven't heard from you since you visited. How is the business? Steph's final surrogacy just ended, he wants to talk to you."

Ugh, of course he did. The last weeks before I was done had been full of terror, excitement, hope, all of that fucking hope that would be ground into powder to be snorted at dirty clubs over the next year. Steph would suffer the same fate.

With difficulty, I got back to work.

"Yes, this is Ember Dawson, calling in response to your query about a console upgrade? Oh, I see. Okay, no problem. Yes, please keep me in mind for future electronic needs."

I tapped the keyboard to end the call, and dialed my next lead.

"Hello, this is Ember Dawson ..."

The evening began with a few mostly guaranteed gigs for me to look forward to. I ate a salad slowly, trying to enjoy every nuance of real, fresh food. My mind flashed to Jess as I licked the vinaigrette from the bottom of my bowl. I swallowed down the longing with the earthy oil. Where was he now? Would he think of me at all?

Could I accept that it was truly over?

The next day, I visited a doctor who praised whoever had set my bones and advised me to keep to my six-week schedule with the sling. When I asked about working out, he said it would be pointless until I could stretch and move without pain. The worst part was that I knew he was right.

So I returned home, sat at my desk, and the monotony of my life threatened to consume me. Conversing with clients, repairing electronics, spending too many creds on injections and food. It was all the same as it had been for years, except for my absence from the gym. The walls of my apartment seemed to close in, trapping me, forcing me to confront the tedium of my existence following the madness that had been the Outskirts.

After almost a week, I fled outside to retrieve a new video card for a client. Mascs glanced at me as I walked through the mall, though whether it was myself or my sling getting their attention, I wasn't sure. Regardless, my skin crawled. I wanted to hide; the crushing sameness of my apartment was better than their narrowed eyes.

Trace's eyebrows rose when I approached him.

"Is that where you've been?" he asked, gesturing at the sling. "Who did that to you?"

"Long story," I admitted, avoiding his gaze.

"You'll have to tell me sometime."

It was hard to say who did this to me. Marin for keeping me alive, the scavenger for shooting me, Jess for putting me in danger, myself for taking the gig? I blamed myself, but the rest still haunted.

When I returned to the supposed safety of my desk, I stared at my console's screen and the absurdity of trying to carry on as I had been before constricted my chest. How could I ignore that it all happened? My sling and ongoing discomfort didn't let me forget getting shot, so why should I sit here and forget about being loved? Forget about the risks he'd taken to save me?

I couldn't forget. And now the memories of the last few weeks bubbled up my throat and tingled down my arms and legs until I clutched the sling and sniffled. My mind swirled with his touch, the sound of his voice, the stories he had shared, and it all condensed into pangs of nostalgia.

I yearned for him in a way I could not describe or justify. And I had left him. I could have stayed, I could have fought, but I hadn't. It had all been too much, and I likely destroyed any chance we might have had to be together. For him, yes. To try to give him his life back. But what about me?

Shit, I'd made a terrible mistake. I shouldn't have pushed him away. But now . . . it was too late, wasn't it? What could I possibly do to fix things? Email him? My muscles tightened at the thought, then I forced out a bitter laugh. It wouldn't be enough.

But less than an hour into a console upgrade, the idea of reaching out had escalated into an all-encompassing need. The acidic doubt had been overpowered by a screaming voice that said, *If you don't email him, you will spend the rest of your life wondering what-if. And every moment you wait makes him more likely to ignore you.*

No, I couldn't let that happen. With a tingling rush of determination, I opened my email, and addressed a message to him.

Jess.

I fucked up. I shouldn't have left, and I miss you.

I want to make this work. You and me.

What's our next step?

Ember.

I stared at the words until they lost all meaning. Held my breath. Pressed Send.

I forced myself to keep working as waiting for Jess to respond stretched from hours into days. Every job I did took twice as long due to the sling, but I was thankful for that. The distraction, the concentration, passed the time. But while repairing a keyboard display unit, memories flooded through me: voices and touches, the stink of acid. My fondness for Jess had devolved into a frustration that constricted my chest. Maybe he hadn't yet decided on what to say.

At least, that's what I told myself six days after sending my message, as I tried to convince myself to get out of bed. The dull metal ceiling still reminded me of waking up with the scavengers, that moment when my life had changed.

Then Niche spoke through my shut door. "Hey, Ember! Come to the gym today. I'm sure you can handle it by now."

I grumbled into my pillow.

"I'm serious. Even if you just walk on the treadmill."

Like walking with the metal leggings, my feet squelching in the muck. I raised my head.

"If I'm gonna go, I'm gonna do my regular shit."

"Let's do that, then."

The sling had held my discomfort at around the same level the past few days, so I could surely handle something. I joined him in the hall, and he patted my back.

"The bruises are gone. You're lookin' good."

"As good as a scavenger," I mumbled in return.

Soon, we stepped into the moist, sweaty air of the gym, and I felt flickers of my old self. I folded the sling into my gym bag, headed to the free weights, and lifted the lightest ones there, stealing glances of Niche's smiling face. My muscles strained, but I pushed through, keeping my pace slow and trying to ignore the toned bodies around us, as well as their derisive glances. When I changed weight levels on the machines, the soft clicking of the metal transformed into a bolt pulling back, and shot panic down my spine. Glancing at the mascs around me, the anxiety churned in my gut, telling me how weak I had become.

"I want to take my chances with the treadmill," I announced.

"Totally." Niche led the way. "I took Zell out here a few times while you were gone."

I scrunched my face.

"It was kinda fun not being the slower one for once," he laughed. "Ready?"

Only a few minutes in, I stumbled off, gasping painful breaths and clutching my shaking arms to my chest. Niche kept running while I swallowed down the sticky lump in my throat.

When Niche was finally done, he hit the showers, and I waited for him outside the changing room. Realizing that I was holding my bad arm tight to my chest, I gave up and pulled out my sling. But as I fastened it in place, a movement past my fingers caught my focus—shoes of someone standing a few feet away. I scanned up past toned legs and crossed arms to find Loren leering at me.

"It's bad enough having andros here, but an injured one? You look at someone the wrong way or something?"

My breath caught from the hatred flooding my system, but with my tensed muscles came the reality of my current weakness—an ache soaked in fear. I lowered my head, and bit my tongue so hard I tasted blood.

"Hey, I'm talking to you."

"I was just leaving." The timidity of my tone sickened me. A far cry from the last time we met.

"You were? But I didn't get the chance to try breaking your other arm."

"Leave him alone," Niche called from the changing room doorway, and I flinched in surprise. He took a step toward us. "Please, he's not bothering you."

Niche, no! I stood frozen, tongue-tied.

Loren chuckled and faced him.

"Ah, but now you are." He lunged forward, grabbed Niche's wrist, and threw him to the floor—I stepped back as he crumpled, feeling helpless and useless. "Next time your kind want to work out here, do it when we're not around."

Loren went into the changing room, and with shock reverberating through me, I knelt at Niche's side. *Please don't be badly hurt . . .* Niche groaned, his hand gripping his shoulder and his face scrunched up.

"Did he dislocate it?" I asked, touching his shoulder with trembling fingers. He hissed, but didn't cry out.

"How can I tell?" As he crawled onto his knees, I sighed with relief, and then helped him to his feet.

"He didn't, or you wouldn't have been able to put any weight on it. But I bet it's gonna hurt like shit for a few days."

"Damn, okay." He shook out his arms and winced. The pain on his face tore through me; I had failed him—stood there and watched while he was assaulted. How was I a man if I couldn't stand up for myself, let alone my friends?

"Let's get out of here," I muttered, leading the way back home.

I collapsed into my desk chair, humiliation and helplessness coursing through me. Niche shouldn't have had to take the hit for me. And with my abysmal performance today, how long would it take before I could defend myself again?

Fuck, this was unfair. I couldn't think of any point since I'd become an andro when I hadn't been able to fight, or at least react fast enough to get out of harm's way. Except in the Outskirts. I recalled Jess justifying their weapons, the memory of his voice twisting my gut: *"The scavengers negotiate with bullets, so we have to speak their language."*

If in Atlanta the mascs negotiated with fists, would bullets be that much more effective?

The idea of owning a gun felt wrong. *Unnecessary.* But it would make a masc think twice. *Dangerous.* That would be the point. *But what if I used it . . .* Then it would justify the purchase.

As Niche left for work that afternoon, his careful movements and stifled hisses as he pulled on his jacket fueled a deep guilt within me. If he was targeted on the bus, in the mall, at work because of his weakened state, it would be my fault.

No one else should ever again take the fall for me. Not after Jess saved my life by ruining his. I could not do that to anyone else—I had to be responsible for myself.

Braving the humidity, I traveled to a nearby mall that had a pawnshop. And within an hour, I had curled up on my bed, a silver pistol surprisingly heavy in my hand, a box of bullets by my side, and my bank balance missing a fourth digit.

My fingerprints smudged the polished metal. I flipped the safety back and forth, which clicked softly. Pressing another button popped the magazine out of the handle. It was empty. With only one hand free, I held the gun between my knees and pulled the slide back; the chamber was empty too. Pushing the magazine into the handle clicked it into place. I picked the gun up, squeezed the trigger, and nothing happened. Flipped the safety. Squeeze, *snap-click*. It sounded so quiet and harmless. Quite unlike that shattering *boom* the first time I had shot the rifle. I pointed the weapon at the wall ahead of me—flip, squeeze, *snap-click*. Twisting the gun around, I peered down the dark barrel. Exhaling, I pointed it at the wall again. Flip, squeeze, *snap-click*.

I thought I'd say to myself: *let those mascs come, I'll be ready for them now.* But I didn't think that at all. My mind remained as cold and silent as the weapon in my hand. My fingertips rubbed the metal slowly; my heart thudded through the fabric of the sling.

Soon the gun went with me whenever I left the apartment. I analyzed the fluctuating price of groceries with my hand warming the handle. I traveled to the mall to buy equipment from Trace with my fingers caressing the trigger. There was a comfort in having it, a sense I remembered from my rifle in the Outskirts.

And as the silence from Jess stretched from days to weeks, the vague familiarity of carrying a weapon became one of the few memories of that time that didn't hollow out my gut. I was long past hope, long past anger. His silence was his answer. He had moved on, and so should I.

It hadn't yet been six weeks when I took off the sling. If I wasn't healed by now, I never would be. With my newfound freedom allowing me to feel normal again, I yearned for companionship. And in that yearning came a desire for Jess. I shoved that back down into my gut as well as I could. There was another option, if he'd have me.

I left him a message. *Hey, Trace, you want to hear that long story tonight?*

My Common chimed only a moment later. *Not the best night, I'm not sure when Iren will be home.*

I narrowed my eyes, I had never liked this particular boyfriend. Regardless, I typed back, *Please?*

I had gotten through most of the upgrade on a client's Common before my own chimed again.

You're damned bold. See you at 17:00?

That was more like it.

I prepared my injection, though suspicion of the substance threatened my resolve. I pushed in the plunger anyway, and forgot my doubt when my mind flashed with Jess's sultry voice: *"Can I watch?"*

Damn it, don't think of him. Just move on. Soon I stepped out into the muggy air of an Atlanta evening, and a short bus ride put me in reasonable distance to Trace's place.

After a quick walk from the bus stop, I escaped into Trace's apartment complex, and took a deep breath of the conditioned air. I let it out with relief, excitement blossoming and my limbs trembling as I approached the right door. Trace answered my knock, echoing my smile.

I strode past him, pulled off my jacket, and collapsed onto a couch tightly upholstered with dull-gray fabric, the gun in my thigh pocket smacking against my leg.

Trace leaned on the back of the couch, and I admired his features, upside-down from my vantage point. He had shaved since the other day, though he'd left a sparse mustache on his lip. His brown eyes narrowed as I shifted my hips.

"You just shot up, didn't you?"

"Yeah?"

"What happened to telling your long story?" He pushed up from the couch.

"I still can." My mind flashed with images that made my breath catch, and I pressed my feet against the floor hard to stop my legs from shaking. Trace put on some music, a sort of distorted dance with a strong beat. I bobbed my head, swallowing down spikes of sorrow as the burning flourished. He settled next to me.

"I know that look in your eyes." He raised an eyebrow. "You remember last time you tried this?"

Two years and three boyfriends ago, I had received a black eye and bruised ribs. I rubbed my side. "Worth it."

Trace's chest rose and fell. He half smiled, which I took as enough incentive to lean forward and pull myself onto his lap. I kissed him, the prickling of his mustache, the slickness of his mouth erupting flares of pleasure. Then his hands pressed against my chest, and I withdrew.

"Don't kiss me," he muttered, averting his gaze. This was how a masc really behaved. I slipped off of him and onto my knees on the floor, unbuttoning his pants as I went. It didn't take long for him to relax into my change of location, and as his body responded to my touch, I tasted relief and satisfaction to the rhythm of the music. For a few moments I pretended he was Jess and reveled in every inch of him.

We failed to hear the door's lock turning, but I saw it swing open out of the corner of my eye. The adrenaline fueling my excitement changed into fear as I pushed away from Trace and flopped onto the floor.

"What the fuck is this?" At the door stood a well-built masc, with dirty-blond hair and tanned skin. Trace pulled up his pants with shaking hands, his face flushed with shock.

"Iren, it's just Ember, I told you about him, remember?" Trace took a few wobbly steps toward him. "I'm just letting him have fun; it doesn't mean anything."

My gut gave an uncomfortable jolt as Iren glared at me with disgust.

"The fucking andro. I can't believe you'd let that thing near you, let alone blow you!"

Trace mumbled a response and Iren shoved him with enough force to make him stumble. Then Iren started toward me.

"Get up!" he growled, and I complied, wiping my mouth on the back of my hand. "What do you think you are, fooling around with my man?"

"I'm just another man," I said, my teeth clenched.

"I don't think so." His fist flew, and I couldn't react in time. Pain exploded in my cheek. I stepped back, my nerves crackling with anger, and Iren lunged forward. Then I did the only thing that made sense with my head still swirling: I pulled out my gun.

"Stay away from me!" I growled, before racking the slide. Iren froze in his tracks, his face flushed and his arms twitching, and waves of excitement and fear crashed in my gut. *What am I doing?*

"Ember, fucking damn put that thing down," Trace managed in a squeaky voice.

But the thrill of power kept my grip steady. "And what, let this asshole beat the shit out of me?"

Iren exhaled forcibly, his gaze still on the gun. "Get the fuck out of here. I don't care what toys you have."

My cheek throbbed, and I kept the gun trained in Iren's direction as I skirted past him and picked my jacket up off the couch. The flames that still licked up my abdomen clashed with echoes of gunfire, the ghost of a bullet wound stabbing my shoulder. I was wide-eyed but giddy, and through my panting breath my shoulder panged, and I couldn't tell if it was real.

I shouldn't shoot him—this wasn't the damn Outskirts! But aiming at a masc felt so good. Why would I like something so horrible? None of this made any sense.

"Sorry, Trace," I muttered, before slipping through the still-open door. And as I traveled home, I fought off lingering excitement that left me shaking and confused.

Crazy things had occasionally happened when I injected, but they had never gone this far.

A week passed with enough business to keep me occupied, to serve as a distraction from Jess's silence. I kept trying to let him go. But he remained in the back of my mind as a half recollection. Out of sight but on the tip of my tongue.

My confrontation with Trace's boyfriend hadn't stopped me from keeping the gun close. Just in case. At least it had worked, right? *Yeah, and at least I don't yet have blood on my hands.*

What a great attitude I was in to inject tonight.

Then, just to further complicate things, Dad called again. I balked at his caller ID, gave up, and answered.

"Hey, Dad. I know it's been a while. I'm fine. No really, I'm fine. How's Steph? Yeah? Oh, I know. He's going to be a great man. Yeah, okay."

Then I was talking to my brother.

"When's your first shot?" I asked him.

"Whenever I want. I have everything I need." His soft voice seemed both excited and scared. The innocence in it gripped my heart. "But Ember . . ."

"Yeah?"

"Can you show me how?"

I had shown Sable; it figured he'd ask me too. "Yeah. What are you doing tonight?"

After saying good-bye I paced my room, anxiety churning in my gut. I pushed it down as best I could. If Steph was anything like I had been, he'd been looking forward to this night for years. This was a well-anticipated evolution in his life, something expected and celebrated. Regardless of what my gut tried to tell me.

Steph arrived in the late evening, after Niche had left for a night shift, and well after my first craving. I welcomed not my little brother but a budding andro into the apartment. He had already undergone surgery, his chest relieved of its unnecessary organs. His naked chin let me see his full, excited smile. He looked me over, and the smile faltered.

"You lost a lot of weight. You stop working out?"

I shrugged my right shoulder. "Kinda had to."

He gave me a solemn nod, and then excitement crept back into his face as he bounced on his toes.

"Look what I got!" He dug through a backpack, and laid everything out. Four vials, four needles, a sharpening and cleaning kit, a tourniquet strap: all together about a few thousand wattcreds from a dealer. All those creds . . . it made me sick. My gaze flickered from the needles to his arms and everything Marin had said lurched up my throat. *Could I actually do this? Of course I could, I had to—*

"The store clerk said there's different grades of testosterone. I got regular. Was that right?"

I nodded. "That's fine. The heavy stuff will make you spike and put you in the hospital."

Because of the J-thirty-two? *No, because too much of a good thing is always bad. It shocks your system—we even learned that in school.*

"Has that ever happened to you?" he asked, and I shook my head. He removed his jacket and revealed a skintight, red and purple tank as if he were going to a club after this. A thin layer of fat clung to his stomach and hips. He would lose that after a few weeks of injecting.

"My boyfriend's brother spiked. I'm never gonna be that stupid," Steph announced.

I had started toward my bedroom to get my supplies. "Boyfriend?" I called back, my voice breaking in surprise.

"Yeah, Lexis. Ran into him a few times at doctor's appointments. We got to talking, you know, typical hookup." He laughed. "We've been going out for almost two months. He'll be able to start injecting soon, too."

I forced a smile as I returned. "That's great." Why had that never happened to me? Because I had never seen other Y negatives as anything more than freaks? I grimaced at my needle as I sharpened it. After a moment, Steph noticed what I was doing.

"Wait, wait, tell me how!"

"Come on, already," I taunted, trying to put on the face of a good older brother, even when the doubt made me clumsy enough to drop my sharpening stone.

By my prompting, he mimicked me as I sterilized my needle, and I summarized how and when the cleaning kit should be used, stopping to steady my voice more than once. *I have no proof that anything Marin said is real. Then, damn it, why is this still so hard?*

"So. When you've been doing this as long as I have, you become an expert at using either hand to inject. But we'll start with your dominant hand."

I slipped the strap up my left arm, trying to move that arm as normally as possible despite its stiffness. Steph followed my lead.

He laughed nervously as we filled our needles. "I feel so awkward."

"Practice. You'll get lots of it, don't worry."

He grinned at me and my gut flipped. *Fucking stop it, Ember. Stop thinking there's something wrong when there's not. This is Steph's reality, as it is yours too.* Sucking in my breath, I held up my filled needle, and flicked the air bubbles out. Showed him how to do the same.

"And now the hard part . . . Slip the needle in, just a little bit, right there." I pointed at his arm, the rest of my fingers digging into my palm. "I know you've gotten dozens of shots for the surrogacies, and it's just like that. You won't even feel it."

He gasped as the needle pierced his skin. I looked away and shuddered. *You piece of shit, keep yourself together!*

"Okay," I rasped. "Now push."

In the time it took him to carefully empty his needle, I had switched my attention to my arm, pierced, and injected, all on automatic. He finished and smiled.

"Loosen the strap already or you'll bleed it back out."

"Oh!" He complied, and then tapped at the tiny red dot on the crook of his elbow. "And now I'm an andro."

"Now you're an andro." My throat seized, and I bit back tears.

"And then clean it again," he said, and we cleaned.

I taught him to take the flat edge of the needle and swipe it across the sharpening stone, and then rub the tip against a soft cloth. I inspected his needle with a magnifying glass from my console repair kit, and gave him a nod. Then we packed our supplies into our respective bags. What was done, was done. *And I didn't say a thing.*

He sighed. "When will I be able to feel it?"

"About twenty minutes."

"Hmm." Steph pulled out his Common, tapped on it for a few moments, chuckled. "That's before I can join Lexis at Santana's, then."

"So you are going to a club."

He nodded happily. "I better start painting." He grabbed his bag and headed for my bathroom. I followed him, and watched as he brushed colors as bright as his shirt across his cheeks. Damn it, he reminded me too much of myself five years younger. He painted his lips black, and then painted red and purple streaks radiating out from them.

"Is that your style?" I asked. He smiled into the mirror.

"Fuck yeah. Bright and bold. Here, try my favorite flavor." He held the brush out to me, and I pinched some of the crimson paint off and stuck my fingers in my mouth. It tasted like cherries, sweet and tart.

"Now if that's not a 'fuck me' flavor . . ." I mumbled.

"Exactly," he giggled.

Anger grabbed my chest. "Please don't throw all your creds away like this."

His pleasant disposition faltered. "What?"

"Just . . . try to save. Don't go out every night. Don't give in to the latest trends. Try to get a solid job. Okay?"

Understanding dawned on his face with the furrowing of his brow. *Now look what I fucking did . . .*

"How long?" he asked. "How long have you been broke? Not just the one time you asked them for help, huh?"

I shook my head. "Years."

"I don't get it. Why couldn't you . . ." He gripped the sink. "Whoa, everything spun."

"Forget I said anything," I insisted, hoping the first effects of his injection would distract him. "You're gonna have a great time tonight. Okay?"

"What's wrong, Ember?" He embraced me. I awkwardly returned the hug, the movement shooting pain up my arm. "I never hear from you anymore, and I miss you. Are you okay?"

I couldn't meet his eyes. "Don't worry about me." I went to wave my hand dismissively and couldn't hide a grimace from the motion.

"Wait, are you hurt?" His face was half skin and half chaos, and the rush would hit him any minute now.

"I'm fine. You don't have time for this. We can talk more later."

"Fuck that." He tapped at his Common and a Y negative's voice came out of it a few seconds later.

"Steph, where are you?"

"Can you pick me up at my brother's? I'll send you the address."

"Sure, man, see you soon."

Steph typed for a moment, then narrowed his eyes at me. "We can talk more now."

"I . . ." I raised my hands in defeat. My left went no higher than my waist. "I haven't been working out because I'm recovering from being shot."

Steph's eyes widened. "What?"

I pulled down my collar so he could see the scar.

"Fucking damn, Ember! How did that happen?"

"Wrong place at the wrong time during a gig. Damn bad luck."

Steph regarded me with shock, but then his eyes shut tight and he gripped the sink again. He breathed deeply, his head lowered. "Shit." He giggled. "This normal?"

I felt it too, with a pang of hurt at losing his attention. "Yeah."

"It almost feels like a high."

Fuck. I stuttered, shut my mouth. Why did he have to say that? Out of a desperate attempt to think of something else, I said the first stupid thing that came to my head.

"There's this guy." I leaned on the bathroom doorframe. "Who was on the gig with me. He took me to a doctor when I got shot."

Steph nodded solemnly. "Saved your life."

"We had spent the few weeks prior . . . He had told me—"

"You love him; I see it in your eyes."

I blushed and stared at the floor, and a wave of burning swept through me. A few moments later, Steph stifled a moan.

"Oh fuck," he said airily. "This happen every time?"

"Yeah, it does. You know, you should finish painting."

Steph giggled again, and soon had beautiful abstract art on his face. I sat at my desk, and his arms were shaking, and his breathing was deep as he leaned against it.

"You haven't seen this guy since?" He smiled.

"Haven't had the chance."

"You know . . . when I was younger, and you used to tell Dad how hard it was, I didn't really want to believe you. Yeah, I'd get the shit punched out of me. Yeah, I'd cry, but I always had someone there, helping me through it. Nathe back in school, Brynn and Jackie and all the boys who suffered with me, we kept each other strong. And now Lexis—he's taught me that no matter how much the surrogacies and the mascs have ravaged our bodies, we're still men, we still want to be loved. He helps me stay strong. So this guy. You care about him? Does he give you strength?"

I nodded.

"And he cares about you?"

I shut my eyes. I couldn't quite nod to that.

There was a knock at the door. Steph squealed and bounded for it, opened it up, and flung his arms around his boyfriend. The Y negative had blond hair brushing his forehead, his clothes and paint in shades of yellow and green. They kissed passionately.

"We're smearing our makeup," Lexis complained. They kissed again.

"I don't care. Fuck, this is amazing. You're gonna love it."

"Be safe, you two," I called. Steph smiled at me, the paint around his mouth indeed a smeared mess.

"Thank you, Ember. Now get your ass off that chair and go claim your strength." Then they left.

"But Steph . . ." I whispered to the shut door. "He doesn't want me."

CHAPTER 26

"**N**iche, I gotta ask you something."

Nothing was adding up. Steph's behavior after injecting yesterday, my overreaction at Trace's place, it wasn't right. I needed to prove that Marin was wrong before I lost my mind.

Niche looked up from his granola and strawberries and raised an eyebrow. "Shoot."

"What if there were drugs in our testosterone?"

He puckered his lips. "That's . . . quite a conspiracy theory. What made you think of it?"

"One of the scavengers told me," I admitted.

"That weird Y negative?" he asked, and I nodded. "That guy was crazy, don't believe him."

"But what if it were true?"

Niche laughed. "I think I'd know if I were taking a drug every week, especially something like a J-series. The testosterone rush is just what it is—pure nectar making this bitter life sweet."

"You been writing poetry again?" I joked, and he smiled and returned his attention to his breakfast.

And I resumed staring at my desk with a hand in my pocket, rubbing the warmed gun barrel under my thumb, going over every high I had ever experienced. Obviously, they had felt different than J-seven. My head wouldn't spin with injections. My skin wouldn't go numb. But both turned me on, made me reckless. Made me happy. Could that be a drug or just the psychological benefits of the hormone?

Why am I even contemplating this? Niche said what anyone would agree with: Marin was crazy.

Yeah, but what would it mean if he were right?

Niche left for work a few minutes later, and the front door had barely shut before my Common chimed.

Thanks for showing me how it's done, bro! You'll have to come to the club with us sometime.

If Marin was right . . . it would mean that I got Steph addicted.

No, I couldn't accept that. So I opened up a query for Marin's fabled J-thirty-two. A website showcasing hundreds of recreational drugs listed it as more easily addictive than other drugs in the J-series, and with unpleasant withdrawal symptoms. They were exactly what I experienced when I'd been late. Seeing the list made my skin crawl.

A simple search querying J-thirty-two and testosterone turned up other andros with the same questions I had, but no leads. So I searched for where the testosterone vials were produced, but once the trail led overseas, I hit a dead end. I couldn't search networks on other continents. There had to be some other way.

"Maybe, the distributors," I mumbled. "If they aren't black market groups."

But most of them weren't; they were legitimate companies with websites that unfortunately didn't reveal much of use. So I opened up a command prompt, and my hands hesitated over the keys. I shouldn't be doing this, but . . . I had to know.

My requests bounced through the servers of local businesses before hitting one of the websites with a piece of code that would dig up log-in information from other users. Once I got a log-in, I queried the site simply using the word "testosterone." Almost everything required special access, but after a few more requests, and a few more moments of waiting, I freely scanned a list of documents. There were correspondences with overseas manufacturers, and schedules of shipments, including records of payments for more wattcreds than I had expected. Surprisingly, these records went back almost a century. If the vials were laced, how long had it been going on?

Five years ago, ship schedules read: "Ten thousand vials of testosterone grade five, standard cocktail." There was that word again, "cocktail." I opened up a schedule twenty years old. Standard cocktail. Forty years, the same. But at sixty years . . . the phrase wasn't even there. It just read testosterone, and listed the grade. I raised an eyebrow at this, but couldn't really come to any conclusions. The other distributors had similar results.

Time for a different approach. I queried the sites for J-thirty-two. One of the distributors was a branch of a pharmaceutical that had researched its effects. My gut lurched when I scanned one of the article summaries.

"The Benefits of the Injection Cocktail." It was fifty-seven years old.

> Studies on the transitioning population of Y(-) individuals, more commonly known as 'andros,' has found intriguing results when this population's steroid use is mixed with that of various J-series insufflators. Subjects report having to inject more often, once a week instead of a more typical ten days, due to the mixing of these substances. However, the complimentary effects counteract the increase of injections. Subjects describe increased euphoria and libido following an injection/insufflator combination as compared to one or the other separately. This study proposes the effectiveness of combining these two substances into an 'injection cocktail' not only to increase the injections per year of the 'andro' population, but also to attract more Y(-) individuals to this habit.

I couldn't read anymore. Pushing my chair away from the desk, I wrapped my arms around my stomach and tried to breathe through my tight throat.

My whole adult life . . . the life of every andro I knew, of every andro that had carried us within them, defined by an addiction rather than a choice. Marin had been right, and I had denied it—I had denied it and got Steph addicted. I was no better than a masc.

But wasn't that what I had always wanted to be?

Fucking damn, not like this! I don't want to be a masc like this!

It was all wrong. All the pleasure, the confidence, all a fucking lie. I buried my face in my hands and felt reality crumbling through my fingers.

"Not like this . . ." I pleaded, my voice breaking. "I can't . . ."

I can't keep injecting, not now that I know the truth.

And all I wanted to do was curl up into a ball and sob, curse Marin, curse Steph, curse all the stupid andros that came before me and didn't know. Pulling myself to my feet, I strode into my room, where there were strewn clothes and stacked electronics and everything that was mine, the life I had tried to build all based on lies.

I sat on my bed, grabbed my bag of supplies, and picked up my next vial, which I had bought early thanks to a multi-console gig the week before.

"Fuck you," I hissed, squeezing the vial in my fist, craving the drug, but desperate to throw it against the wall.

Damn it, get ahold of yourself.

I took a deep breath, wrapped my bad arm around my waist. No, I wouldn't inject this.

But there was another way to remain myself.

For the first time in my life, I called up the closest pharmacy and asked what the going rate of medical testosterone was. Of course the pharmacist was an andro.

"Oh, I don't get that one too often," he said. Yeah, I bet he didn't. "Looks like fifteen hundred wattcreds a month for the prescription. If you tell me your medical number, I'll have it cleared with your doctor."

"Fucking damn," I muttered. Twice the price. Twice the damn price! That was impossible.

"Hey," the andro said, his voice hushed. "I get mine for half that. I can give you the guy's name. I've taken the medical grade before, and this guy's stuff has so much more of a kick."

I hung up, shuddering. That was exactly how andros had gotten into this mess.

My day to inject came and went and every time I thought about injecting my mind shut down. So I kept working. But when the edge of the inevitable withdrawal started grating against my body, things got difficult.

Tremors had set deeply in my limbs by the time I restocked my food supplies for the week, carrying bags of beans and oats up the stairs to my apartment with weakened arms and wobbly legs. When I pushed open the front door, I came face-to-face with Niche and his boyfriend. As I dropped my burden onto the kitchen counter, Niche nodded in greeting, though Zell hardly gave me a glance before striding past me toward Niche's room, a translucent blue scarf around his waist flowing behind him. Niche followed, and his door shut.

I put away my groceries and got back to work. But soon Zell's presence was inescapable thanks to thin walls. My legs shuddered and I pulled out my gun and fiddled with the safety as Niche's occasional laugh or moan splintered my thoughts, sending nightmarish flushes of anxiety across my skin. The pleasure they were experiencing seemed impossible to me now, at the brink of bodily collapse. When the withdrawal ended, it wouldn't change the fact that Jess hadn't responded to me. And I couldn't be satisfied with an andro—I wouldn't lie to myself like that again. Not for the sake of being normal, fitting in. There was no normal for me now. I couldn't even call myself an andro anymore. So what was I?

When the andro lovers finally emerged from their hole, I dropped the gun into my lap and resumed working on a hard drive that sat by my console, digging for the right size screwdriver as Niche gave Zell a kiss and bid him farewell. When we were alone, he turned to me.

"Zell was telling me the other day he knows a guy you'd get along really well with."

"Why are you two talking about me?" I challenged, taking apart the hard drive one screw at a time, my hands staying steady out of pure willpower.

Niche leaned on my desk. "Because I've noticed you've been more off than usual?"

I let out a "pshh," lining up pieces of the hard drive, organizing the screws in tiny straight rows.

"Ember," he said. I met his questioning gaze. "What the damn are you doing?"

I . . . I have no idea. "I don't want your help finding a guy; I don't want you guys talking about me."

Niche crossed his arms. "And here I thought you wanted to be with a masc."

My gut twisted. "Zell knows a het masc?"

"Yeah, the guy thinks het is kinky."

A memory of Jess's body against mine melted into the drug-induced haze of a masc yanking my hair toward him to shove his dick deeper down my throat. I shuddered.

"Been there, sucked that. Not quite what I'm going for."

"You make no sense." He pushed away from my desk. "I thought that's what you wanted."

I swallowed down the longing, the loneliness, and almost yelped as the motion churned up a wave of nausea. "Stay out of my business."

"Go ahead and brush me off. But don't ever claim I didn't try."

Fine, I wouldn't. I kept my eyes on the scratched metal desk as my gut roiled.

He sighed. "Whatever."

He left me, and for a moment I thought my composure would crumble, but I just sat there, my mind buzzing like the cicadas: meaningless noise. My body tensed with the growing waves of nausea, the bile pushing at my throat, and I was stuck, hiding somewhere inside.

The apartment was so quiet that the *click* of the air conditioner switching on seemed loud. Sweat broke out on my forehead, and I lifted the gun from my lap and laid it gently on my desk.

And then with a suddenness that reminded me of morning sickness, I gagged, stumbled from my chair to the kitchen sink, and threw up.

"Damn, Ember, it's been a couple days . . . you still have the flu?"

Yes. Leave me alone. All that came out of me was a grunt. I rubbed my forehead, waited for more of Niche's muffled words from beyond my door. But they didn't come. I slipped back into a daze of stabbing hunger and throbbing headache.

When the withdrawal finally subsided, there was nothing left of me. I lay in bed for long hours, my mind static, my fingers fiddling with the silver gun, tracing the lines engraved on its sides.

I kept my business alive, but barely, as I forced myself to talk to shitty clients, handle the sporadic business. There was no joy in the tinkering, no anger in the haggling. Just . . . nothing. Buzzing. Blank. Not enough business was coming in because I was no longer fighting for it, so my stores of food dwindled. I didn't even dread the imminent chalky supplement; at least then I wouldn't have to summon the energy to cook.

The ability to work out still eluded me—I tried running again, but a stabbing pain gripped my chest immediately, leaving me doubled over and wheezing. I had never felt so weak and broken.

And every day, at least for a fleeting moment, I thought of Jess. Even if it was just to remark that he still hadn't responded. Steph's innocence and Niche's ignorance had only served to point out how wrong our relationship would have been. That's why I had pushed him away. That's why he hadn't replied.

There was a truth in his silence; and the silence seeped into me like my body heat into the metal of the gun. And once it was in, warm and ambiguously one with me, I saw how quiet and numb I had become. My mind was a sheet of metal left out in the rain. Slowly rusting.

CHAPTER 27

A dull-gray sunrise brightened my room enough to wake me. I sat up, and the gun slipped off my chest. With a sigh, I put it on my nightstand, the movement rekindling the soreness of my muscles. *Damn, I don't think this pain is ever going to go away.* Slowly stretching my arms, I shuffled to the bathroom, twinges of discomfort shooting up and down my back enough to knock the rest of the sleep from my system.

It had been a few days since I cleaned up my beard, so I pulled my razor out of a drawer and looked up at my reflection. My raised hand hesitated—there wasn't much to clean up. *Wait.* I ran my fingers along my cheeks, a dump of adrenaline quickening my breath.

My beard had stopped growing? Not this soon, no, please, the testosterone couldn't be wearing off this soon!

"Fuck, I'm not ready for this!"

I scrolled through my Common and struggled to do the math in my head—did I have enough to buy—fuck, maybe? Striding back to my room, I pulled on whatever clothes I could reach, all the while the desperation in my chest tightening, constricting. I couldn't breathe. Would the hair fall out? Would I lose what muscle remained? Would I . . .

I buttoned my jacket and left the apartment. Memories of being twelve years old threatened to strangle me—sitting on the bathroom floor, crying as I held a rag between my legs.

I couldn't. Fucking. Breathe.

And as I rushed past shops, all around me mascs and andros went about their business with no idea what was seething beneath the surface.

Damn it, why did the pharmacy have to be so far away?

A masc jostled past me, bumping my bad shoulder. I winced and kept on, willing the shop fronts and the glass ceiling to stop closing in on me. Begging for every fucking person to shut up so I could think. Oh, but think of what? About how my life was falling to pieces and how I wanted to scream and tear myself apart?

Finally, I made it to a brightly lit pharmacy, passing rows of remedies and toiletries as I shot toward the back counter.

An andro with curly hair and a white frock eyed me as I stopped in front of him and pushed my Common across the counter, already open to my medical ID.

"Medical grade testosterone," I snapped. "Please."

He raised an eyebrow. "You have a prescription?"

"Make it happen." I waved at my Common.

He typed in my number, and I hugged my chest tightly, still trying to take a full breath. "It takes a day to fill that kind of prescription," he said.

"Don't you have anything back there now?"

"I might." He eyed me again. "What do you want the medical grade for?"

I grimaced. "The black market stuff is laced."

He let out a chuckle. "That conspiracy. Got it. I'll check the back for you."

As I waited, my skin crawled, and my clothes itched, and I begged myself to believe it wasn't too late.

The pharmacist returned with a small white bag, and my heart hammered as I gripped the counter. He put it down and typed at the console, scrolled, typed, hummed, and if he didn't get on with handing me that white bag I was going to grab it and run.

"It's your lucky day, friend. The system's letting me use your original prescription from after your surrogacies."

I exhaled, the relief lessening some of the pain in my chest. Dad had made me submit all the forms, even though we both knew I wasn't actually planning on claiming it. I never figured I would five years later.

"This stuff is every ten days, not every seven. Got it?"

I nodded.

"That'll be four hundred creds for one. That's all I have in stock."

The number was like a bullet wound. I blinked back tears, and waved my Common over a sensor.

There went most of my creds for food. But at least I'd still be a man, right?

Twenty minutes after I injected myself with clean steroids for the first time in my life, reality hit me.

No rush. No flutter. No arousal. Just sameness, stretching on minute by minute, and then hour by hour.

The world had lied to me. Here was my reality. My sober, shitty reality.

Hunger pulled at me. My shoulder throbbed dully. I wouldn't lose my beard now, but what did it fucking matter?

The day wore on and I sat on my bed, attempting to lose myself in my favorite Dirty Code songs as I fiddled with the gun in my lap. I took it apart and marveled at the inert metal in front of me, and then put it back together just as quickly and effortlessly as any electronic device I had handled. I loaded it. Every piece fit together perfectly. Had a purpose. Achieved a goal.

Which was infinitely more than I had ever achieved in my life.

I turned the gun over and ejected the magazine, popping the rounds out one at a time, laying them out in a row. Eight. I wasn't a man. Not to the mascs, not to the andros, not to my family or friends. I glanced in the magazine, in the chamber. Empty. I counted the rounds. Eight. I wasn't an entrepreneur; my business was as dead as the Outskirts were supposed to be. I clicked the magazine back in place, flipped the safety. Squeezed the trigger at the wall. I listened to the *snap-click* for longer than I could gauge, the pulsing trance of the music helping me float. I wasn't a lover, the silence from Kansas City proof of my failure to hold on to anything I cherished. I brought the barrel gently to my temple. *Click. Click. Click.*

I couldn't even cry. I felt nothing.

In ten days I'd be lucky if I had enough gigs to pay for rent and my next shot. And that wasn't even taking food into account. I popped the rounds into the magazine to the rhythm of the music, my fingers working on automatic. This testosterone was too expensive. But I couldn't go back to how I lived before. It was an impossible decision, with an impossible answer—and end—that I just couldn't commit to.

The Dirty Code album finished, and as I played with the safety on the gun, my Common moved on to the next thing in my music library.

Suddenly I was confronted by the melody of an old pop song that had defined my teenage years. It was sung by a young masc who had inadvertently taught me that I should find him attractive, but that there was no place in his world for people like me. As the first verse started, it brought back all the hurt of lessons learned through bruises, friendships lost through blood, and I gripped the gun in my lap and my vision distorted with stinging tears.

I thought I had come so close to being a man. But there was so much further I could never go. So what else could I do, when faced with my past, and my future, but sing along? I croaked out the first verse, not used to the strain of singing, my throat wavering as the tears slipped down my cheeks.

"'I'm not the little boy you knew back in school,'" I sang to my window, shades open to reveal a clouded yellow sky.

"'You say I'm not ready for it all, not ready to be a man?'

"'If you only fucking knew all the shit I've done to get here!'" I hissed. Ruined Jess's life. Ruined my own. Because I couldn't stay in my place?

"'You're trying to keep me down, I know it—you're trying—'"

I shut my eyes tight, my breathing reduced to a wheeze. I hated my deviance, I hated my dependency, I hated the love still hiding inside me that just wouldn't die. I closed my fingers around the gun. Chorus time.

"'Is there any fucking way . . . to step out from within your shadow?'" I pointed the gun toward my window and flipped back the safety.

"'Is this the only way to show you who I am?'" I shoved the barrel against my head.

"'Is this . . . the only fucking way . . .'" I sobbed, thrusting the gun forward. "Well fuck you!"

I squeezed the trigger.

Gunfire exploded in the small room, and I shrieked and scrambled back on my bed until I hit the wall behind me, the gunshot reverberating into the now-familiar ringing. The gun had been loaded? When had I— Hadn't it been— My heart pounded, and I touched the side of my head.

"Fucking damn . . ." I dropped the weapon from shaking hands, and blinked away tears. I hadn't known . . . I hadn't meant . . .

"Ember? Ember, are you all right?"

Niche shoved open my door and gasped, and I followed his gaze to the broken window, where shards of glass littered the floor.

"Shit, I thought you had offed yourself."

I let out a whimper. Our eyes met, and his expression softened.

"Do you want me to leave?"

I shook my head. He sat next to me, and put an arm around my shoulder. With a shuddering sigh, I did the same.

My life could have been over in a split second. One mistake, one more ounce of bad luck.

Several minutes passed before the shaking stopped, and Niche sat with me the whole time in silence. The ringing in my ears faded enough for me to hear traffic through the broken window.

"What happened?" he asked quietly.

"I forgot what I was fighting for."

"And what's that?"

"Myself. My right to exist. Because if I don't fight for it, who will?"

This was a step in the right direction. I headed back to my apartment with a satchel over my shoulder, its contents having changed from sculpted metal to liquid in glass. My almost-finality exchanged for a month of life? I'd take it. And I'd have a few weeks to figure out my next move, maybe work on my advertising angles.

I greeted a client outside my apartment, and we discussed different upgrades available for his Common as I stepped inside and woke up my console with a tap of the keyboard.

"They've actually just come out with larger hard drive options," I explained, my gaze focusing briefly on the tiny "1" over my email inbox. I still thought of Jess. It had been three months since my email, and I still thought of him.

"And they'll fit in the case?"

I forced my eyes up. "Oh, yeah. Most of what's in that case is a battery. The electronics take up hardly any space at all. Here, let me show you."

It was another half an hour before the client left, his hard drive in my loaner Common until I could do the upgrades on his model. Finally, I sat down, and opened my email.

The message only had four words. But those four words changed everything.

PART 6
JESS
XX

CHAPTER 28

The workday was over, and free from Father's offices, I sat at my desk at home. Immediately, the guilt started in on me again: I had waited too long.

How many times I had brought up his email, read his words, and then closed it again out of fear for our future? Fear for Ember's life should I return, and for my own as well. Still, I kept coming back to the email, and every time I did, I felt the sting of Father's slap and the ferocity—the disappointment—in the way Father had talked to me then, the way he still talked to me. Dad had told me to fight for what I wanted, but what I wanted and what I needed and what everyone expected of me didn't line up. I didn't know what to do, and I missed Dad more than ever. He would have understood. I wanted to believe that he might even have accepted Ember and me. Or maybe I was being naïve.

I had done what Father wanted by taking a tech lead position, but he breathed down my neck every day, a constant reminder that I could lose my job, the roof over my head, who knew what else, if I reached out to Ember. My shame grew as the time passed—*I should have responded immediately, or within a day, or for fuck's sake, within the month*. Soon thoughts of Ember paralyzed me as badly as Father's piercing stares. So I had done nothing, until I finally couldn't take the loneliness anymore.

I miss you too.

Damn it, I was pathetic. I could have told him I wanted to see him again, that I wanted to figure this out. But those angles lost their meaning when time dilated from "maybe he meant it" to "maybe he'd remember." The phrase that had become my mantra after he left was the only phrase I could muster the courage to say.

I refreshed my email again. And again. Three whole days and there was nothing but my own reply, lost to the ether.

"Damn it, Ember," I whispered, his name enough to make my limbs tremble. But I didn't know why I expected him to email me back. After my long silence, he probably figured I had moved on.

And I was too much of a coward to tell him I hadn't.

Half an hour after I got home, the front door pushed open and several voices echoed. Pascal, Brent, and their friends? Damn it, having the place to myself tonight would have been so relaxing. Not that it was completely awful living with other CamCo guys; it beat living with Father. And it wasn't like Heath was still an option; from what Pascal had shared of his dating habits, he had moved on, and quickly too.

I rubbed my temples, and sought to ignore the talking and laughter drifting my way, by scrolling through news articles on my console. "Solar Panels Increasing Output with New Advancement in Technology." Well that was wonderful.

"Norman Collen Running for Reelection in the Fall." That wouldn't be too bad; he welcomed research and development.

"Increase in Scavenger Attacks in Recent Months." My stomach dropped, and I flipped past the article.

Then from down the hall, there was a knock. The conversation hushed, and someone opened the door.

"Oh, can I help you?" Brent asked.

"Yeah. Um, does Jess Cameron live here?" Recognition punched me in the gut. *No fucking way.*

I pulled myself to my feet. My heartbeat pounded in my ears as I turned into the hall to find Brent leading a slender negative into our apartment. His eyes met mine and his hand flew to his mouth.

Suddenly I was blinking back tears. "Ember?" I managed. "What are you ...?"

Ember's hand trembled as he let out a sob. "Hi, Jess," he said, and I couldn't help but laugh. One of the guys asked what an andro was doing in the apartment, but I ignored him completely.

"You're here!" I exclaimed, my cheeks hot. "I'm sorry it took me so long to reply ..."

"Better late than never, right?" His voice cracked and I stepped toward him, hardly hearing the agitated voices of the men beside me. Ember took a deep breath. "I know I'm not how you remember."

He was so skinny, all his muscle gone, his hair buzzed short, his wounded arm hugging his waist. I had forgotten how he never slouched like I did. I had forgotten how gorgeous he was. "You're exactly how I remember."

I touched his arm, and we collapsed into each other, and even though he whimpered when I squeezed him, I kept squeezing. Against me, his body expanded with his breaths, the warm air in the crook of my neck, and I shut my stinging eyes. He shuddered and hugged me back.

"Waiting for you to answer was torture. When I got it . . . I couldn't stay away. I'm so sorry."

"Why be sorry? You were more of a man than me. You took the risk. I've been hiding here. Hiding from my feelings. And for what?" I spoke into his shoulder. His hands took fistfuls of my shirt as he shook his head.

And then a deafening whistle made me wince. I looked up to see Brent removing his fingers from his mouth. "Seriously, Jess, what the damn is going on?"

The others were scowling, and Pascal stood with his arms crossed, his raised eyebrow suggesting he already knew the answer to Brent's question.

Ember and I separated, and his pale-blue eyes were wide. I had seen that look before, in the Outskirts. He was terrified, and it sent a chill down my spine.

How could I explain this? Especially since the "oh he's just a brother" excuse was completely out in the rain after our embrace? Ember had changed stances, now with his eyes on the floor and his hands clasped in front of him. Like a "well-behaved negative." Like no man should have to act.

This angered me enough to say the second most dangerous thing I had ever said, second only to telling my Father that I loved Ember.

"He's my boyfriend."

Their reactions were immediate as Brent and Pascal's friends burst out laughing.

I gulped down my humiliation. "You got a problem with that?"

"Your boyfriend's a baby machine?" Pascal asked, and I glanced over my shoulder. *Please don't react* . . . Ember kept his eyes on the floor.

"I don't understand," Brent said. "It's a negative."

"He means he's a pervert," one of the guys said. Shaved head, large shoulders. Marc.

"I heard there's medication for that sort of thing," the other added. I had only met him once. King?

Pascal shook his head, giving me a cold smile. "I knew you were off. I didn't know you were completely off your shit."

"Says who?" I defended, my heart hammering so hard they could probably hear it. "It's not illegal."

"It's also not illegal for you to jump out that window. You gonna do it? Just 'cause you can?" King chuckled.

"Look at the scrawny andro . . ." Marc taunted. "I bet he'd squeal if you held him up and—"

"Don't you dare talk about him like that!" I snapped. The men laughed. "We don't have to take this shit from you guys. Leave us alone."

I took Ember's hand, and turned toward my room.

Pascal sidestepped ahead of us, his arms crossed and a smile on his face. "So let me get this straight. You think you can tell us this thing is your boyfriend, and just walk away like nothing's wrong?"

"Yes." I stood up straighter, and stared him down. "Our lives don't affect yours once we leave these walls. I want you to give me one reason why I can't do whatever the fuck I want when I'm out of your sight."

"Because that's not the way the world works," Pascal said, glancing behind me. Ember yanked my arm hard, pulling me out of the way of a lunge from Marc.

Again, the others laughed, and I stood there shaking.

"Let's get the fuck out of here," Ember hissed.

"He even bosses you around?" King asked.

I swallowed hard. "If he wants to, yeah."

"Wait till this gets to the office," Pascal said. "We've confirmed the boss's son is fucking a vicious little cunt."

"You let him fuck you with his pseudo too?" King called. Ember growled, and I gripped his shoulder.

"We gotta just ignore them," I whispered.

Ember took a deep breath, and when our eyes met, he appeared surprisingly collected. "Jess, what do you think about moving out? Right now?"

"I think you're reading my mind." I motioned for him to follow me. "Help me pack."

"No, no. Enough of this nonsense," Pascal said. "That thing isn't staying here another second. If you want out, you handle that on your own."

Brent frowned, and stepped toward us. "Hey, man. Let him help the guy pack."

Pascal gaped at him, and Marc shoved Brent hard enough for him to splay his arms.

"I'm serious," Brent said, shooting a look at Marc. "Jess is right. Let him leave and you can all forget about it."

"How can you side with them?" Pascal accused, and as Brent attempted to defend his position, I took the opportunity to lead Ember to my room.

Once out of eyesight, we embraced.

"I'm so sorry about that," I whispered.

"No worse than I'm used to," he whispered back.

I grabbed my luggage from my closet, and handed a bag to him. "Empty my dresser into it?" I asked, before starting in on my desk with the other. "Do you have any plans for what happens now?"

He shoved clothes into the bag and shook his head, the hint of a smile on his lips. "Ideas? Yes. Plans? Nothing past getting the fuck out of this apartment as soon as possible."

"Where will we go?" I asked.

He sighed. "If we go back to Atlanta, I can keep my business."

"That's a start."

Our gaze met again, and I couldn't help but be drawn to him. We kissed, and the soothing release of it relaxed my tight muscles. This was right; he was right. It had been too long . . .

But thankfully not too late.

"Do you want to leave for Atlanta now?" Ember asked as we drove in his rental car. "And I'm not sure about you, but I'm starved."

I thought for a moment, our freedom just starting to register as a tingling in my skin. "Yeah, let's find a place to eat. The highway's right up this way, then take exit 3A and get on Forty-third Street."

As he got on the highway, he filled me in on what he'd been through while we were apart, and then the conversation turned to his brother, and the truth about the testosterone.

"I can't believe Marin was right," I said.

Ember shook his head. "I just wish I could have told Steph before he injected."

"You still can. You can tell him how much safer the untainted hormone is."

"If he'll believe me. If he can afford it." Ember groaned. "I don't even know how I'm going to afford it."

"We'll make it work," I said. "Are you definitely going to keep injecting?"

"Of course. I was miserable as a Y negative. I felt disgusting. I felt wrong."

I could understand this, with how easily men talked of the inferiority of negatives. But that didn't stop men like Marin. "There's nothing inherently wrong with being negative."

Ember sighed. "Besides how mascs make it wrong? I guess not. But many of the Y negatives in school looked forward to injecting as an accessory, whereas I looked forward to shedding that identity permanently. Injecting the medical grade . . . I hope I've freed myself from one level of masc control. Maybe now I can just be me."

By this point he had reached Forty-third, and I gave him directions to a restaurant a few blocks from my old secondary school.

I smiled. "I'll get something to go for us."

"I don't have many creds . . ."

I waved my hand. "It's on me."

An andro took my order as I thought of what Ember had told me. This guy didn't know he was drugged. My jaw clenched with how unfair that was. But could one man do anything to expose the truth? Could two?

I returned to Ember with a bag of veggie wraps, and the aroma of the restaurant's signature sauces filled the car.

"Okay, now up this block a ways and make a left on G."

He complied, and I instructed him to stop at a hotel. He pulled over and looked up at the sign, then gave me a shocked expression.

"I'd rather start the drive in the morning, wouldn't you?" I said.

"This is the kind of place where rooms are called suites. Can you afford this?"

I nodded, and as he idled, I went inside and rented a room. Would I be able to spend like this forever? No. But a few days wouldn't hurt me. I soon climbed back into his car.

"You should . . . I mean, let's go through a side door or something." I blushed. It didn't feel fair, but I didn't want to take any risks.

"Yeah, that's a good idea."

He parked in a lot around back. Thankfully undisturbed, we stepped into our room. I scanned its large bed, sleek metal desk, and mutely colored couch, the stillness of the atmosphere allowing me to hear my heart thudding.

"I feel like I'm a spy in a televid," I told him, shutting the door and flipping the lock.

"Oh, but Mr. Cameron," Ember said in a dramatic voice, picking a wrap from the bag and peeling back the paper. He sat on the bed. "How else are you to capture the criminal and save the world?"

"How about I start with saving the man I love?" I asked, trying to emulate that same voice.

"Pff, like I needed you to save me."

I laughed. "Yeah. You saved me."

We ate, and he told me about Atlanta—his clients, his roommate, and his usual haunts. It sounded good. It might just work, as long as the mascs in the area didn't target us.

"I assume we'll find a new place to live."

"Yeah, I think we'll have to. There aren't enough mascs in my complex for you to blend in."

"So we'll find a place with a good mix, where we can hide that we're together."

"As long as we're not stupid about it," he chuckled.

"Where no one will know what happens behind shut doors," I said softly.

A smile blossomed on Ember's face as he nodded, and his gaze darted down my body. "I think we're in that situation right now, too."

Before I could take a deep breath we were in each other's arms, his stubble tickling my lips as I took in as much of him as I could. He let me lower him to the bed as we shared a kiss that for once stretched on as long as we wanted. And it all went so naturally after that, as we peeled off clothes and I reveled in the electricity of his skin on mine. As he moaned my name and I got lost in his differences, in his similarities. As I forgot where I was and who I was until he told me in the way he gripped my back, the way he gasped and laughed.

And he told me again and again until I fully understood and made it a part of who I'd always be.

CHAPTER 29

Three months later

"Thank you, Mr. Ranford. Come back soon." I smiled as the client left, and then I shut the front door and scanned our living-room-turned-office with a sigh. The bookcase of our extra stock parts looked good by the window. Professional.

Against the back wall was Ember's desk, where most of the time clients didn't bother him and addressed me instead. I pulled up a chair next to him and curled my fingers around his waist.

"So this processor's gonna go right there," Ember said, pointing at the spot on the circuit board with a pair of tweezers. "It connects at the three points on the left side and the fifteen on the right."

I watched and listened. Commons and consoles were a bit more complicated than sensor arrays, but I was learning. In the past few months I had learned enough that Ember now trusted me with the little things. And it was great having the knowledge to answer customer questions.

"Okay," Ember started, once he finished that project. "So I was poking around the news networks this morning."

"And?" I asked, squeezing his hip.

"I think I can get through. I can't use my log-in grabber, but I don't think they have a defense against brute-force."

"Meaning?"

"I set up a program to keep trying passwords until it gets through."

I snorted a laugh. "That simple?"

He smirked, but shook his head. "If it works, and assuming I can get past whatever posting restrictions there may be, we should be able to upload everything I found to the front page of each site. Everyone checking the news would see it, at least. It will get taken down fast, but hopefully it'd be enough to get people talking. It'd be a start."

He'd post everything about the drugged testosterone, and all the companies that had been keeping the secret. The world had to know—not to mention our personal stakes. "And then maybe your brother will believe you."

Ember's shoulders slumped as he rested his head on his hand. "This is a lot bigger than helping Steph. This is about helping all of us wake up."

I rubbed between his shoulder blades and he arched his back toward my touch. "It's more than just waking people up. We're fighting for your equality. Your autonomy."

"That's a tall order for two guys."

I shook my head. "There's no way only the two of us want this."

There was a knock at the door. We exchanged hopeful glances, and I kissed his cheek and stood.

When I opened the door, my jaw dropped.

Heath stood in the hallway wearing a button-up shirt, a week-old beard, and a cautious smile.

"Heath. . . what are you doing here?"

"CamCo's meeting with an Atlanta research team. Working out a merger. Figured while I was in town. . ."

Something behind me caught his attention, and his eyes widened. I glanced back. Ember had joined us, his expression unreadable.

I regarded Heath. "Come on in. It's good to see you."

But Heath's gaze lingered on Ember as he stepped forward. "So the rumors had some truth to them."

"Probably. And a lot of lies too," I said. Ember stood by my side, and when I touched his arm he grabbed my hand. Heath flinched, and kept his eyes on me.

"You have more balls than I thought," he said. "After the hold Hale had on you when we came back from the stations, I really didn't think you would ever leave the company."

"And be stuck at a desk until I retired?"

He let out a laugh. "Well, yeah! You would have had an easy life." Shaking his head, his gaze slipped back to Ember. "Instead you chose the hard road."

He wasn't just talking about CamCo now, and of course, he was right. But my response formed without me dwelling on it. "I would never have been happy."

Ember and I met eyes briefly, and he gave me a smile.

"And are you happy now?" Heath asked, gesturing at the room, ending at our clasped hands.

"I am."

"I don't know if I'll ever understand it," Heath admitted.

Ember beat me to responding. "But can you let us be?"

Heath glanced at Ember, but then spoke to me. "If you're happy doing your own thing, then . . . then I want to respect that."

The tension lifted from my chest, and I let myself smile.

"Could we get you anything to drink? Do you want to join us for lunch?" I asked.

Heath rocked back on his heels as he waved a hand. "No, that's all right. I actually meant to give you these."

He proffered a pair of discs, and I took them and was instantly blinking back tears.

"They're my dad's encyclopedias," I said, running a thumb over Dad's neat handwriting on small labels. "I'd figured I left them at Father's."

"Found them between couch cushions."

"Thank you," I managed, sticking them carefully in my pocket.

He gave me a slow nod. "I gotta get going; I'm due across town."

"Well, good luck." I held up a hand, and with a chuckle, Heath shook it.

"Take care of yourself," he said, and he went on his way.

As I shut the door, Ember ran a hand through his hair. "Did that really just happen?"

"I think it did. Except. . . Heath acted like a human being." I stifled a laugh. "Maybe I'm dreaming."

Ember raised an eyebrow and danced his fingers up my arm before pinching me hard. I yelped, and he snorted, wrapping an arm around my waist.

"Is it a dream?" he asked.

I slid my hand around his shoulder, and we pulled into a kiss. The warmth of it tingled through me.

"Nope," I admitted, resting my forehead against his.
"Good. I'm done dreaming. I wanna live."

Dear Reader,

Thank you for reading Kelly Haworth's *Y Negative*!

We know your time is precious and you have many, many entertainment options, so it means a lot that you've chosen to spend your time reading. We really hope you enjoyed it.

We'd be honored if you'd consider posting a review—good or bad—on sites like **Amazon, Barnes & Noble, Kobo, Goodreads, Twitter, Facebook, Tumblr,** and your blog or website. We'd also be honored if you told your friends and family about this book. Word of mouth is a book's lifeblood!

For more information on upcoming releases, author interviews, blog tours, contests, giveaways, and more, please sign up for our weekly, spam-free newsletter and visit us around the web:

Newsletter: tinyurl.com/RiptideSignup
Twitter: twitter.com/RiptideBooks
Facebook: facebook.com/RiptidePublishing
Goodreads: tinyurl.com/RiptideOnGoodreads
Tumblr: riptidepublishing.tumblr.com

Thank you so much for Reading the Rainbow!

RiptidePublishing.com

ACKNOWLEDGMENTS

First of all, a huge thank-you to my husband, who helped me brainstorm the initial draft of this story, and who is always there when I want his opinion, regardless of the hour. And thank you for doing the dishes all those nights I was glued to my laptop. Yes, I'll do my share now.

Second, thanks to all the family and friends who read early drafts of this book and offered advice and encouragement, including all my friends in the writers' groups, the Davis Writer's Salon and Stonehenge Writers. Thank you especially to Robert Gmelin, my screaming buddy, who helped me through all the drafts and rejections. Look! I did it, and you're next!

And of course a gigantic thank-you to Riptide Publishing and editor Carole-ann Galloway, who took the risk on what I always had feared was too niche a story, and helped me shape it into a book that I am both amazed by, and proud to share.

ABOUT THE

Kelly Haworth grew up in San Francisco and has been reading science fiction and fantasy classics since she was a kid. She developed way too active an imagination as a result, thus, she started writing. Being genderfluid and pansexual, she loves to write LGBTQ+ characters in genres such as science fiction with diverse aliens, and urban fantasies with shifters and fire sorcerers. With degrees in both genetics and psychology, she works as a project manager at a genetics lab. When not working or writing, she can be found wrangling her toddler, working on cosplay, or curled up on the couch with a good TV show or book.

Website: kellyhaworth.com
Twitter: twitter.com/KellyLHaworth